Journal *of a Lounge* Lizardman

BOOK ONE

Written by Mick McArt
Cover Art by Matthew McEntire

MICK ART PRODUCTIONS LLC PUBLISHING
www.mickartproductions.com

This is a work of fiction. Names, characters, places, and incidents are a product of the author's imagination. Locales and public names are sometimes used for atmospheric purposes. Any resemblance to actual people, living or dead, or to businesses, companies, events, institutions, or locales is completely coincidental or being used for parody. The author has represented and warranted full ownership and/or legal right to publish all the materials in this book.

Journal of a Lounge Lizardman, Book One
All Rights Reserved
Copyright © 2022 Mick McArt, Mick Art Productions
V1

This book may not be reproduced, transmitted, or stored in whole or in part by any means, including graphics, electronic, or mechanical without the express written consent of the publisher except in the case of brief quotations embodied in critical articles and reviews.

ISBN: 978-1-948508-12-4

Published by
Mick Art Productions, LLC
www.mickartproductions.com

PRINTED IN THE UNITED STATES OF AMERICA

THIS BOOK IS DEDICATED TO
E. GARY GYGAX
AND
WEIRD AL YANKOVIC,
WHOSE INFLUENCE YOU'LL SEE
THROUGHOUT THE BOOK.

REVIEWS FROM THE REALMS

"I really dug these stories; each entry was a true nugget!"
– Doug Tunnels, Dwarven Mining Times

"So many smash hits!"
– Rock Bolder, Throwing Stone Magazine

"Each entry kept me on the edge and had me falling for each one!"
– Cliff Burdon, Skyfall Press

"Just reading the words to the songs had me tapping my foot,"
– Max Caffiend, Coffee Shop News.

"All these wonderful songs seem so familiar to me,"
– Melody Mocktune, Hit Charader Magazine

REALM OF GASPENFALL
REALM OF FARLONG
REALM OF DARKMIST
REALM OF CLOVEROSE
PROVINCE OF RUSTWOOD
PROVINCE OF BARRENDRY
PROVINCE OF ELDERWHELP
PROVINCE OF THUNDERFUSS
PROVINCE OF WINTERSPRING
PROVINCE OF SLAPHAMMER
PROVINCE OF EAGLESPAW
PROVINCE OF RIPPENWIND
PROVINCE OF MOONWINK
PROVINCE OF DARKENBLEAK
PROVINCE OF DRAGONSHELM
PROVINCE OF SUNKENSOD
LAKE NETHERBOTTOM
LAKE UNDERGLUB
PURGEWATER LAKE
HOKTU MOUNTAINS
FAERWOOD FOREST
TANGLEWOOD FOREST
MUFFLEMAN FOREST
ELFLANTIC SEA
N
W
E
S
THE UNREMEMBERED REALMS

THANK YOU'S

God, my late father Mickey McArt; my wife Erica, my sons Micah & Jonah, & my daughter Emerald. Chuck Bailey for giving Scales a voice along with wonderful parody music; My mother Marilyn McArt; Curt "Spaceburt' Coker; Kristen Coker; Brian Green; the Bila family; The Amazin' Mitten; Bruce Shields; Tom Adams; Andy Schiller & Family; Ernie Gygax, Jr.; Justin LaNasa; Jeff Leason; Lee T. Maker; all my new friends at the Dungeon Hobby Shop Museum in Lake Geneva, Wisconsin; all of my Kickstarter supporters; Jennifer Bouchard who is an editing wizard, and a huge thank you to the evergrowing fan base of the Unremembered Realms who inspire me to keep building this world!

Mick Art Productions Publishing
www.unrememberedrealms.com

Journal of a Lounge Lizardman - Book 1
Written by Mick McArt
Cover Art by Matt McEntire
Back Cover by Josh Williams
Map by Justin Andrew Mason
Editing by Jennifer Bouchard
Proofing by Erica & Micah McArt

I want to thank (and apologize) to all the musicians and artists who are parodied in this book. It is done out of a heart of love and admiration. Music has always been something that has moved my soul, and I'm grateful for all the influences that inspired me for writing the character of Scales and his band of bards, the Marshtones.

Entry 1

Life on the road isn't easy for the band and me. Playing shows, arguing with tavern owners over the pay, dodging rotten fruit- all the usual nonsense bards like us have to deal with. It's all worth it though, once when you have built a name for yourself. Seeing crowds gather outside the tavern, buying your merch, and eventually singing your songs back to you from the audience is the best part.

Within every crowd, though, there is always someone looking to spoil the fun for everyone else. The most common one that I face is the heckler. They are also known as "anti-bards." These killjoys ruin the fun for every patron in the place. Sometimes, a corrupt tavern keeper will secretly hire hecklers to disrupt an entertainer's show during the last set. If the bard gets upset and quits, it voids his contract, and he doesn't get paid.

Professional hecklers usually get half of what the entertainer would have. Sure, it's a slimy way to do business, but it's such a common practice that nobody questions it. Hecklers eventually formed guilds of their disruptive expertise. They are also skilled in backstabbing and light forms of magic. Their famous motto, "The show must go off!" is the bane of every bard in the Unremembered Realms.

Hecklers are the main reason I appreciate Maul Chafer, our slap-happy half-ogre who loves to have violent conversations with these critics. Maul usually stands off to my right, playing his trusty Warshburn bass tub and scanning the crowd for these pests.

I remember the first night Maul played with us. It was at the Scarf & Gobble, a well-known tavern in Thudbunker. Some noobie heckler tried ruining our set. "Hey, songbird," he yelled from the crowd as our song ended. "Are you sure you're not a buzzard? That last song sounded like you were choking on a rotting carcass!"

Maul quickly cracked his knuckles before diving into the crowd. After a few slaps and screams, the half-ogre returned to the stage with a big grin. I remember the night fondly; we ended up getting a standing ovation, especially once Maul glared at the crowd and cracked his knuckles once more!

Entry 2

One of the biggest thrills for the Marshtones and I was when we hooked up with a famous manager. His name was Colonel Crom Parker. He was an older golden-scaled Dragonborn who came from the southern swamps, just like me. He was also highly respected by many for managing Elfis, the most famous bard in all the four realms.

Elfis was incredibly popular back in the day and a big inspiration for me. The crooning elf was getting older now, though, and had packed on a bit of weight. Rumor had it he would eat an entire turkey dinner by himself before going on stage. His first song, "2 Minute Belch," was usually followed by three or four of his classics before having a sit-down.

The downside to being managed by Crom was that the Marshtones and I were usually booked in the venues that Elfis wouldn't play. One time, we played the graveyard shift in the town of Slabstone, in the northern tip of Darkenbleak. It wouldn't have been so bad, but the town's population was entirely made up of the undead. I complained about playing there, but Colonel Crom insisted that we prove ourselves before getting bigger shows. "Bring a little life to the place," was the quote I remember him saying in his thick Widowsmarshian drawl. I found this an odd thing to say because no one in the Marshtones was a cleric, and we couldn't cast any Raise Dead spells.

We played the show, but I don't think they liked it; talk about an unlively audience! First off, we didn't click with the skeletons; they just chattered through our whole set. The mummies weren't much better. They didn't even look up from their tables, because they were too wrapped up in their conversations with one another. The Banshees were encouraging, though; they screamed the whole time we were on stage. The best ones, though, were the zombies. They dug Ghaspers bongo solo at the end! They all gave him multiple hands, literally. I know this because I had to dodge them as they were thrown!

We should have ended our set right then and there, but, being the showman I am, I decided to do an encore. It was a cover of "The Sun Shine Inn" by the Experience Points, another band of bards I admired. The song didn't go over well with the vampire couple in Section AB, and they started to shout slurs at us. All I heard, though, was blah, blah, blah.

I've developed a deaf ear hole over the years when it comes to complaints.

In the end, we left them wanting more, especially after I cut my finger when one of my lute strings broke. The whole audience became deathly quiet at that point and focused on me. I knew I would win over the crowd, eventually. Some of them were so delighted they even started drooling!

Entry 3

You don't often get to meet your heroes in person, so it's something you don't tend to forget once you do. One night, as we were setting up our equipment at the Doublewide Tavern in Shamptown, I heard the voice of a halfling. "What's the realms is going on here?!"

When I turned around from our magical enhanced amplifiers, I saw an older halfling, with his hands on his hips, looking up at Maul, who was holding a half-eaten sandwich. "That was mine, you oaf," the halfling barked. "Do you always eat everything in sight without asking?!"

"Yes," the rest of the band responded at the same time.

Maul pushed the rest of the sandwich into his mouth and scratched his backside. He then turned around and walked to the stage, ignoring the halfling following him. "Hey," I said in shocked surprise. "Aren't you Mel Gormay, also known as the Velvet Smog?"

The halfling looked me up and down for a minute. "I used to be," he quipped. "But I'm retired from music now. I bought this tavern so I wouldn't have to deal with weirdos or monsters stealing my now-famous sandwiches!"

I was blown away. My mother used to sing me Mel's songs when I was a kid, and here he was standing right before me! "Hey guys," I said, "Mel is the true master of singing love songs. By the end of his set, this little crooner had all the females in the audience eating out of the palm of his hand!"

"They never eat out me hand," Maul commented, wiping sauce that was still on his hand onto his vest.

"I can see why," Mel remarked with a look of disgust.

"Could you teach me some techniques?" I asked, hopeful that he would forget our bass player's thoughtlessness.

He looked me up and down. "I don't know," he said. "Lizardmen like you eat halflings, and I find that incredibly rude!"

The halfling was right. In my village, halflings were a staple part of our diet. "I've sworn off halflings," I told Mel while putting a claw over my heart. "The only thing I crave now is music!"

Mel rubbed his chin and seemed to be thinking. "Hmm," he said. "If it works for you, then other lizardmen might be influenced and eat less of my people. You have a deal!"

The halfling shook my claw and had me pull up a chair. As Mel talked about vocal techniques, I happened to sniff the claw he had shaken. It made my mouth water. I started to drift off to memories of halfling stew on the hearth, pickled halfling innards in mustard sauce, and many other delicious foods that Grandclaw used to make. By the time I snapped out of my daydream Mel was patting me on the back. "And that is how, dear lizardman, you can sing through all the octaves with little or no effort!"

I couldn't believe it. I had one of the greatest singers in all the realms reveal his great musical secrets to me, and all I did was daydream of eating him; I never heard a word!

As Mel turned and walked away, Maul stepped up next to me. "Mmmm…that halfling made a good sandwich."

"I bet he would," I said to myself as my stomach grumbled.

Entry 4

People often ask me why I became a bard in the first place. The truth is, I started as a low-level fighter, protecting my home swamp just to the north of Floptover in the Province of Sunkensod. Although my heart and childhood dreams were all about music, my parents were pushing me in the direction of spear fighting. That is until my cousin Tegus was found dead in Widowsmarsh. Not only had he been killed, but his head was smashed flat, and his left hand had been cut off!

This incident was one of many that convinced my family to let me try music and find a better way to make a living. Like many others in my village, my cousin thought he'd get rich by raiding caravans, but it only got him killed. A goblin bard named DeCasio played at his funeral, and everyone seemed to appreciate the lovely song he had written for the eulogy. I think that made a good impression, which helped me get approval.

DeCasio's music was good but seemed kind of repetitive. The funeral attendees didn't seem to mind, though; there wasn't a dry eye in the place. "I could do that," I thought to myself as I watched the funeral director hand the ugly creature a small sack of gold. I could only imagine that if a handsome lizardman like myself was doing the same thing, I could make some big coin!

I asked DeCasio to give me a few lessons, and he accepted. He had me try different instruments before I eventually settled on a long-neck lute that I named Tegus in honor of my cousin. He would have taught me more, but he was hired by my village to play at a costume party. Apparently, his halfling costume was a big hit, and maybe a little too real looking. He was never seen again.

Entry 5

After a decent turnout at the Moonring Tavern in Neverspring, I was feeling pretty good. The band had just been hissed off the stage by a large group of snake men called Pythogoreans. I was told this was a good thing considering they hissed at everything. The half-snake men were really into mathematics and dug our numbers. Around that time, Colonel Crom Parker decided we were big enough to have a warm-up act.

The groups' name was Ghoulie & The Banshees, and they were an all-female quartet of up-n-comers that were slaying audiences all over the realms. I first met them after their warm-up at the Rumbletuff Tavern in Dociletoff.

Ghoulie smiled at me and gave me a wink. I must admit, although I'm not attracted to humans, Ghoulies green skin and bald patches made her a lot more appealing to a lizardman like myself. Her band, The Banshees, were creepy and undead like she was and just floated around backstage tuning their instruments. Ghoulie seemed pretty cool; she was always complimenting the Marshtones. Ghoulie said she respected our ability to paralyze an audience with our unique sound. The sunken-eyed crooner told me she hoped to do the same.

I felt peckish, so I offered to buy them lunch at a café down the road, but they said they'd wait to eat at the show. This statement didn't make much sense to me, so Peavus, Maul, Ghasper, Rhody, and I shrugged it off and left for a quick bite before our set.

We had lost track of time over the meal, so we had to hotfoot it back to the tavern. Ghoulie and the Banshees had just finished their set. Ghoulie gave me a high-five as I passed her in the hallway on the way to the stage. "The crowd was great," she beamed before letting out a cute, girly belch.

I looked down at my claw and noticed it was spattered with blood. I didn't have time to think about it because I was eager to get to the stage. When the Marshtones and I got out there, it took a moment for our eyes to adjust. The stage lights, which were magic light spells cast on some directional light lanterns, were blinding at first, but then we noticed the dead bodies scattered over the floor after our eyes adjusted. All the patrons had become withered husks that were clutching their ears. It looked like their souls had been sucked clean out of their bodies. Some poor elf had been ripped in two, and something had snacked on his guts.

"Well, that's a fine how-do-you-do," I turned around and said to my band. "Another dead audience."

"What a rip," Peavus stated.

"We only got paid for the first half."

"It's okay," Rhody shouted to us from the floor. "The gutsy elf was the tavern keeper. He has the remaining half on his remaining half!"

Our roadie held up a small, bloodied coin bag and pinched his nose. "Man, do elf guts stink!"

After packing our gear into our tour wagon, we hit the road, heading to our next stop. I was starting to grow suspicious of Ghoulie because the next show turned out to be just like the first. Another dead audience, with the tavern owner deceased on the floor. I was going to say something to the undead songstress, but the show after that ended any chance of that happening.

It turned out that Colonel Crom had booked us at the Paladine, an elegant, upscale clerical temple in Lhentil Keep. I guess the audience of high-level clerics didn't care for Ghoulie and the Banshees and turned on them. By the time I got on the stage with the Marshtones, all that was left of Ghoulie and her band were piles of dust. In honor of the fallen group, we opened our act with our song, *Another One Turns to Dust*.

(Sung to the tune of Another One Bites the Dust by Queen)
Old lichy couple hobbling down the street
With an aching in their bones
Scaring everyone that they meet
Multivitamins ready to go

Can you hear me? Hey, turn up your aid
Are you putting in both rows of your teeth?
Out of the crypt with broken hips
Brought along a cleric with me

Another one turns to dust
Another one turns to dust
And another one gone, and another one gone
Another one turns to dust
Hey, I've got a holy symbol on you
Another one turns to dust

Why do you think that I'd play a club
Without a cleric in the crowd?
You could drain me for every ounce of life
And drop me to the ground

Are you hungry, unsatisfied?
I'm not brunch, a nosh or treat
I've got a gallon of holy water on me
If you're feeling just a little thirsty

Another one turns to dust
Another one turns to dust
And another one gone, and another one gone
Another one turns to dust
Hey, I've got a holy symbol on you
Another one turns to dust

There are plenty of ways that you turn a lich
And bring him to the ground

But you can't beat him, cheat him, or damage him bad
Without a magical item in your hand

Are you hungry, unsatisfied?
I'm not brunch, a nosh or treat
I've got a gallon of holy water on me
If you're feeling just a little thirsty

Another one turns to dust
Another one turns to dust
And another one gone, and another one gone
Another one turns to dust
Hey, I've got a holy symbol on you
Another one turns to dust

The show went well, and the clerics seemed pleased that night. It was just too bad things had to end the way they did for our opening act. I'd like to say I missed Ghoulie, but I prefer to play in front of a live audience!

Entry 6

Before we hired Ghasper on bongos, we had gone through several percussionists. Some were lame, like Milktoast the Drab, who played the same tired rhythm over and over. Then there was Ratatat, a were-rat who played wonderfully but smelled bad and ate out of our garbage.

The one I had the most hope for was a Rhuddist Monk named Kickdrum. The tall, gangly elf was covered with bruises, stitches, and scars and was very enthusiastic about pounding on the bongos. Rhuddist Monks are trained to stir up trouble and start many fights for those who don't know. One of their most famous quotes is, "However many angry words you graffiti or taunting words you may speak, what damage will you cause if you do not act upon them?"

Eventually, the violent elf revealed why he got the name Kickdrum. It wasn't because of any instrument he played; it was because he liked to kick people in the eardrum when they were trying to sleep! I remember the last time I saw him; he was giggling to me about pulling a prank on

Maul Chafer, who had just gone to lie down after a gig we did in Rippenwind.

Entry 7

I used to catch a lot of flak from the other lizard boys for reading comic scrolls and hanging out with other races down at the Treasure Hoard, a little shop on the outskirts of Floptover. My parents didn't mind much, but I think my father was disappointed that I wasn't focusing on my spear training as much as my older brother.

It was always fun for me, though, especially on new comic day when the latest issue of One Man Bard came out. It was my favorite. Rumor had it that it was even based on a real-life person! I was OMB's number one fan, and just one glimpse into my part of our family's swamp hovel would prove it! Drawings, carved action figures, logo-ed tunics; you name it, I had all the merch!

Since I saw myself as an upcoming musician in my own right, One Man Bard had a lot of appeal to me. Sure, I had other musical influences, like Mel Gormay and Elfis, but OMB was different. He was also a hero, someone who could fight all the neer'-do-wells and save those who couldn't defend themselves. Although hoping not to pursue a warrior's life, I still enjoyed the spear training and defense techniques that my father taught me.

After a day of training, my biggest thrill was lying down in some hay and reading the adventures of my hero. One Man Bard had started as a typical human bard making his way as a stand-in musician in all the taverns of the realms. He played with groups like the Fifth Dimensional Doors, the Prismatics, and even the soulful Earth, Wind, and Fireballs.

As he was a fill-in, he learned many musical instruments, and then one day, he disappeared. The scuttlebutt was that he had been taken captive by a music-loving evil wizard who was trying to build a super-group of ultra-talented bards and take over the realms. No one knows what became of the wizard, but we know that when One Man Bard appeared at a tavern somewhere in Farlong, he brought down the house with his powerful array of instruments and the beautiful melodies he could play.

This multi-talented human played a classical lute with a kazoo fastened on the top. Then, there was a kick drum slung on his back, which reacted to the movement of his elbows due to a nearly invisible wire harness. He had knee-knocking symbols, a tambourine belt, and zip clacker boots he could use by running a heel over. He also had an airbag under each arm, which would blow out a trumpet or tuba sound depending on which one he needed. The harmonica around his neck was held up by a small metal device that also had a whistle and a mouth harp that he strummed with his tongue. I'd say that was the whole shebang, but that's what he called his magic boots, which gave off drum sounds; his left foot was a snare, and his right foot was toms. His high hat was just that. It sat above his head and even had a tiktokky metronome that helped him stay on time.

One day, as I sat reading my latest issue of the comic, I heard screams coming from the direction of the main village. When I ran out to see what was going on, I saw the vast body of a black dragon flying overhead, roaring and spewing out its deadly breath weapon. I grabbed a spear, but my mother held me back as my father and other village colleagues took off after the creature. It did not sound like things were going all that well when I suddenly heard the most beautifully orchestrated music coming from outside. We listened to the death cry of the dragon, and then all became quiet.

Later, the lizardmen of the village discovered the decimated corpse of the black dragon. Parts of it were turned to stone, and others burned. The corpse had its belly split open, and its guts had spilled out over the ground where it had fallen. The village ate well that week; black dragon is tasty if you ever get a chance, even though it is a bit spicy. Everyone had theories about the dragon slayer. Was it a wizard? A group of warrior heroes? Nobody seemed to know, but I knew who it had to be. I heard the music. Not only had this musical hero saved my people, but he inspired me to reach for the stars!

Entry 8

Sometimes life on the road is outright dangerous. The Marshtones and I are always on our toes for one reason or another. Maybe we played a song that offended someone, or maybe Maul sat on somebody by mistake, crushing them. It's just part of being a band touring the Unremembered Realms.

One of the weirdest encounters we've had to deal with was when we were in the town of New Orc City; a popular monster hangout in Darkmist. We had been playing through our usual set at a tavern called the Ecto Chamber when four powerful clerics walked in and started causing a scene. I don't think they were there to harm us specifically, but I call what happened a case of being in the wrong place at the wrong time.

It didn't take long for these clerics and the undead patrons to get into an all-out brawl! We watched and played through most of the violence, trying to use our music to give the battle a little climatic exuberance. The four holy men looked determined to wipe out every undead they could. They worked efficiently as a team and even wore cool matching armor!

Their holy symbols represented the different temples they hailed from, and the colorful beams emitting from them were disintegrating ghouls, zombies, and even ghosts! The tavern owner was quite upset by the loss of his customers, so, being a mage, he tried to raise a golem to stop them. The problem was that there was no suitable material for him to cast the spell upon, so he had to grab whatever he could from the kitchen. It was a shipment of marshmallows!

The marshmallow golem grew large, and it attacked the clerics, tossing them all about but not causing much damage. I thought the mallowy beast would tear them apart, but the cunning clerics did something that I had never seen before; they crossed the beams of their holy symbols to roast the golem and turn him a nice golden brown. Maul could not help himself and ran to the dying creature, biting off huge chunks of it. The marshmallow golem never made a peep.

When the creature finally collapsed, the four clerics were all high-fiving and getting ready to leave. The tavern owner yelled at them about the mess but then ran into the kitchen to hide. "Great work, boys," I said, giving them a thumbs up.

"Where to now, Sprangler?" one of them asked.

"I guess there's been some trouble in New Orc's main gate," Sprangler began, pocketing his holy symbol. "Some undead fool's claiming to be the new gatekeeper. We better go check it out."

That's when they noticed Ghasper hovering behind me, holding his bongos. "Hey, Begone," one said. "Is that a ghost?"

"Don't be afraid of him, boys," I said, holding up my claws. "He's with the band."

They quickly drew out their holy symbols again, but the tavern owner ran back out with a large bucket before anything could happen. The four clerics were taken by surprise as he tossed the contents onto them. "Aahh!" Sprangler yelled. "We've been slimed!"

They were right; the bucket had been full of goopy green slime, one of the grossest monsters in the realms. "I had Slimy hid in the back," the tavern owner shouted. "That will teach you!"

The clerics pulled at the slime but were having a lot of difficulties. That's when Ghasper flew over to them one at a time and drained the life force from every bit of the gooey creature, which then fell to the floor in a grayish puddle.

"I can't believe it," Begone said, looking at Ghasper. "A phantasmal force for good! I've never seen anything like it."

"He's a great drummer, too," I said. "I was trying to tell you!"

"We've misjudged this ghost," Sprangler said. "Maybe we shouldn't assume the undead are all evil."

"That's what I was trying to say!" the tavern owner stated angrily. "Some of them just haven't been raised right!"

The undead busting team of clerics swore an oath to do better and thanked Ghasper for opening their eyes. They even made him the official mascot for their team. When we met them later at other venues, they showed us their new team symbol for their armor that featured a likeness of Ghasper on it.

Entry 9

Staying on my all-vegetable diet while on the road is tough, especially being a lizardman faced with all sorts of culinary temptations. As most of you know, halflings are a favorite food for most lizardmen. To this day, I have warm memories of celebrating Fallfest around the table with my family. Everyone would ooh and ahh as our den mother would pull a freshly baked halfling out of the stove and set it down before us.

I always remember my cousin Tegus and I each got a leg, but it wasn't my favorite. That honor goes to the big jar of pickled halfling feet Grandclaw used to make. Nothing was better than curling up around his feet as he'd recall stories of his past while gnawing on the hairy foot of one of these delicious creatures.

I'm only bringing this up because I almost ruined my diet after playing at the Brown Cushion Tavern in Port Laudervale. There was a table full of halflings, and my mouth wouldn't quit watering. Why do they have to smell so appetizing? People often ask me why lizardmen find them so tasty, and it's a legitimate question deserving a legitimate answer.

I can easily understand why people would ask such a question, why I, being such a talented performer, would waste any of my valuable time craving anything so ridiculous as a puny halfling. The look of these humanoids is a bit deceiving. They appear skinny, scrawny, stringy, unappetizing, anemic, ugly, and misbegotten. Ah, but how little do most know about halflings. You see, to the taste buds of a lizardman, they are what filet mignon, caviar, and chocolate fudge are to the taste of a human.

You see, the halfling delicacy is completely without waste. Each bit of the runt comes in a variety of flavors: bananas, asparagus, papaya, licorice, vanilla, sponge cake, celery, candied yam, caramel, chop suey, noodles, pork chops, cheddar cheese, bratwurst, pistachio, and pudding. Mmm...so good. I personally know over 4,000 recipes for the hairy-footed little creatures. There's a filet of halfling smothered in poinsettia sauce, barbecued halfling stuffed with pickled broccoli pears, brazed halfling under shatterproof glass, diced halfling ragu served on a wagon wheel, or just plain old sour halfling squab, just like den mother used to make.

I tossed and turned that night before I snuck out and hit the streets, determined to break my diet. As luck would have it, I stumbled across a little halfling selling maps. I grabbed him and ran into an alley, hoping to satisfy my hunger with just a toe or two when he convinced me to let him go. His name was Robbie, and I found him charming. He even gave me a free map for some secret treasure, but I lost it that night because Maul grabbed it and ran to an outhouse after eating at the Brown Cushion.

That didn't bother me, though. It wasn't the type of wealth I longed for, anyway. The only treasure I truly pursue is the applause from my audience and maybe a halfling toe now and again.

Entry 10

Before the Marshtones and I ever signed with Colonel Crom Parker, we used to play anywhere and everywhere that would take us. That included playing for dancing bums on street corners, crying brats at their birthday parties, and even a wedding or two. I don't remember too much about those gigs, except we cycled through many drummers at these events before Ghasper came along.

One wedding that sticks out in my mind was when we played for a newly married couple of werewolves. We played the reception and thought we were doing pretty well, performing covers of songs we thought the couple would enjoy, like Please Don't Wear No Silver by the Inhuman League and Merry Moon by Red-Eyed Rick.

Things were going fine until our drummer, I believe his name was High Hat, had let the cat out of the bag. I mean this literally! He had a cat named Ziljan that he carried around with him everywhere. He said it was a therapy cat, whatever that means. Well, it didn't work that night. The cat got out onto the dance floor, and the groom went crazy, chasing it around barking at it.

The room erupted into chaos, and our song was interrupted as the giant lycanthrope nearly knocked me over while chasing the frightened feline. Before I knew it, the bride had jumped on High Hat and was devouring him amid the chaos! By the time the hubbub ended, all that was left was a smashed-up reception hall, one of High Hat's thumbs, and Ziljan, who escaped by hiding in the back in our tour wagon.

Entry 11

On the west side of Omer is a small village occupied by a sect of gnomes called the Nommish. They are highly technical and are advanced above all other gnomes with their inventions. They usually don't let outsiders into their village, but they don't know anything about music. So, when they have a celebration, they like to hire a group of musicians like us to come in and entertain them at their favorite tavern called the Metro Gnome. I remember a Nommish gnome with round spectacles came up to me after a show in Miftenmad. He tugged on my sleeve, looked up at me, and said, "Now is the time when we dance."

The emotionless little guy tried to make a smile when we agreed and said: "I am joyful, like a little girl."

He said his name was Sprokkut. I usually enjoy playing for just about any crowd, but this group of societal outcasts were just plain weird. When we played at their event, the whole audience was dressed in all-black bodysuits. The little weirdos danced funny during all of our songs, like they were convulsing to mathematical equations or something. At the same time, their faces stayed in the same unemotional state. When the song finished, they would all sit down without making a sound.

The last song we played was called *Whole Lotta Blood*, it was about a vampire who always overate. We figured a scary song about a creature like this might stir up some emotion from them.

(Sung to the tune of Whole Lotta Love by Led Zepplin)
Hey fat vampire
I see you drooling
Drank too much type-A
Now your belt needs loose-nin'
Look at that waistline
Belt buckle goes shooting!
Not gonna give you my blood
I'm not gonna give you my blood

You drank a whole lotta blood
Drank a whole lotta blood
Drank a whole lotta blood
Drank a whole lotta blood…

You've been thirstin'
For a jugular bursting
But now you're too fat, vampy
Need some calories burnin'
Shifted into a fat bat
Lying on the floor, out of flaps!
Not gonna give you my blood

I'm not gonna give you my blood

You drank a whole lotta blood
Drank a whole lotta blood
Drank a whole lotta blood
Drank a whole lotta blood...

After the song finished, the gnomes got up from their chairs and left the building in a single file, showing no emotion whatsoever. Sprokkut came up with a sack of gold coins and coldly instructed us to go. "We are complete," he stated. "Thank you for the pain."

Entry 12

I hate song pirates. I remember this show in Port Laudervale, where the band and I had Sleeping Dust thrown on us, and we woke up somewhere in the Elflantic Ocean on a pirate ship. It turned out the Marshtones song that we played that evening, *Cursed Ring*, was the pirate captain's new favorite. He had heard us play it in the Brown Cushion Tavern, and he wanted to listen to it, over and over again, or else! Not given much choice, we set up on a makeshift stage and played it.... a lot. It went like this:

(Sung to the tune of Wild Thing by the Troggs)
Cursed Ring
You are just bad bling
You came from mount doomy
Cursed Ring
Cursed Ring, I think I loathe you
Is amputation the cure?
Something doesn't seem right
I must remove you

Cursed Ring
Bought from a halfling
He ruined everything groovy

Cursed Ring
Halfling, I think you tricked me
Now I gotta find a cure
Now I become a were-cow at night
You mooed me

Cursed Ring
You're udderly bad bling
I now eat everything grassy
Cursed Ring
Come off, come off,
Cursed Ring!

I think we played it over 33 1/3 times before I called for a halt. The pirate crew and the captain were not happy about it and quickly surrounded us. By their "plank" expression, I could tell that they were determined that the band make a splash, either musically or physically. We caved in to the pressure and played the song around 45 more times before they all fell asleep, and we escaped in a rowboat.

"Me think we broke record," Maul whispered to us as he rowed. "Song played most times in a row."

"Scratch that," Peavus replied. "That records held by the Repeat-les, who played the same song one hundred and eighty-five times at the Murky Cup Tavern in Thudbunker."

Maul stopped rowing. "Let's head back," he stated. "Me want to give that record a spin!"

We all gave Maul "the look," and he repented of his plans. The worst part about the incident wasn't even the repetitive song playing. Later that month, we found out the captain had stolen our tune and formed a group called The Abominable Showmen. The pirates only knew one song, and they sailed around to all the different ports playing "Cursed Ring" and claiming it was theirs!

Entry 13

Most of the time, our lead lute player, Peavus Calloway, is pretty chill, but onstage, there's no holding him back! I've seen him bust into solos where his lute bursts into flames because of his high-velocity fretwork (with maybe a Fingerflame cantrip mixed in).

I've also seen him do high jumps off of our magically enhanced Marred Skull Amplifiers, only to land while doing the splits back onto the stage, never missing a note. One crowd went crazy after witnessing this and had to be subdued by bouncers in white outfits. Peavus thought this was incredible and has bragged about it ever since. I don't have the heart to tell him that the crowd was actually crazy, and the venue we played at was an insane asylum called Jabberbabbles Discount Sanitarium.

The craziest thing Peavus will do usually happens on our closing number. If the crowd is riled up enough, he'll end the song by guiding us into a big crescendo, then start smashing his lute on the stage, causing the audience to go crazy! I mean, WHO does that!?

Entry 14

As someone who appreciates good music, I love being the opening act for some of the best bards in all the realms. Warming up the crowd for more well-known talent is an honor and a great way to open doors. We'll perform for just about anyone, too; it is one of the Marshtone's greatest strengths.

Then there are times when we open for groups that leave us scratching our heads. Like the time we opened for the Heartridge Family in a place near Shamptown. I believe the band was named after the tiny hamlet of Heartridge, or was the town named after the large family that resided there? The concert seemed more of a family reunion of some sort because all the people there looked alike. Everyone called each other "cousin" as a greeting. They were not the brightest group of people in the realms either, but they sure loved music.

At the end of the show, everyone there said we should join their family, but Peavus kept demanding we go quickly. One gal kept following Peavus around, trying to get his attention. "I don't know which one of her eyes are looking at me," he said, freaking out a bit. "She bit the head off of a chicken a few minutes ago. I think she's trying to impress me!"

I didn't understand why he was complaining. When someone in my home swamp bit the head off of a chicken, it meant romance was in the air. But I knew Peavus didn't want to settle down; he loved being a bachelor.

Another group we opened for was Manilli Ice, two ice elves from the Hoktu Mountains. They danced well but used backup singers to cover their lack of singing talent. I guess everyone should have caught onto their fakery sooner, especially since their two hit singles were *All Our Fans Are Fools* and *Pointing All The Blame*.

Either way, the Marshtones and I like our life on the road. It sure beats crawling around dirty, smelly dungeons and getting pummeled senseless by crazed monsters. Wait a minute; I think I just described the last tavern we played!

Entry 15

The Marshtones and I were playing a gig for a company called Winkdodger Investments. It was for their annual motivational seminar, and things were going well, except when our act was interrupted by a loudmouth wizarding accountant named Garflunkle. His tone-deaf singing voice kept drowning out mine. "Excuse us, sir." I'd say between songs. "Would you mind keeping it down?"

"Why should I?" the red-faced number cruncher hissed back. "I'm making your songs better!"

Thankfully, the audience disagreed. "Shut up and sit down," fellow employees would yell out. "Stick to singing to the boss, you brown noser!"

Garflunkle furiously kicked over his chair before pulling at the graying tufts of hair he still had. "I'll show you," he screamed. "I'll show all of you!"

When we played again the following year, Garflunkle showed up with a lute. He tried playing along with the band from his seat in the audience, even busting in with an off-key solo. It was apparent the pest had been practicing and was attempting to show us up. "Me want to slap this poser," Maul grumbled, getting ready to climb down the raised platform of the stage.

But it was the boos and jeers from his co-workers that had the bard wannabe storming from the room in a huff, once again.

The following year, Garflunkle didn't show up at all. The gig went wonderfully, and everyone had a good time. Winkdodgers management even gave us a nice bonus. We asked where "You know who" was, and they informed us that, as far as they knew, Garflunkle had left the company to study a newer style of magic. Everything finally seemed to be going smoothly for our arrangement with this investment firm. That is, until the following year.

While in the middle of our set, the doors to the room exploded open and a menacing lich stormed in, holding a lute. "Get off the stage," he said in a haunting tone.

Being a lich, we all stepped down, except for Ghasper, who just yawned and crossed his arms as if not impressed. "My name is Muzack," the lich stated before starting to play his lute.

The lich played steady and without soul. "This is bland," Peavus whispered to me, looking unimpressed.

The management team at Winkdodger was frowning at the music of Muzack! The rest of the office personal seemed turned off too, but what could anyone do? After all, this was a lich! As the undead musician played on, we began to realize that the songs he was playing were watered-down versions of our music! Peavus and I looked at each other and stated, "Garflunkle!"

Muzack turned to us and hissed. "You're just jealous that I'm better at your numbers than you!"

"Hold on a minute," I said, climbing up on the stage. "Are you telling me that you gave up the glorious life of an accountant, studied death magic, then turned yourself into a lich just so you could play your weird style of music for all of eternity?"

Muzack stared at me with his glowing red eyes and nodded. "Yes."

"Well," I replied. "How can anyone argue with that? Anyone who loves music that much deserves our help! Let's get up there, boys!"

That night we did backup for the loony undead accountant. Winkdodger's team seemed happy, and the deathly smile of Garflunkle never left his skull face. It was some real onstage magic; I'd even dare to say the music we played somehow brought Muzack to life!

Entry 16

One of the craziest performances in my life was at the Battle of the Bards held at the Torchstick Arena in Lhentil Keep. The place is huge and can seat up to 10,000 realmsians. It is supposed to be run by a local board of city officials, but everyone knows that sleazy hobbyists and mob bosses secretly fund it. I found out later that this year's Battle of the Bards was being run by none other than Elfalfuh himself, the largest and most muscular elven mobster in all the realms!

The only reason I got involved in one at all was because of Elfalfuh's thugs. They are two human rogues named Apichat and Onquay. They had kidnapped me one night after a gig at the boring yet occasionally violent Scufflebored Tavern.

They approached me, pretending to be autograph seekers as I was on my way back from the outhouse. "Excuse me, Stales," one said in a gruff voice. "Could you sign my parchment?"

"Mine too, Snails," the other agreed, nodding his head. "We're your biggest fans!"

Being thrilled at being recognized for my talent, even though they got my name wrong, I let my guard down, and the more massive human grabbed me. I'm pretty strong, even among other lizard people, but this human was amazingly stronger!

"You're gonna make a fine contestant in the battle of the bards," said the smaller, wiry one named Apichat.

"But I don't like to fight," I explained, trying to undo my claws from the rope they had used to bind me. "Music is about bringing everyone together."

Onquay, the larger of two, pushed me forward. "Everyone will be together tonight," he laughed. "Watching you sing your last song!"

They brought me to the arena and pushed me down a dark corridor. I was shoved into a dimly lit cell before the Onquay untied my hands. They threw a lute at me, which I caught easily. "You better play well, lizardman," Apichat said, grinning. "Your life may depend on it!"

I wished Maul was here. His giant fists would have knocked out these two foul-smelling thugs before they could blink. I knew I shouldn't have gone to the outhouse without, at least, Ghasper there to scare off any neer-do-wells.

So there I was, sitting in the cell, practicing a few songs, wondering what would happen next. When I paused from playing, I could hear other bards through the walls practicing, as well. I even caught a dwarf yodeling. Something told me this was going to be a long crazy day.

As the hours slowly dragged by, I practiced song after song, figuring out which would be the best one to play. I even did some stretches, getting my muscles ready in case I had to fight. I may be all about the music, but I had also been trained for fighting since I was hatched. I'm very capable of defending myself with a spear, sword, even a small painted turtle (I'll have to explain that in a future entry).

A loud horn blew, and I heard the distant sound of a crowd cheering. That sound always made me happy. As a bard with a band that regularly toured, I just couldn't get enough. When a couple of guards came to fetch me, I was already excited to get on stage and play! After being led down a few long tunnels, I could hear the crowds getting louder. Finally, we stopped at a double-sized door, which led into the arena. I could see the sunlight pouring in from under it.

I also noticed the faint smell of blood. "You ready to battle?" a voice came from behind me.

When I turned around, I saw a dwarf wearing colorful leather armor. He had a braided brown beard and wore the top part of his long shaggy hair in a top knot. "I don't care about the battle," I said. "I just want to make sure everyone's entertained."

This statement must not have been what he was expecting to hear. He looked me up and down suspiciously. "My name is Scales," I said, trying to introduce myself. "What's yours?"

"Warblinn Offkee," he grunted back. "But it's soon to be the Warblinn "The Champion" Offkee. Understand?!"

Before I could respond, the guards pushed me toward the doors, which were pulled to either side by some pulley system. The bright sunlight warmed my scales as Warblinn and I were marched out into the arena to thunderous applause. Sadly, the clapping and yelling wasn't just over me; other bards were being led out from all around the arena. There must have been over fifty in total.

In the middle of the ring was a raised circular wooden platform. On it were a few arena musicians who must have been there to play back-up for whatever bard was onstage. There was also every instrument you could think of, mandolins, ukuleles, a piano, and even a few I had never seen before. Behind the stage, about thirty feet back was a catapult. The huge device was aimed at a makeshift wooden wall with a bullseye painted on it.

Then, I noticed, 20 feet in front of the stage, was a long table with three humanoids who sat there talking with each other. It was obvious they would be the judges that determined all of our fates. I knew the big guy in the middle; it was none other than Elfalfuh himself! "The frowning human on Elfalfuh's left is Iva Scowl," Warblinn stated. "He's tough to please."

"Who's the gal on the right?" I asked. "She's got a nice smile."

"Her name is Bella Donna," the dwarf said with a smirk. "Believe it or not, she's the deadliest one up there."

It wasn't long before the first bard was brought up to the stage, and the show began. Each bard was given a chance to sing a song and be judged. You were either selected for the next round or eliminated, and by that, I mean, drug off the stage and killed! The first act up was a group called the Leech Boys. Their gimmick was to cover themselves in leeches and play until they passed out. Their harmonies were amazing while they were conscious. Iva voted them down after their act, but Elfalfuh and Bella Donna liked them, so they moved on to the next level.

The next act was a massive hit with the audience. It was a group called Three Dogs and a Knight. The dogs, led by the knight, barked their way through a funny rendition of some holiday song everyone knew. I had to admit, it would be hard to compete with that! They would have won for sure, but during the applause, people from the audience started to cheer and whistle. The dogs all took off after hearing the whistling, and they couldn't find them after that. The hapless knight was drug from the stage, put in the catapult, and flung at the bullseye where he missed the center only by a few feet!

The judges all held up numbers chalked on pieces of slate, a 6, 7, and 9. The audience went crazy! "I can do better than that," I thought to myself.

I was going to make a comment to Warblinn, but he was shoved forward to the stage. He picked up the ukulele and started to sing. I figured Warblinn Offkee must have been part Cagin' Dwarf because of his southern drawl. Whatever Warblinn was, though, he had the whole crowd singing along. He was crooning a song about being in a jailhouse or something. This topic must have touched a nerve with Elfalfuh the Crimelord because the giant elf held up an open palm and nodded along to the last chorus. Bella Donna smirked, but Iva, as usual, gave it a thumbs down.

Many acts followed the successful dwarf. Iron Maven, the Familiar Shop Boys, Black Sackcloth, Darth Brooks, the Chuck Bailey Band, and even a screeching banshee named Wailing Jenny. Whether they moved on to the next round or ended up splattered on the target wall, I noticed Iva had given them all a thumbs down. This situation had me fidgety by the time it was my turn to take the stage.

I nervously walked up and spoke into the magic amplification wand after adjusting it on its stand. "Good evening, everyone," I began, already noticing a frown on Iva's face. "I'd like to play you a crowd favorite at all the gaming establishments. It's something we can all identify with; It's called *Cursed Dice O' Mine*.

(Sung to the tune of Sweet Child O Mine by Guns-N-Roses)
"There are twenty sides, and it seems to me
That rolling good should come naturally,
But it always ends up with the worst number on the die

Now and then, when I need you most
My character winds up with the Holy Ghost,
And the GM blushes when I break down and cry

O woe woe, cursed dice o' mine
O woe oh woe cursed all the time

Dragons blaze, and my heroes rise
Hoping to stop their reign,
I'd hate to misroll all of my saves and absorb that breath of flame

I bought these dice at a gaming place
Where me and my friends abide,
And play through the morning till the night til the weekend passes by

O woe woe Cursed dice o' mine
O woe oh oh woe Cursed rolls of mine
Oh oh oh oh Cursed dice o' mine
Ooohh oohoh yeah, Cursed rolls of mine
Oh oh oh oh Cursed dice o' mine
Ooohh oohoh yeah, Cursed rolls of mine

How will I roll now? How will I roll? How will I roll now?
How will I roll? How will I roll? How will I roll now?
How will I roll? Cursed Dice o' mine, How will I roll now?
Cursed dice, cursed dice o' mine

I thought things were going well because I could see most of the crowd swaying along to the chorus and clapping along at the right moments. I was even enjoying it, too, forgetting that I was in mortal danger! Iva did not seem happy, though. I was just about to end the song, and the music curmudgeon wasn't changing his expression. Iva kept eyeballing the bloodied target wall, and this made me nervous again.

Just as I ended my song, I bowed my head, waiting for the crowd's applause and the judges' decision. But none came. As a matter of fact, it had grown deafeningly quiet! When I looked up, I noticed all three judges with their jaws hanging open. Their wide-eyed expressions seemed to look just past me. I slowly turned around and finally saw what the non-fuss was about.

Towering above the stage was an ugly, bald, and partially toothless fog giant. "Me name is Zham Leaf," he began. "Me could hear music. Me love groovy sounds. Me want to play, too!"

I quickly bolted off the stage and past a small group of human guards who were too scared to move. Elfalfuh looked back and forth at the other judges and gave the giant a nervous grin and a thumbs up. Zham Leaf gave the elf a big smile and broke out into a song that was so bad I had to cover my ear holes. I watched with delight as Elfalfuh and Bella Donna pretended to enjoy the out-of-tune warbles and what seemed like off-key belches. Iva, on the other hand, just couldn't handle it. He climbed up on the table and defiantly gave Zham Leaf a double thumbs down.

"You're terrible," he yelled out. "That was, by far, the worst attempt at singing that I have ever heard!"

With tears forming in his eyes, the red-faced fog giant clenched his fists into balls. "It sounds like you're strangling a manticore!" Iva continued. "Get off the stage; you are a big loser; make way for some real talent!"

"Me try something else," Zham Leaf said, reaching out and grabbing Iva Scowl by the waist. "It called Human Beat Boxing!"

Within moments, the giant was punching Iva's upper torso in a rhythmic beat that had the whole crowd getting into it! Then, Zham grabbed the other human guards and smashed them around, causing different sounds. The now fascinated audience went crazy! I had to admit that I, too, enjoyed the sounds and began to bob up and down to the rhythm.

Noticing that everyone was distracted, I decided to make a break for it. This situation was one time I didn't mind tucking my tail between my legs and scampering off. Living to play another day is always worth it! I just got to an arena door when it swung open, and standing before me were Elfalfuh's two ornery bodyguards. "Where do you think you're going, lizardman?" Apichat asked, with a look of disdain on his face.

"Yeah," Onquay laughed. "We don't remember giving you permission to leave!"

"Sorry, fellas," I began. "But a good bard knows when to take a bow."

As I took a bow, I heard something fly over me; and as I glanced up, I saw the torso of Iva Scowl crash into the two thugs, knocking them both off their feet! I quickly unbowed and gave the two a thumbs up and a big smile. Without hesitation, I made my way out of the arena; I didn't want to get hit with any more human debris!

I eventually found my way back to the Scufflebored Tavern and informed the Marshtones about what had happened. Later that evening, the band and I caught word that Zham Leaf had won the Battle of the Bards. It was not a shock, but I did feel a twinge of jealousy. Maul commented that he liked the idea of that Human Beat Boxing, but I wouldn't let him do it. I consider it bad luck to beat your audience half-to-death. The music may be good, but stunts like that can be a real crowd killer!

Entry 17

Many non-musicians don't know this, but most bands need a soundboard and someone skilled enough to use it. I can't remember how many times I've had to signal to Rhody, our dwarven roadie, to work the device to help with the show. It's such a wonderful thing to see him carrying the large piece of wood over to where the heckler is sitting and cracking the loudmouth over the head with it. The sound of the board thumping over a skull usually quiets any further heckling for the night.

Entry 18

One night after a show, we were sitting around the Dim Sun Tavern in Achincorn. It was during the winter season, so we were all feeling a bit festive until the doors flew open and a few adventurers carried in a frozen fighter. "Somebody bring us some chicken soup!" one of them screamed.

"Soup ain't gonna help that poor sot," Peavus chuckled. "He's frozen to the core!"

"Looks like another group from Sunkensod," I stated, munching my flavorless salad. "Another group, going after Frostbite."

"That dragon flies into this town every year," Peavus laughed. "Then freezes every knucklehead dumb enough to try to face it!"

"Me saw postcard at souvenir shoppe," Maul stated, daintily dabbing a few smears of deep-fried chicken guts off his chin. "Go to Achincorn, it read. Kill Frostbite, be hero!"

"Welcome to our winter wonderland!" I laughed, nearly spitting out a crouton.

Then a song idea hit me, and I scribbled it down on a napkin, which is where most of my songs wind up. I titled this one *Running from an Ancient White Dragon*.

(Sung to the tune of Winter Wonderland by Jeremy Stuart Smith)
Slay bells ring
are you listening
in the cave

scales are glistening
A frightening sight
we're now all affright
Running from an ancient white dragon

Gone away is our defenses
Our fighter has leaped 'over the fences
He'll freeze to death
From Frostbite's popsicle breath
Running from an ancient white dragon

In the shadows, we can build a good plan
Then we'll send in good ol' Parson Brown
He'll say I'm a cleric, not a barbarian
But we'll say: Go, man!
You can do the job
If you're not chowed right down

Later on
we'll conspire
as we cast spells of balls of fire
To fulfill unafraid
the plans that we've made
Running from an ancient white dragon

After his breath, we'll all look like snowmen
still alive but frozen 'yond our knees
We'll be picked up as snacks one by one
I hope we can at least give him brain freeze

When exploring
Refrain from
killing
White dragons when they're chillin'
It'll frolic and play
Then cone of cold spray
Running from an ancient white dragon

"Good lyrics," Peavus stated happily. "Perhaps we can play it to thaw this sap out."

That's when we heard the crash. The fighter had been leaned against the wall by the fireplace and left alone while the others ordered off the menu. The scattered bits of fighter slid across the floor in every direction.

"Glad me not janitor," Maul exclaimed, cracking a joke. "But he can brag to wife that he mopped floor with fighter today!"

Entry 19

One night at a talent show at the Falling Star Tavern, we saw a horribly coordinated effort by a band known as the Dratz. It didn't seem like they were bards at all, just a quartet who were hoping to make a few bucks, even if placing last. None of their instruments were in tune, and their lyrics were awfully depressing.

Their lead singer, a gray-haired halfling named Eew, sang off-key. Their lute players, Wilby Understone and Hangdog the Glum, had some missing strings, and their drummer, a blue female Dragonborn named Kolly, looked utterly lost. "This next song was a hit with the Goth giants of the Hopeless Pines," Eew said to the crowd, which started tossing food at him. "It's about being trapped in a dungeon. It's a cover of an old Twisted Cistern song called *We're not going to Make It*. One. Two. One, two, three, four...."

Only Hangdog the Glum started playing. It took a few chords before the other two realized they were supposed to play after the count. Eew shook his head and started singing, almost lining up with the rhythm.

(Sung to the tune of We're Not Gonna Take It by Twisted Sister)
We're not gonna make it
No, we ain't gonna make it
We're not gonna make it to the door

We've had a path to choose, yeah, and boy did we just blow it
It's game over, man, and we're going to die!
We fought with powers poorly, now our backsides hurting sorely
We should have known, so why even try!

*We're not gonna make it
No, we ain't gonna make it
We're not gonna make it to the door*

*Twisting hall's deep descending, this dungeon's never-ending
We won't get nothing, not a thing, from you
Our lives are just ill-fated, depressed, and eliminated
We're not the best, and that just won't do*

*We're not right, yeah
We'll flee, yeah
We'll scream, yeah
aaaaiiieeeeee, yeah*

*We're not gonna make it
No, we ain't gonna make it
We're not gonna make it out the door
We're not gonna make it
No, we ain't gonna make it
We're not gonna make it out the door
We're all worthless and weak!*

I think they had planned a few more choruses, but Eew was hit by a moldy potato and fell on his rump. I hate to see stuff like that, but Eew seemed to like it. It was the only time when the audience cheered. I've been there a few times myself, so I knew the feeling.

After the show, I walked up to their table at the tavern and asked if they didn't mind if the Marshtones and I covered their song. "I don't mind at all," Eew stated, eating some of the food that was thrown at them. "I didn't think it would work out for us anyway; the message is too positive."

The rest of his band nodded in agreement. "This trial of being in a band turned out worse than we thought," Wilby Understone stated sadly. "I told everyone here last night it would fail."

"Are you kidding," I said. "You got a free meal, didn't you?"

"Yeah," Peavus chimed in. "You may see that moldy potato as half rotten, but I'd like to remind you that it's half-ripe!"

The others of their band just shrugged in acceptance. "I wouldn't give up yet," I advised. "We've played plenty of worse venues than this."

Eew stood up in his chair and raised his fist, "You hear that guys?" he chimed. "Things can get a lot worse!"

They raised their hands in unison. "For worse times ahead," they cheered in unison.

We left them to their meal. To this day, I had never met a more depressing group of people.

Entry 20

One of the worst weeks on the road for us was when Colonel Crom Parker had scheduled an opening act for us named Bomb Tombadill. This solo artist liked to sing acapella songs about hugging trees, bird watching, and walking around through the woods. I think he was a druid before he decided to try his hand at being a bard. He was especially fascinated by moss, so most of his songs were centered around that very subject.

His opening song, Watching Grass Grow, was a real snoozer, and Peavus and I would stand behind the stage curtain watching audience members falling asleep or ordering extra tomatoes with their meals.

By the time he ended his set with Between Your Toes, where he had sung about a random foot disorder, he was covered with all sorts of thrown edibles. These performances always drove me crazy because the audience would leave or be in a foul mood by the time we started to play. Plus, we'd slip all over the stage from the greasy chicken or cold soup that was thrown at him. By the time we kicked him off our tour, all our costumes were stained from all the times we fell on mashed grapes or gravy.

I don't mind writing about Bomb Tombadill right now, but if anyone ever writes a documentary play about the Marshtones, the guys and I agreed to leave him out of it!

Entry 21

One day, at the Randum Tavern in the city of Dankpond, Rhody burst through the door with a large sack over his shoulder. He tossed it on the table, right smack on top of our dinner leftovers. "Fanmail!" he yelled out happily.

Everyone scrambled at the letters, snatching as many as they could scoop to their side of the table. The Marshstone's favorite thing in the world is hearing from our fans. Maul even liked the occasional hate mail. He tended to take those to the outhouse. I quickly tore open the envelope of the first letter I could. "This one is from a fan named Ooga Igga Egga Ogga Oge," I began. "And it's a question for Maul. She asks, 'Since you're a half-ogre, would you only date humans and ogres? Would you consider a going with a scabby half-goblin, hint, hint, hint?'"

"Oo, la la," Peavus said, winking at Maul.

"She's impressed with you, Maul," I said. "The envelope smells like fish heads, and under a P.S., she says that you are dreamy."

Maul pulled his finger out of his ear and wiped it on the table. "You hear that, boys?" he stated proudly. "Me dreamy!"

"Here's a question for you, Peavus," I said after opening another letter. "From a Polly Pimpleton of Humderum. She wants to know about what you eat on the road."

"Hmm," he said, tapping his chin. "I do tend to enjoy tossed salads of all sorts. I wish audience members would toss up a bit of dressing, with the lettuce and tomatoes they normally throw!"

"Did Ghasper get anything?" Maul asked.

"Just more junk mail from life insurance companies," I commented as I poked through the bag. "I think it's a bit late for that. Plus, I don't think he'd pass the physical. The cleric would be there for hours trying to find his pulse!"

"Unnhh!" Ghasper groaned while pointing at a gray envelope.

"Hey, wait. Here's a real one," I said, picking it up and opening it.

The letter was long and eloquent, describing how much they adored our drummers playing. It was written better than any fan mail I'd ever seen. Ghasper sat in his chair beaming. "Wait a minute," Peavus said, taking the envelope from me. "There's something else in the envelope!"

Peavus shook the envelope upside down, and a receipt fell out. "Hey! He hired a ghostwriter!"

Ghasper groaned in shame. I could tell he was embarrassed because the mist around his face turned slightly red. Usually, our ghostly friend got letters from zombies, which were hard to read because it was just bloody scrawls on paper that smelled of dried brains.

"I got a whole bunch of letters," I said, opening them and reading them out loud quickly. "Scales, you're great! Scales, you're handsome! Scales, you're super talented! Scales, are you coming home around Fallfest…."

"Wait minute!" Maul grabbed the envelopes from me. "These all from your mother!"

"I can't help that she's my biggest fan," I replied, somewhat embarrassed. "…and she can't help that she has great taste in music!"

"You guys are all crazy," Rhody laughed while munching on a breadstick. "I love fanmail day! You guys get the weirdest stuff!"

"Look," Maul stated, pushing an opened envelope towards Rhody. "A letter for you!"

Rhody never got any mail, so he nearly dropped his food. "Really?! Wow! Somebody finally noticed my contributions!"

The dwarf reached in and grabbed the slip of paper out, and unfolded it. His smile disappeared, and then he looked up at us all. "I got the bill for the meal?!"

"You do?" Peavus stated. "Thanks, Rhody!"

"Me love fanmail day," Maul laughed as Rhody stomped off to pay.

Entry 22

Dealing with invisibility is one of the hardest things in the Unremembered Realms. I've heard many tales from fighters, clerics, rangers, and rogues about how difficult it can be to find someone who has either drank a potion or cast a spell on themselves.

I agree it's not something I'd want to deal with in a dangerous dungeon, but I have to tell you, the type of invisibility the Marshtones and I have to deal with is much more powerful. You see, when it comes to the end of the night, and we go to collect our gold from the tavern keeper, they disappear into thin air. The waitresses shrug when asked of their whereabouts. You'd think these sneaky tavern keepers stepped into another plane of existence!

The only way to ever locate these invisibility masters is to shout,

"Okay, Maul. Go eat all the food in the kitchen."

These powerful magic words work well, because by the time Maul has eaten half their wares, the panicky tavern owners miraculously appear out of nowhere and reluctantly pay up.

Entry 23

In times of desperation, the Marshtones and I have to go into dungeons to make a little money. Like this one time when we were heading north to Skull Hollow, we found a headless corpse lying outside a cave. "Is he dead?" Rhody asked, poking it with a stick.

"Of course he dead, bean brain," Maul grumped. "His noodles off the plate!"

"I know that," Rhody retorted, stroking his beard. "I just thought he could be a zombie or something. Look, he is holding something."

I reached down and pulled a piece of parchment from his fist. "It's a treasure map!" I stated happily, "I bet there's a secret dungeon inside this cave. I bet we'll find all sorts of goodies."

"Look," Rhody said, standing on his tip toes to see the map I was holding. "There's a name on this."

"Robert the Rogue, Esquire," I read. "Sounds official. What do you think, Maul?"

The half-ogre went back to our wagon and grabbed his tree-stump warhammer named Mable. "Me wouldn't mind making a few hits," he smiled, with a sparkle in his black eyeballs. "Me am a musician after all."

"I'll get my torch," Peavus giddily stated, running over to the wagon as well.

The former wizard turned bard pulled out a short wand that had been previously charged with Light spells. He tapped it on his left hand a few times, and it blinked to life. I always felt bad for Peavus because he was just a human and didn't have infravision like the rest of us.

I got my spear, threw my lute on my back, and led the others into the entrance. We didn't have to go far before spotting a crude door. Maul didn't want to wait, so he just pushed past us and opened it. "Hey!" Rhody complained. "I didn't put on my adventuring helmet to have you knock it off before our first battle!"

The half-ogre ignored him and strode into the room, with Mable in hand. Standing around inside was a group of eight skeletons who saw us and held up their swords. "What's the password?" one cackled.

"Me don't know," Maul growled, looking for a fight.

I grabbed Maul's arm and quickly threw out an idea. "We're the band that your boss ordered for the secret party."

"Secret party?" one questioned. "What secret party?"

Peavus started to play along. "If your boss told you, it wouldn't be a secret, now, would it?"

The undead soldiers started muttering amongst themselves. "Will there be cake?" one of them asked.

"We just band," Maul grunted, lowering his weapon. "We don't' cook squat. Well, unless me killed it, then we cook squat."

"Have you ever eaten squat?" I asked Peavus because I had no idea what that was.

"I heard it ain't nothing," Peavus replied before turning back to the skeleton who seemed to be in charge. "Can we go?"

"Just follow the corridor," one said. "Through the storage room, and beyond that, we just don't know; we're never allowed past there."

The door was locked when we got there, so Ghasper floated through it and unlocked it from the other side. Our ghostly bongo player also switched off the trap that was waiting. "Thanks, Ghasper," I said, looking at the poison darts hidden in tiny holes in the door frame.

We went through the storage room, picking little bits of items here and there. It was mostly M.R.E.'s, which is Monster Ration Edibles. Maul swears by these, but I think they are too salty, and I was raised in a salt marsh! Maybe that's why Maul's blood pressure was so high. His cleric warned him about overdoing it, but the half-ogre's response was to always chase him around, trying to slap him. Needless to say, our band mate never had a family cleric long.

"There's another door," Peavus said. "What does the map say?"

I unrolled it and pointed, "Look, there's a corridor that goes about fifty feet, then there are three rooms that shoot off of it, and those are filled with the treasure!"

"Are you sure," Peavus asked. "That doesn't make any sense. Where's the kitchen, the restrooms, the dining hall, or even the big bosses' quarters?"

"Well, if we can't trust Robert, the Rogue, Esquire, who can we trust?" I responded, even though I was beginning to feel a little doubtful.

The door was unlocked, so we opened it. The torches lining the corridor were unlit, so once again, Peavus used his magic torch. We walked carefully to the other end, brushing cobwebs from the path the entire way. The door at the other end was locked, so we had Ghasper float through it once more. When he did, an alarm started ringing, and we could hear stone scraping stone behind us. When we turned around, we could see six secret doors opening, three on each side, and two driders coming from behind each of them. Driders are creepy-looking creatures with the bottom half of spiders and the top half of dark cloud elves.

"Fresh blood," one said. "Thanks for trying to raid us guys. We're so sick of M.R.E.'s. The cheapskate wizard who runs this place never splurges for fresh vittles."

"Whoa there," I said, holding up my claws. "We're with the band."

My stall tactic didn't seem to sway them because they all held up their crossbows and fired at us all at once. I closed my eyes and braced for the piercing of the bolts, but all I heard was the clacking of bolts hitting the floor. "Great shield spell, Peavus," Maul remarked as he brushed by me, heading toward the driders.

The first two driders jaws dropped as they were not expecting us to live past their first assault. They were not prepared for the headache Maul gave them as he smashed their brains out with Mable. Talk about a mind-opening experience! I took out the third one with my iron spear, and Rhody slid under one with his dagger and impaled it from underneath. "Argh!" the dwarf yelled out as the guts from the creature's stomach gushed out all over him. "I'm going to reek of elvish guts!"

Ghasper was back through the door now and draining one of its life force while Peavus whipped out his lute and started shredding on some chords, which seemed to heighten our abilities. Peavus was an amazing bard and knew dozens of musical spells, so by the time he broke into his massive solo, the rest of the Driders had scrambled out through the supply room door and were gone.

"Phew," I laughed. "A fight like that brings back memories. We need to do this more often!"

"That's easy for you to say," Rhody said, wiping a drider spleen off his shoulder. "Even their blood is sticky!"

We took a moment to search around in the hidden drider rooms but didn't find much; mostly webs, bones, and some web mail, which were parchments left on their webs from their families. "Driders may be bloodthirsty killers," I told Peavus, as we poked around their stuff, "but they have beautiful handwriting."

Peavus nodded. "Their poetry is terrible though; look at this," he stated, handing me a letter he found.

The letters were calligraphic masterpieces, but he was right; the poetry stunk.

"*Here in my cavey wavey,*
 with eight long hairy leggies,
we share a feast under the moon
and chew the guts from what's cocooned."

"Uuunnnnnhhh," Ghasper moaned, shaking his head.

"Me write better than that," Maul stated. "And me terrible!"

"Can we move along, please," Rhody said, pointing to the sundial on his wrist. "We have a show in Skull Hollow tomorrow, and I'm going to need a shower before I set up the stage."

"I hope our gear is all right outside in the wagon," I said to Rhody, feeling worried.

"Don't worry, boss," the dwarf stated smugly. "I put a 'do not steal' sign on it so nobody should mess with it."

That had me feeling a little better, so we finished our search and started to head for the door at the end of the corridor. "Did you see anything through there, Ghasper?" I asked.

The ghost shook his head and groaned, so I figured the coast was clear.

When we went through it, we could see the corridor divided into two different directions. We studied the map for a minute and realized that except for the entrance and first couple of rooms, this map wasn't reliable at all. "What a swizz," I said, throwing the map to the floor. "If I see that Robert the Rogue, I'm going to strangle him!"

"Which way do we go?" Peavus asked.

"We should split up," Rhody stated before the rest stopped to stare at him like he was nuts.

"What?!" he said, looking frustrated with both of his hands up. "What did I say?"

"Never suggest a band splits up," I hissed. "It's bad mojo!"

Rhody frowned for a moment, rubbing his beard. "Oh, okay. How about we all move forward....but in different directions!"

"Mmm, yes," I replied, "that is more doable."

Before deciding who was going where a couple of slobgoblins appeared from around a corner down the corridor to our left, they looked shocked to see us at first, but we acted natural. "Hey, guys," I greeted them casually, "Wuz' up?"

They both set down the buckets they were carrying and put their hands on their very sharp-looking swords. "What are you doing here? And what's with the human?"

I noticed that the buckets they were carrying were filled with bloody guts. "We're here to see the boss about a job," I replied. "Umm…this human is our prisoner. What are you two doing."

The slobgoblins looked at each other and shrugged. "Got to feed the driders," one stated. "Belfry gets angry when we forget."

Then the one pointed to all his facial scars, "See."

"Those are from a Mind Slayer," Peavus whispered to me. "They are pretty powerful. Their tentacled mouths wrap around your head and destroy your mind. The singer of the last band I was in was the victim of one. He had the brain of a radish."

"That's not good," I whispered back. "Radishes are awful."

"How do we get to Belfry?" Rhody asked. "We're kind of late for our meeting."

"Go down that corridor, past the big green door and open the blue door," one explained. "Once in there, you'll talk to Belfry's secretary. She'll let him know you're here."

"What's behind the green door?" I asked.

"There's a trap door in the floor with a Jelly Cube in it," one replied while picking his buckets back up. "It's how we dispose of all the garbage."

We thanked the slobgoblins and headed down the corridor. We went past the green door, opened the blue one right after that, and walked in. We all stood in a 20' x 20' room decorated like the office of any business. A female orc with an under bite and horn-rimmed glasses sat behind a wooden desk, jotting down notes. I stepped up and asked, "We're here to see Belfry, my name is Scales, and this is my band, the Marshtones."

She opened a little booklet next to her and read through some things. "You're not on the schedule," she stated. "Would you like to make an appointment and come back later?"

Maul stepped up and showed her his fist, still covered with drider blood. "Here be our appointment!"

The secretary rolled her eyes and pushed his fist to the side before standing up. "Let me see what I can do," she said before exiting the room through a door next to her.

We all looked at each other and shrugged. We sat down in some chairs and breezed through some boring monthly scrolls about monster health or how to invest in the stock market (which I never do because I hate torture devices). After a short wait, the secretary came back into the room and stated, "Belfry will see you now."

I thanked her, and we all went through the door. The room we entered was just as large as the last; only this one had a few tables in it with two humans and an elf strapped onto them. The humans were dead, but the elf was still twitching as Belfry, the Mind Slayer, had his tentacled mouth over the poor slob's head.

Belfry stopped absorbing the elf's mind for a moment to say, "Hold on, guys, I'm just finishing lunch."

I clutched my spear and was just about to move forward when Peavus grabbed my arm. "Be careful, Scales. Mind Slayers are extremely powerful."

I looked at Maul, who also looked anxious to kill this brain devourer. "I hear you're a band," Belfry said after a burp.

He wiped his mouth with a napkin. "I heard you are here to play, or can I have you quilled in as my next scheduled meal?"

"We're here to play," I said, trying to think of something. "Do you like music?"

"I love it!" Belfry beamed. "I never get to go out anymore. Too much to do around here. Running a dungeon, feasting on brains, you know how it is."

"Sort of," I stated. "The Marshtones and I wander from dungeon to dungeon, entertaining others, hoping to gain fans and make a few coins."

"That's wonderful," Belfrey stated, pointing to a treasure chest behind him. "Because I just came into some money."

He looked at the three corpses on the table and belched again. I knew we had to play something quick, or we might end up on those tables later as well. "It just so happens that we wrote a song about a Mind

Slayer just like yourself," I told him while pulling out my lute. "It's called *Living with a Slayer*. It's about a time when I was down on my luck in Skull Hollow and desperately needed a roommate."

With that said, we started playing:

(Sung to the tune of Living on Prayer by Bon Jovi)
Could barely 'ford a new pair of socks
My shows had dried up
And we were stuck on the road
It's tough, so tough

A mind slayer seeks a mind for its prey
But Skull Hollows not the place
If you're hungry for the brains
It's true, so true

I said, "Hold on, I know we just met
But we're both having trouble just making the rent
If we room up together, we could save a lot
There must be a way to get out of this rut."

Whoa, it may sound weird
Whoa, rooming with a slayer
Don't take my mind, or I'll kill you, I swear
Whoa, rooming with a slayer!

My lute and its strings were in hock
Along with my band, we played the docks
And waited for our break
To get on the stage, up on the stage

The mind slayer dreamt of owning a cave
With a buffet of brains and drones to enslave
He'd gripe from the couch
Browsing want ads all-day

Now we'd mop floors and do dishes all-day

Whatever it takes to put some food on a plate
I hate the way he stares at me in that way
I just wish he hadn't slain his last five room mates

Whoa, I have to beware
Whoa, rooming with a slayer
Sometimes he gives me a headache, I swear
Whoa, rooming with a slayer
Rooming with a slayer!

During the song, Belfry was getting into the groove. He sang along and air luted along while thrashing his head up and down. He dropped to his knees during the last part, and raised his fist in the air as we held the finishing note. It was at this moment that I signaled to Ghasper, who quickly flew behind Belfry, then placed a hand on his shoulder.

The Mind Slayer shook as Ghaspers ghostly grasp started draining the life force from him, and then Peavus ran up and smashed his lute over Belfry's head, shattering the instrument to pieces! Maul happily followed up with a slap so hard I could hear bone crack. Belfry hit the floor in a shuddering heap. "Mind Slayers cute when sleeping," Maul remarked before throwing Belfry over his shoulder. "Now me take out trash!"

Peavus and Rhody grabbed the treasure chest then we walked back out into the secretary's office. "That's just great," she snarled, standing in front of us with her hands on her hips. "He was the first decent boss I've had in months. I've got mouths to feed, you know!"

I reached into the groaning Mind Slayers robe and took out a set of keys. "Here you go. You're the boss of this place now."

She smiled and shrugged before waving her fingers at Belfry, who was groggily blinking at her. "Ta ta!" she laughed.

We watched a few moments later as the Jelly Cube behind the green door slowly absorbed the now flailing Mind Slayer. Before we left the dungeon, we played a small show for the skeletons as we promised. They clacked along happily without a care in the world. Even the leftover Driders, and Slobgoblins showed up and joined in on the fun. None of them minded being rid of Belfry!

Entry 24

One time on the road, we got stuck opening for the band Sandbox Charlie & the Murder Hobos. It took us a few shows to realize that this group either had no idea what they were doing or didn't care. Their Tour Manager, or TM, would constantly come into our rehearsals and yell at them for not sticking to the tour plans he had laid out. The band would nod in agreement, then do whatever they wanted.

We never knew what show we'd be playing next, and half the time, the Murder Hobos lived up to their name by killing whatever creatures happened to be at the show that night. "You know, Charlie," I'd say. "The Marshtones and I try not to make it a habit of killing our fans after our gigs."

The crazed-looking human would smile at me and say, "You think killing the audience is wrong?"

"It's not good for repeat performances," I warned. "Not many come back to the show after they are dead. It's bad for ticket sales."

"Some do," Charlie stated, looking at me with bugged-out, crazy eyes. "But they are zombies, and that's when things go helter-skelter!"

We quit the tour a few shows after that. We had reached our limit when Charlie showed up with a peace sign tattooed in the middle of his forehead and suggested we do the same….or else. A few kind words and a severe beating from Maul helped Charlie change his mind and release us from our contract!

Entry 25

After a particularly rough night at the Fistacuff Tavern in Floptover. I wandered over to the garbage can by the front door and started digging through the trash. After finding what I was looking for, I went to the table where the rest of the band was relaxing. "Great news, guys," I began. "I found 24 of our business cards that had been thrown away."

"Why is that good news, Scales?" Peavus said. "People always throw away our cards, and then you recollect them. That's nothing new."

Maul grunted, and Ghasper groaned in agreement. "That's right," I began. "But earlier tonight, I had set 28 cards on our merch table. That's means at least four people took them home!"

Everyone cheered and high-fived before turning to Rhody, who had just walked up to the table. "I'm glad to see everyone in such a happy mood," he grumped while cautiously lowering himself onto a chair.

"What's the matter with you, Rhody?" Peavus asked.

"Paper cuts," he replied. "The bathroom ran out of paper, so I grabbed a handful of our business cards. We need to invest in a softer, more absorbent, paper stock!"

Entry 26

The greatest thing about warmer weather in the Unremembered Realms is that we get to play our music outside. One of the best venues is wherever creatures all gather to take a dip, like a river. Maul calls these events "streaming" because they are by flowing water. There's nothing like cooling off in the water after a good show. I must admit, though, that not every music stream goes swimmingly. One time we were playing on a grassy knoll, under the shade of a large willow tree, performing for a small crowd who were dancing along with their feet in the sand.

We ended our short set with a real sing-a-longer, called *Teenage Lycanthropy*, which had the crowd chanting along.

> (Sung to the tune of Teenage Lobotomy by the Ramones)
> Lycanthropy! Lycanthropy! Lycanthropy! Lycanthropy!
> An ugly beast put the bite on me
> Now I am a were-wolfie
> Guess I'll have to just get used
> To eating flesh and chewing shoes
> All my friends are covered in fleas
> I'm a teenage lycanthropy
>
> Silver really does a job on me
> Got fur but still pimp-ul-y
> Attacking villagers when I smell em'
> Fetchin' sticks when someone throws em'
> Gonna tinkle on a tree

I'm a teenage lycanthropy!

One listener in the crowd stood out more than the rest. It appeared to be a skinny halfling wearing a fake beard. I guess he could have passed as a small dwarf, but the bare hairy feet had me thinking otherwise. "That's our set," I said after the clapping died out. "Any tips are appreciated. It was great to be here in the city of Blinkfizzle!"

After collecting some of the coins, buttons, and leftover foods thrown in front of us, we decided to wet our feet in the stream. "I don't know how you can eat other people's leftovers," I said to Maul. "That's just wrong."

"What?" he replied, tossing a soggy half-eaten sandwich into his mouth. "Me washed it first!"

I just shook my head, trying to get the thought of that weird-looking dwarf out of my mind. It sure smelled like a halfling. I've never had my mouth water over a dwarf before; just the thought of that grossed me out. "How'd we do, Peavus?"

Peavus usually kept the money. Ghasper didn't care about it, since he was already dead, Maul has trouble counting past four, and Rhody likes to gamble with it, then complain about cheating casinos. Me? I don't care about the money; I'm more about the applause. Peavus, being part wizard, keeps a stern eye on our budget, making sure we don't live above our means.

"Not bad," he replied cheerfully. "We got two gold, sixteen silvers, twenty coppers, a chewed-up button, and a rock with a smiley face painted on it."

"That's not bad," I told the gang. "Let's go get some lunch, then come back for another set. This music streaming is paying off!"

After a quick bite from our tour wagon, we walked back up the grassy knoll, only to find out that our instruments had been stolen! "Me Warshburn bass!" Maul hollered angrily. "Me will kill whoever took it!"

We ran around frantically, trying to see if we could find any clues. "Unnnnh!" Ghasper yelled out, pointing downstream. There, on a raft, was a group of dwarves, holding our instruments. With them, was the weird dwarf I had seen earlier. On the raft, was a flag with a dead willow tree on it. "Song pirates!" I shouted before giving chase with the rest of the band.

Song pirates were the bane of any musical act. They stole instruments, copied songs, and would sell them off to other groups, hoping to make a quick bit of gold. I must admit that I've almost bought a few songs from pirates, myself, but I fought the temptation and stuck to writing my own music. I have played covers, but it's always with permission from the other bards, themselves.

"Those aren't ordinary song pirates," Peavus huffed as we ran. "See their dead tree logo with the broken seed on it?"

"It looks like an evil eye," I replied.

"It's a bad seed that grew large and became an evil tree," he explained. "That's the Black Willow gang!"

I had heard of the Black Willow gang. They were known troublemakers and were tough. Even with Maul with us, I was beginning to think that getting our stuff back would not be easy.

"I don't think we're going to catch up with them," Rhody huffed and puffed. "The current is too fast."

"I can fix that," Peavus claimed as he reached into his long beach shorts and pulled out a small vial of glowing blue powder.

"You bring spell components in your swimming clothes?" I asked, amazed.

Peavus just grinned at me, then turned to face the fleeing raft. With a few mumbles and a toss of the powder, a white cone of snow appeared around the raft, freezing the water and locking it into place. Maul laughed while punching the open palm of one hand with his fist. "Me go smash them!"

By the time we caught up, the dwarven gang was still trying to smash holes in the ice in an attempt to break themselves free. "Hold it right there, music thieves," I said as we approached the edge of the now frozen water. "Those are our instruments!"

A stocky, balding dwarf with a squint looked at me smugly. He smacked his hand with a leather riding crop as he stepped forward. "We're not thieves," he began. "We found these abandoned on the side of the stream. Finders keepers, ya' know."

"You tell him, Quade," a handsome-looking muscular dwarf chimed in.

"Shut up, Chook," he spat before returning his gaze to us. "However, we're fair. We're willing to sell these gorgeous instruments back to you at a fair price."

"What?!" Maul erupted. "Me want to hold bald one's head underwater!"

"But the water's frozen," I replied.

"Me smash his skull through first," Maul explained. "Me not dumb, you know."

With that said, Maul began to step forward. Then, with a groan, the burly half-ogre sank to one knee. "Unh!" he cried out, sweat forming on his brow. "What be happening…poison?"

Quade laughed as the suspicious-looking dwarf with a fake beard stepped forward, holding an empty bottle of Flying Bull, a magical energy drink that was also a powerful laxative. "Good work, Skole," Quade laughed before shouting at Maul. "Didn't anybody teach you not to eat other people's food left on the beach?"

Maul quickly stood up and looked around. He spotted a patch of bushes and ran as fast as he could while shouting. "Get me Warshburn.... and soft tissue!"

I shook my head and turned back to Quade, who just stood there with his arms crossed. "You think Maul is all we have? Hey Ghasper, give the little guy a hand…."

Ghasper immediately floated over the stream and almost reached Quade. As he held out a hand to drain the dwarf of some life energy, a dwarf in a horned helmet stepped in between them, holding up a tuning symbol in the shape of their Black Willow logo. Our drummer placed his hands over his eyes and floated back, groaning. "Great work, Pacoyma," Quade laughed before looking back at me. "Now, will you pay up?"

"Listen here," I began to say, then Peavus stepped over to me and whispered in my ear.

I nodded in approval of his suggestion. "Okay, Mr. Quade," I began. "We hardly have any money; that's why we were here playing for tips. So, if it would be okay with you, we'd like to sing something to entertain you to earn our instruments back."

Quade smirked for a moment, then signaled for his gang to huddle around him. They murmured for a few seconds, then fell back to their defensive positions. "Okay, lizardman," the dwarf stated. "But you'll have to sing it acapella. And no funny business or you'll face the wrath of the Black Willow gang!"

"You sure this will work?" I whispered to Peavus, as he and Ghasper both gathered around me.

"Sure thing," he said under his breath. "I incorporated a Slumber spell into the lyrics, for emergencies like this"

"You birds better start to sing," yelled Quade. "This ice isn't going to last forever."

We could hear the noises from Maul over in the bushes and knew this would be our only shot. So, I did four finger snaps to set the pace, and we started to sing our song, Mr. Sandgolem.

(Sung to the tune of Mr. Sandman by The Chordettes)
Mr. Sandgolem, made by the stream (bung, bung, bung, bung)
Made by a wizard with an evil dream (bung, bung, bung, bung)
Then it picked tulips, some roses, and clover (bung, bung, bung, bung)
The wizard screamed, my career is over!
Sandgolem, nobody knows (bung, bung, bung, bung)
Your magic power to make people doze (bung, bung, bung, bung)
Please turn on your magic beam
Mr. Sandgolem, give them a dream

Mr. Sandgolem, give them a dream
You're not like the other golems that I have seen
You may look like a sand dune rover
They'll wet their beds before the night is over

As the three of us were harmonizing, I could see that the song spell was having an effect. All the seven dwarves were getting sleepy. Some of their eyelids were drooping, and they were all yawning. So, we kept going.

Sandgolem, they'll have no clue
It's off to dreamland, off they will scoot
Please turn on your magic beam
Mr. Sandgolem, give them a dream
Mr. Sandgolem, (yes) give them a dream
Make their eyes droop and their mouth dribble
Til' it flows down and forms a puddle

Mr. Sandgolem, it's now time to go (time to go)
Back to the beachy before we're too old

So please turn on your magic beam
Mr. Sandgolem, give them, please, please, please
Mr. Sandgolem, give them a dream

As we finished the song, we heard the dwarves slumping over from where they stood. "Whoa, Peavus," I said quietly. "It worked!"

Peavus laughed and we all walked across the ice to grabbed our gear. Then, we dragged the dwarves who were on the ice and placed them on the raft. "They're going to be out for a while," Peavus stated. "You know, we could have a little fun here."

"I'm listening," I replied.

Peavus found his travel pack that the dwarves had grabbed, reached in, and grabbed his shaving razor. Peavus held it up with a grin. "What do you say we shave off their eyebrows," he chuckled.

Twenty minutes later, we stood on the edge of the stream as the raft broke free of the now melting ice. We all watched as the dwarves floated downstream to whatever eyebrow-less future awaited them. "They're not going to be pleased when they wake up," Peavus stated, smiling.

"I don't know why," I said. "I don't have any eyebrows, and it doesn't bother me."

Entry 27

The first time I ever met Maul Chaffer was at a carnival in Dockport. The half-ogre had set up a booth with the word 'SLAPS' painted on a sign over the booth's counter. It also had the words 10 Copper Pieces with a red stripe over it, crossing it out. Next to that was written two copper pieces. That, too, had been crossed out; the only word left uncrossed was freshly painted in blood. It said FREE.

Peavus and I only walked up because the booth had no customers, and the big guy was looking sad and playing a washtub bass. "He's pretty good, Scales," Peavus said to me. "We are looking for a bass player for our band."

I tapped my claw on my chin for a second. "He's awfully big," I replied. "He might scare off customers."

"Or hecklers," Peavus shrugged.

"Hecklers are half our audience at this point," I reminded Peavus. "I wonder if he can sing?"

We walked up to the booth and Maul stood up, cracking his knuckles. "Finally," he said. "Got me some customers!"

"No, no," I said, holding up my claws. "We're not here for the slaps. We heard you playing and noticed that you've got some musical talent."

"Music keep me calm," he stated matter-of-factly. "That and giving slaps."

"Would you be interested in becoming a Marshtone?" Peavus asked.

"What a Marshtone?" he asked.

"We're a band," Peavus stated. "Scales is the singer, and the Marshtones are his backup."

"Me no bard," Maul said. "Me a fighter."

"I'm a former wizard," Peavus replied. "But I'm learning the ways of the bard."

"Yeah," I agreed. "It sounds to me like you're a natural."

The half-ogre scratched his head for a moment. "Me tempted."

"Can you sing?" I asked.

A big grin grew on the monster's face, revealing his short bottom fangs. "Oh, boy, can me," he said.

Maul jumped out of the booth, grabbed a passing druid, and started slapping him senseless while singing at the same time. "You know," Peavus said to me. "If he can sing like that while slapping the strings of his washtub bass, I think we have our next member!"

We both gave Maul the thumbs up, and he dropped the discombobulated druid and shook our hands, being careful not to crush them. "We can't pay much now, but I'm sure we'll be the next big thing," I said.

"Me don't mind," Maul replied. "As long as there be an audience to slap."

Entry 28

Down on the coastline of the province of Dragonshelm lives a community of ogres called Ogaville. These violent creatures kill and eat anything that wanders in, most of the time, but because Maul was with us, they let us come and go as we please. For the most part, they live normal, happy lives, that is, when not ripping people limb-from-limb. So, as usual, we play music at their gatherings in which we've grown quite popular.

Maul's favorite part of visiting there is picking up the latest copy of the fan scroll Ogateen Beat, which features all the village celebrities. Teen ogres go crazy over this and usually pin the drawings of Maul up on their bedroom walls. During interviews, the reporters ignore the rest of us and focus on our half-ogre bassist. To my surprise, even though he does like the attention, Maul doesn't like playing Ogaville very much. I asked him why one time, and he leaned over and whispered, "Is it just me, or do you find ogres kind of ugly, too?"

Entry 29

One of my favorite bands is the Traveling Elderburys. The group is made up of five elderly bards who have joined together to form what I consider to be a super group. But, as great as they are, they don't stay the same band for very long. The Elderburys change members often because one or more of them tend to kick the proverbial drum kit, if you know what I mean.

Sure, it's sad, but secretly it's every bard's dream to one day be a replacement member of the band, even if it's just for one final tour of the realms. I hope to one day join the Elderburys, then molt away into oblivion, peacefully, of course.

Entry 30

Living on the road isn't easy, especially when you have to share the tour wagon with an eclectic group like ours. There's a violent half-ogre, a human with lots of wardrobe accessories, like magical platform shoes, a grumpy dwarf who snores (even when he's awake), a ghost who's always groaning about something, and our pet cat named Ziljan, who refuses to share his mice.

Our horses, Haul and Oats, seem to be of a positive disposition. We hardly hear a neigh out of them. The duo will haul us from province to province, city to city, and then there and back, again.

The wagon we have is a used beater that we got from Crazy Barmey's Discount Wagons. It is a patchwork of repairs that has managed to hold together over the years. Its creaks and groans remind us of our audiences at some places. The noises it makes have grown louder over the last couple of years, significantly after we added the equipment cart, which is attached via the hitch on the back. We'll probably never get rid of our beloved jalopy, though, because of the cool spell that was placed on it by a couple of wizards who were hitchhiking to Neverspring.

The old humans were so thankful that they cast a Time and Relative Dimension Inside Spell, or something like that, but it made the wagon huge on the inside. I don't understand how it works, but it's wonderful having a bedroom to yourself inside this mysterious and magical tour wagon. From the outside, it appears normal, but inside, it's got corridors and two separate floors with a staircase! The downside is that, because it's a bachelor pad, it can sometimes be a bit whiffy, especially in Maul's area.

One of the nice things we have is Ghasper. The ghost hardly sleeps in his urn and doesn't mind hanging out looking after the wagon while we sleep at night. I highly recommend keeping a dead person in your traveling party. His favorite thing is to rise from the floorboards whenever thieves try to wagon jack us by removing the lock bar we keep on the steering bridle. We always hear Rhody complain when he has to clean the puddles on the seats after Ghasper scares off a burglary attempt.

Entry 31

One night, we were booked to play a show in Port Laudervale. It was during Springtime Break, so we knew we'd have a lively young audience that would be filled with enthusiasm. The downside was that it was at the Brown Cushion Tavern, so they would also be filled with their famous gut-bomb chili. We took the stage that night to cheers and belches.

"Good evening, ladies and gents, welcome to the Brown Cushion Tavern," I began. "We're hoping you have a blast tonight!"

"I hope not," a chubby young dwarf shouted. "I didn't bring a change of pants!"

The crowd broke out into laughs, but I ignored them. "You know folks, when the Marshtones and I were invited to play here; I had heard it was going to be a gas. But what do you expect from a place that specializes in chili? But seriously, folks, expect tonight to be full of surprises, and speaking of surprises, here's a little song about a group of adventurers who decided to plunder the cave of a group of slobgoblins. It started well, because the messy beasts weren't even home, but it turned out to be a bust, because the place was a dump! An underachieving den mother ran it. I dedicate this number to her, wherever Mrs. Slobgoblin is now...."

(Sung to the tune of Mrs. Robinson by Simon & Garfunkel)
And here's to you, Mrs. Slobgoblin
Did you teach your husband how to ba
Oh, won't you please, Mrs. Slobgoblin
Teach them how to use armpit spray? Hey hey hey
Hey hey hey

We stalked your camp and thought we'd raid it for a while
Even though it smells of sweaty shorts and gut cakes
We glanced around, knocking over huge trash piles
Old coffee grounds, twice used underwear, and feet

So here's a broom, Mrs. Slobgoblin
Walking around your caverns is such a trip, woe woe woe
Oh, won't you please, Mrs. Slobgoblin
Who puts used hankies on display? Hey hey hey
Hey hey hey

Living in a place where no one would want to go
Don't ever let them offer you a cupcake
That's not frosting, sir, with a sprouting goblin hair
It's such a mess; you can't even find your kids

PU, PU, Mrs. Slobgoblin
Is this some new funky type of mold? woe woe woe
Or did you sneeze, Mrs. Slobgoblin
Is that a stalactite dripping from your nose? Hey hey hey

Hey hey hey

Sitting on a sofa in some heart-print boxer shorts
We sneak right by you on this raid
Scream about it, shout about it
When we step into some goo
Holding back our retching as we scrape it off our shoes

Where have you put all the hand soap?
Our party runs and out the door from you, woo woo woo
What's that you say, Mrs. Slobgoblin
No one ever wants to stay, Hey hey hey
Bring some spray.

The song ended with people dancing in a line in front of the restroom doors. "You see, Peavus," I said. "This audience appreciates our music! They can't sit down!"

"You stink," someone shouted.

I started to feel insulted, but I realized that they weren't talking to me, but other people at their table. "Don't sweat it," Peavus said. "I guess that's a common phrase here at the Brown Cushion."

"Maybe we should go to the next song to take their minds off the effects of the chili," I said. "I have an idea!"

I whispered to the band what I wanted to play next. Peavus looked confused. "Isn't that like stomping on someone's toe when they have a headache?"

"That's the point," I explained. "The pain in their foot takes their mind off their headache!"

Maul nodded. "Me like stomping toes," he stated, "and heads!"

With that said, we broke into an old classic called *Druidic Aroma*.

(Sung to the tune of Winchester Cathedral by Frank Sinatra/
New Vaudville Band)
Oooh, Druidic Aroma, you're filling the room
You stood, and you watched as my baby left town
You could have washed somethin', hey, you didn't try
You're just like peeling an onion; you leave tears in our eyes

Not exactly roses, our lunch isn't sitting so well
You should have gone far away, but instead, you're bringing your smell

Druidic aroma, you're thick as a cloud
You should be ashamed, but instead, you're proud

Hey, druidic aroma, you're clearing the town.
And whenever you stroll by, everyone seems to fall down
It's making my eyes burn; it's even killing the flies
It's just like your trousers; nostrils flare when you walk by

I found a pin for clothes; I'm wearing it over my nose
We're hoping you go far away, to a place that nobody knows

Now, druidic aroma, man, you've brought me down.
You just stood there emanating and clearing the crowd!

At the end of the song, I had to duck a tomato. It sailed over my head and went clean through Ghasper, who just stuck out his tongue at the throwers. It was a couple of druids. "Great shot, Jinglemilk," one laughed. "You got their bongo player!"

"Thanks, Flipflop," the other one replied. "Now, let's get stepping. That half-ogre isn't looking too happy!"

"Copacetic!" shouted Jinglemilk, as they ran for the door with Maul in hot pursuit.

While waiting for the frustrated half-ogre to return, I spotted a group of halflings sitting around a table. My mouth started watering, but I took a deep breath and decided to banter with them.

"Hey, what do we have here?" I began. "Are you the app... uh, I mean, are you enjoying the appetizers?"

"We're on our lunch break," one squeaked. "It feels good to come in and blow off some steam."

"Sounds like you got a lousy job," I said before turning to the rest of the audience. "You know, I knew a group of halflings just like these guys here. Some old wizard hired them to go on a long, plodding journey. They ended up quitting because of all the walking they had to go through, then finding out giant birds could have flown them the entire time. I even wrote a song about what they told me. It's called *Take This Ring and Shove It!*"

(Sung to the tune of Take This Job and Shove it by Johnny Paycheck)
Take this ring and shove it
I ain't walking for you no more
I should have known something was up when I heard you knew
The spell Dimensional Door
Ya better not try to stand in my way
You no good teleport-or
Take this ring and shove it
I ain't walking for you no more

I've been living peacefully in my hole
For nigh on sixty years
Now me and my friends are
Hiding in the woods and feeling totally scared
And I've seen a lot of good folks die
Because of the wraiths
I'd give the tunic off of my back
If I had the guts to say

Take this ring and shove it
I ain't walking for you no more
I should have known something was up when I heard you knew
The spell Dimensional Door
Ya better not try to stand in my way
Shouting, I shall not pass more
Take this ring and shove it
I ain't walking for you no more

The rebellious nature of the song got us a hearty round of applause. "Thank you, thank you," I waved. "It's nice to get a little applause, especially from halflings, who (smacks lips) are a personal favorite of mine."

Peavus knew where this was headed and said, "Calm down, Scales."

I knew our wizard was right, so I splashed a cup of water on my face and changed the subject. "Yes, yes, you're right. So hey, let's take a look at the others here tonight. Hey, who is this? Do you mind if I stroll on down to your table?"

"Um...I'm trying to pick up this lady," the human male growled. "You've just interrupted my best pick-up line!"

"No, you didn't," the pretty female elf responded, rolling her eyes.

"Oh, I'm sorry," I replied. "Here, you go right on ahead while the rest of us watch."

The room fell stone quiet, and Peavus cast a Spotlight spell on the duo. "I can't, now!" the guy yelled out. "Now I'm all nervous, thanks to you!"

"Go on," I said. "Hey, everybody, think about other stuff while this man hits on this poor elf."

The man pulled at his collar and began to sweat while the elf just glared at him with her arms crossed. "Um, uh," he started as we all leaned closer. "Do you know what's on the menu? Baby, it's um, me-N-U!"

The crowd let out a collective groan a moment before the elf gal smashed her bowl of chili in the guy's face and stormed off. Cheers arose, and even the Marshtones and I gave a round of applause. "You know," I said to the audience. "This reminds me of another loser that I just so happened to write a song about; it's called *She Blinded Me with Blindness*!"

(Sung to the tune of She Blinded Me with Science by Thomas Dolby)
It caused a really big commotion
When she turned me down, you see
I used all of my best lines
Which she claimed were all cheesy
then she blinded me with Blindness
(She blinded me with blindness!)
A spell that's used in sorcery, hey-ey, huh, huh.

When I strolled into the tav'
(Blinded me with blindness, blindness)
(blindness!)
I was impressed with her beauty
(Blinding me with blindness, blindness)
(Blindness!)
(Blindness!)

When I used a cantrip on my breath
She replied she'd rather face death
After my wink, she slapped my face
And sprayed my eyes with her magic mace
She blinded me with blindness
(She blinded me with blindness!)
Flailed me, causing injuries

Good heavens, Miss Clerica - you're beautiful!

I...
I don't believe it!
Here I go again!
But she cast another spell, and I can't see anything!
Both my peeps are on fire
And my pupil yolks
And my romantical intentions

Then I stumbled to an alley
When she took my sight from me
Now to find my cleric
And have my sight restored to me
Because he happens to have Cure Blindness
(He cured me of my blindness, blindness!)
He cured me from....blindness!

After a decent round of applause, we decided to end it on a high note. To be honest, we had to quickly depart, because the guy with chili all over him turned out to be a local constable, and he had left in shame, but came back in with a few of his deputies. We made it out the back door just before they reached the stage. The rest of the night had its ups and downs, and by that, I mean visits to the outhouse after eating our complimentary doggie bags from the Brown Cushion!

Entry 32

Something strange was happening at the last few of our concerts. The places were packed, and with every curtain opening, there would be tremendous applause. Then, as we stepped on stage to play, the enthusiasm would die out. Next, to make matters worse, the audience would start throwing things! These strange occurrences happened at the Dubbledover Tavern, the Moonring Tavern, and finally at the Fish Udder Tavern in Humderum.

We eventually figured out the problem when the crowd at the Fish Udder kept chanting, "We want the Marshtunes! We want the Marshtunes!"

Puzzled, the band and I began to ask around, but no one would talk to us after our shows. But then we found a poster that had been torn in pieces and discarded under a table. I carefully put the bits back together. "It's one of the tour posters we ordered," Peavus said. "I'm glad to see the company we bought them from got them distributed."

"Wait a minute," I exclaimed. "The printer got our names wrong! We're not Snails & the Marshtunes!"

"The writing is all redundant on it, too," Peavus stated. "It's like some mixed-up version of common. 'Come look and see the greatest best musical band in the area land!', this is terribly written!"

"Unnnh!" Ghasper groaned, pointing at the drawing of the band in the center.

"You're right," I said, horrified. "That sketch is not even us! It's a quartet of humans!"

"Handsome humans," an elven waitress commented as she began clearing the table and winking at Peavus. "Too bad only one of them only showed up tonight."

Maul slammed his fist on the table. "Me furious! Let's slap idiots who did this!"

"No wonder people were acting weird," I said. "They were expecting something else. I don't understand why they were disappointed, though; humans are so ugly. No offense, Peavus."

"None taken," Peavus replied, flashing his non-fanged white teeth back at the waitress.

"Let's go to Achincorn, where we ordered these, and find out what went wrong," I stated.

A few days later, we arrived at the Max Most Copy Shoppe in Achincorn, and went in to issue our complaint. We were told to wait at the counter while the secretary, a female gnome with extremely thick glasses, shuffled off to find her boss. Five minutes later, an unshaven gnome appeared, carrying a nearly worn-out writing quill and covered with ink stains. "Can I help assist you?" he stated.

I read the name tag pinned sloppily on his shirt, it read Max Most, so it was safe to assume this was the owner. "It's this," I said, un-scrolling the flyer in front of him.

"This looks top-notch great," he observed. "I think I worked on this one myself. Is there a troubling problem?"

"For one," I stated. "All the words on this are redundant; it repeats itself using different words!"

The gnome scratched his chin, "It seems fittingly appropriate to me."

"You spelled our name wrong, too. "We not the Marshtunes, we the Marshtones!" Maul quipped.

"I'm Scales, not Snails," I chimed in. "I hate it when people call me that."

"You must have misspelled it wrong incorrectly," Max said. "You should pay better mindful attention!"

"We didn't write it down," Peavus stated, with his arms crossed. "Your secretary did!"

We all looked over and saw she was writing notes. The secretary's face was so close to the paper that her nose nearly touched it. When she heard that she was being mentioned, she looked up at us. Her eyes blinked at us through the thick lenses, which made them look as big as saucers.

"Did you write down their order, Miss Prince?" the gnome asked.

"A white border? Did you mention say white border?" she said, reaching for a vial of white ink.

"You'll have to pardon excuse, Miss Prince," Max explained. "She's a wee small hard of hearing."

We were all frustrated at that point. Even Ghasper was pulling at his ethereal hair and groaning.

"Listen," I said, biting my forked tongue in frustration. "You didn't even get our picture right. Only Peavus looks anything like the band you have on this poster!"

"Hmmm..." Max said. "Let me fetch beckon our drawing artist."

After he disappeared in the back, Peavus turned to me and said, "I'm beginning to regret ordering the posters here. But they were so much cheaper than the place down the street."

"You mean Ditto Doppelgangers Copy Palace?" I asked.

"Yeah," Peavus said. "They were double the price...and the doppelganger who runs it kept trying to eat me."

Max reemerged with a young female gnome who was covered in ink, as well. She immediately stared at Peavus in awe. "This is Xerocks," Max stated. "She did the sketch drawing."

"I remember recall him," she said, smiling at Peavus with goo-goo eyes. "Isn't he good-lookingly handsome!"

Peavus smiled at her and gave her a wink. "But what about the rest of us? You drew the rest of us wrong! None of us are human!" I raised my voice in anger.

"You're in the music band?" she questioned, never taking her eyes from our musical mage. "I think thought you were entourage...."

"Me can't handle cope with all this redundancy!" Maul cried out, lifting Mable, his war hammer. "Aahh! Now me doing it!"

Maul ran out of the shop with Ghasper floating after him, trying to console the frustrated bassist.

In the end, Max swore he'd remedy the problem and get the new flyers put up all over the realms within the week. I want to say everything worked out well, but after the next disappointing gig, we found one of the new flyers that read. "Smales & The Marchtones. The in-person live show with hearable listening sounds!"

Entry 33

I want to say that the music business is all peace, love, and harmony, but sadly, this is not the case. There is a dark part of the music business that is in every facet of the industry. Once we had gone to the big city of Neverspring to visit Humbuckler's Music & Armory to pick up some strings. It was located next to the Gallowman Temple, so Ghasper stayed in the tour wagon to avoid being seen by the clerics, who were going in and out next door. I always felt bad for Ghasper, all he wanted was to play music and chill out, but even good clerics were skeptics of his intentions.

Once inside the music store, we were greeted by Humbuckler, the dwarven owner. "Scales, Peavus, and Maul! Come on in, boys!"

The dwarf was always happy to see us; we spent a lot of gold there. We'd buy strings, picks, new lutes (after wild shows), and even shields (due to unhappy fans or just violent environments). "What can I get you today?" he smiled.

"Maul needs strings, again," I commented while the half-ogre placed his beloved Warshburn bass on the counter.

"Make it slappy," Maul grinned; it was his favorite joke.

"That joke never gets old," Humbuckler always replied, taking the instrument behind the counter.

"That why me always repeat it," Maul said cheerfully.

I never knew if the dwarf was being truthful about that or just saying it because Maul was huge and scary. "Mind if we play around a bit?" I asked.

"Enjoy yourselves," Humbuckler replied before grabbing a copy of Scrolling Stone and handing it to Maul. "And I can assume you'll be needing this?"

Maul smiled, took the scroll, and headed out the door to the outhouse, which was his favorite way to make some music of his own, as he puts it. In the meantime, Peavus and I found enjoyment fiddling with the more expensive lutes that hung along the walls. We didn't get to play for long before a familiar couple of creepy-looking humans walked in and banged on the counter.

One was thin, oily skinned, and hooded, while the other was large, pale, and had a lot of facial scars. The smaller one banged on the counter bell impatiently until Humbuckler timidly appeared from the back. "Can I help you, Apichat?" the graying dwarf asked.

"You know what we're here for, Hummy," the one called Apichat sneered. "The protection money isn't going to collect itself!"

"Yes, yes," Humbuckler replied. "Make sure to tell Mr. Elfalfuh that I give my best."

Peavus and I stopped playing and looked at each other. We knew about Elfalfuh, the huge Elven Crime Boss from Neverspring. The mafioso had his hands in everything and was not to be trifled with. "What are you two looking at?" the larger of the two said menacingly, noticing us.

I was glad neither of them seemed to remember kidnapping me for the Battle of the Bards, I guess all lizardmen looked alike to them. I held up my claws to show we were not looking for trouble. Then, the larger one turned back to help his partner collect the extortion money. Poor Humbuckler shook nervously as he set sacks of coins on the counter. "Another nice haul, eh Onquay?"

The smiles on the two of their faces didn't last long, as a hand wrapped around each of their throats from behind them. Maul did not look happy. "Robbing me friend?" he asked, in an angry tone.

Peavus buried his face in his hands, and I waved both my claws in the air, trying to signal for him to stop. "Wait! Maul! They are not simple robbers!"

"You're opening a big box of worms," Apichat managed to gasp out while trying to peel back one of Maul's fingers.

Maul laughed. "Me eat worms for breakfast!"

"He's right, you know," I said. "Literally. Every day."

Onquay, being the bigger of the two, managed to hit Maul in the face with his fist a couple of times, which made Maul smile. He raised the pair off the ground and smashed their heads together before letting them fall onto the floor in an unconscious heap. Our mouths hung open as he grabbed each one of their feet and started dragging them outside. "Me take out trash," Maul said before whistling out the door.

Humbuckler was smiling ear-to-ear. "That was amazing!"

"They got off easy," Peavus stated. "Maul must be in a good mood today."

"We didn't mean to cause any trouble," I said.

The dwarf shook his head, "That's okay; I've been looking forward to those two thugs getting their comeuppance. Tell Maul his new strings are on the house, for life!"

"Aren't you afraid of Elfalfuh's wrath?" I asked, knowing this wouldn't be the last of it.

"I make a lot of money," Humbuckler explained. "He'll be around for more, and he's not going to kill the golden goose. You guys, on the other hand, will probably be added on to one of his lists."

Peavus and I looked at each other and gulped. Later, word on that street was that Elfalfuh was furious about what Maul did to his crew. Rumor had it that he used his influence to make sure we were stuck playing only the dive taverns in Neverspring. But the joke was on him because our agent, Colonel Crom, only booked us in those anyway.

Entry 34

One benefit to being a lizardman is that you never run out of picks for your instruments. I'm molting most times of the year and can peel off a scale or two when needed. This ability comes in handy when Peavus or I bust a pick during a lively song. We've both learned that you have to be careful, though, my dried-up scales can be sharp. Peavus threw one to an excited fan, once, and it stuck in their forehead!

Entry 35

The band and I were excited about playing the Oozapalooza, a monster jam festival just south of the city of Brokenpoor. Being mostly made up of what humans call "monsters", we fit the bill perfectly. That is one of the cool things about being musicians in the Unremembered Realms; we get into places that most others can't without a fight. I've often said that even monsters enjoy entertainment, that is, beyond eating, killing, and torturing others.

Oozapalooza was a festival that began a few years back when an evil wizard named Peatree was trying to take over the city of Brokenpoor and needed some gold to raise money for various oozes and slimes to help fortify his dungeon.

The Marshtones and I were in Brokenpoor picking up some bargain rate goods at Dayold's Supply Shoppe when we heard yelling out on the street. As we walked out of the store to load our tour wagon, we saw four humans on the sidewalk outside a small temple. One human cleric was yelling at the three others, then, in one quick motion, slapped all of their faces. As they stumbled back, the one who had done the slapping yelled, "You're fired! Don't ever come back!"

I watched the trio of clerics stumble over each other, trying to get back up. When they did, the one with a bowl haircut pulled on another one's red hair, slapped him, then poked the fatter balding one in the eyes with two fingers. "Me like that guy," Maul commented after watching the slap. "Him got skills."

We all nodded in agreement and then got back to work. It was a hot day, and we were all sweating as we loaded more supplies into the wagon. "I wish Rhody wasn't on vacation," I complained. "These hands are made for strumming, not hauling!"

"Did you say you could use some help, mister?" a voice spoke out. "Because we could use a job!"

It was the three clerics from across the street. They had made their way over to us rather quickly. The one with the bowl haircut hobbled because of a bandage on his foot, and was their spokesman. "I thought you guys were clerics, not roadies," I stated, looking at their clerical garb.

"Not really," the leader answered as all three pulled off their robes, revealing regular clothes underneath. "But we'll do anything to make a few coins for some grub."

"What happened to your foot?" I asked. "I thought clerics could heal people."

The one with the bowl cut shot the fat, bald one a dirty look, "Yeah, they are supposed to heal people. Isn't that right, Coily?"

"It was an accident, Mull, I swear," Coily chuckled nervously, waving his fingers at Mull, who then slapped him.

"Me want to hire him," Maul stated. "Me like his name, too."

"Mull, this is Maul," I said, introducing them. "I guess you're hired."

"That's great news, mister; we won't let you down. By the way, this is Coily, and this pudding brain is Clarence Elfine."

"You can call me Clarey," the red-headed one spoke.

"Speaking of pudding," I said. "We're going to play Oozapalooza. Do you have a problem working around a bunch of monsters?"

"Gold is gold, boss," Mull said happily. "When do we start?"

"Now would be good," I replied. "Can you load these boxes?"

Mull stood up straight and raised his arm, giving me a salute. His elbow hit Coily in the eye, and he fell on his rump on top of one of our boxes, smashing it. "Look what you did, numskull," Mull growled, lifting his bald companion by the ear.

"Sorry, Mull," Coily replied. "I was a victim of circumstance!"

"Take the damages out of his cut of the pay," Mull said, apologizing to us. "This type of thing usually doesn't happen."

Once the three clumsy humans finished loading our supplies, we hit the road. We reached Oozapalooza after a couple of hours and were amazed at the size of the event. Hundreds and hundreds of creatures of every size and shape were milling about, buying merch, refreshments, and waiting in line for autographs from the bands. Some of the biggest names were there, too, along with up and comers. There were the Mighty, Mighty Mosstones, Boots Springleak, Red Hot Chili Powder, and even the aging Black Sackcloth, just to name a few. I nearly fainted when I spotted Mana Turner, one of my favorite singers, waving to the crowd.

Maul guided our horses, Haul and Oats, to the main gate where we picked up our passes. They pointed us backstage, where we immediately went to unload our gear. "This is it, boys," I cheerfully told the band. "Let's get started!"

Clarey, Coily, and Mull tripped over each other while trying to climb out of the back of the wagon and landed in a pile on top of each other. "My bones!" Mull shouted from underneath, "You're breaking my bones!"

"Sorry, Mull," Clarey said, awkwardly climbing off, accidentally pushing away with his foot which happened to be on Mull's face.

"I'm going to moida you," Mull muttered.

"I need you guys to get these magical amplifying boxes up onto the stage," I told our new hires.

We were scheduled for two songs after the married couple of evil clerics known as Leeches and Herbs. The band and I tuned our instruments offstage while listening to the clerics sing their most famous song, *Reanimated*.

(Sung to the tune of Reunited by Peaches & Herb)
I was at your funeral and noticed you died
You were crispy from being fried
That fire spell had taken you from me
Then I realized that I could have you back, hey, hey.

I spent the evening robbing your grave
Dragged you back to a nearby cave

With some components and magic words
Now you're back walking the earth, hey, hey

Reanimated, and it feels so good
Reanimated 'cause we understood
You can only live twice
And, sugar, your touch is like ice
We both are so excited 'cause we're reanimated, hey, hey.

Coily and Clarey got into the song, started dancing together, and circled out into the audience's view. The crowd started laughing at their antics, which made Leeches and Herbs catch sight of them, and they didn't look happy at the disruption of their emotional ballad. "You better get out there, Mull," I warned. "I heard those clerics are powerful. Their encore might spell trouble for your pals."

Mull, looking determined, pulled his belt up and marched out. But as Coily and Clarey spun around in a waltzing motion, they struck Mull, and he stumbled backward into our amps, knocking one loose from the top. It fell and landed on his head, knocking him unconscious. Scared, the two stopped dancing and ran over to him. Coily waved his hand in front of Mull's face, who laid there with a dumb smile and his eyes crossed. "Mull! Wake up! Give me a couple of syllables!"

Mull woke up quickly, grabbed Coily's hand, and then used it to slap Clarey. "Why you split pea brains," he yelled. "Help me up!"

Coily barked like a dog at Mull and ran off the stage, causing a round of laughter from the audience. Clarey took a happy bow but screamed when Mull grabbed him by the hair to pull himself up. A clump of red hair fell from his hand before he chased Clarey off stage, as well. Moments later, Leeches & Herb stomped off the stage and passed us by, shooting us evil looks. I just shrugged back and grabbed my lute. It was time to hit the boards.

"Now, let's have a big round of applause, for Snails & The Marshtunes!" the emcee shouted out to the audience, who lightly applauded.

When I got to the amplifying wand, I corrected the blunder. "It's Scales & The Marshtones, folks, heh heh. We're from the Province of Sunkensod, straight out of Widowsmarsh! Hey, any fellow Marshians out there tonight?"

A few hands clapped, and we got a distant "woo." I was about to speak when we heard a loud crash from behind the stage. "Watch where you're putting all those sandbags!" Mull yelled before another crash sounded."

"Look what you did, Coily, you dope!" Clarey could be heard saying. "Let's find those two clerics. Maybe they can help Mull!"

"Nyuk, nyuk," Coily replied. "Your pretty smart, Clarey!"

I turned back to the audience. "Sounds like there's a bunch of fun and games going on back there," I began. "And speaking of games, our first song is usually one we play at a place like the Dice Tower Tavern. It's about the everyday stress of being a gamer, it's called *The Dungeon Masters Screen*. Ready boys? 1-2-3-4!"

(Sung to the tune of Yellow Submarine by the Beatles)
In the tavern, where we play
sat a man behind a screen
And he rolled lots of dice
Marking maps of where we've been
So we played til no more sun
While we drank some dew that's green
And he told us to roll our saves
From behind a paper screen

We all stare at the Dungeon Master Screen
Dungeon Master Screen, Dungeon Master Screen
We're all there around the Dungeon Master Screen
Dungeon Master Screen, Dungeon Master Screen

Bite our nails until their sore
Our rolls don't count when on the floor
And our team begins to pray...

Tensions in the air around the Dungeon Master Screen
Dungeon Master Screen, Dungeon Master Screen
Shout out prayers around the Dungeon Master Screen
Dungeon Master Screen, Dungeon Master Screen

Went to attack and rolled a 3
A natural twelve was all I need
Then he shook a die of blue (dice of blue) and die of green (and dice of green)
Both with nat crits (behind the screen, haha)
We all glared at the Dungeon Master Screen
Dungeon Master Screen, Dungeon Master Screen
We hear laughs behind the Dungeon Master Screen
Dungeon Master Screen, Dungeon Master Screen

As I was about to sing the next verse, Coily came running out from behind the stage with his bottom on fire and his other two companions chasing him. "Woo woo woo woo," he yelled as the other two tripped over one another and crashed onto the stage.

The audience roared with laughter, so we rolled with the punches and kept playing. "Sit down, yellow ochre brain!" Mull yelled across the stage.

That's when Coily thought he spotted a bucket of water at the front of the stage and ran over to it. "Wait!" I yelled, trying to warn him. "That's not water; it's a pyro drum!"

But it was too late. The minute the Coily sat down, the pyro show began. There was a massive explosion, and colorful fireworks illuminated the stage and launched our temp roadie into the sky! We hurriedly finished our song while the bright lights flared all around us. The audience went wild, and we received a standing ovation!

I want to say that we were a hit with the show's promoters, as well, but the fireworks belonged to W.I.S.P., a musical group of prankenfairies who were supposed to go on after us. "Are you kidding me!" squeaked Blackie Lawfulness, who was floating backstage as we walked by them. "That was our pyro! That's it; we're outta here!"

"That's just great!" the show's promoter yelled. "W.I.S.P. was our final act, somebody needs to get back out there and fill the final part of the schedule, or this crowd will go crazy and rip the place apart!"

The frustrated man turned to us. "You guys need to get back out there!"

"No way," I said, holding up my claws. "That was the biggest round of applause we ever got. I want to end things on a high note. Anything we do on stage after that would just disappoint them!"

The other groups there were all shaking their heads in agreement. "Only a group of idiots would dare go on stage after that!" Peavus declared.

That's when our trio of roadies ran into the area. "We heard you're looking for a group to get out on the stage," Mull said. "Does it pay?"

"Of course it does," the sweating promoter replied. "Can you guys play?"

Clarey grabbed a violin from a nearby pile of instruments and said, "Oh boy, can we!"

"We've been known to shake a leg," Mull bragged. "Let's get out there, boys!"

We all watched as the trio went out on the stage to thunderous applause. Mull had a conductor's wand, Clarey with the violin, and Coily clackered two spoons together in a steady rhythm. We all crept up to the edge of the stage to listen and watch them play their song:

(Sung to the tune of the Swinging to the Alphabet by the Three Stooges)
B—And—B
B—E—D
B—I—beddy-bi—B—O—bow
Beddy—bi—bow—B—U—boo
Beddy—bi—bow—boo

D—And – D
D—Em—Cee
D—M—diddy-die—D—O—doe
Diddy—die—doe—D—U—due
Diddy—die—doe—due

H—And—P
health—4—mee
H—I—Pointy-Pi—P—O—Poe
Pointy—Pi—Poe—P—U—phew
Pointy—Pi—Poe—Pu

A—And—C
Negative—three
M—I—gonna die – O—MY-Y
Critty—why—roll—of just two
Critty—why—woe—two

Rat-da-da-da

I—And—Q
Minus Two
I—I—don't know Y—start to drool
Bibby—lie—low—I—Q—low
(Audience cries out: Coily's a dope!)
Coily chimes in, "Hey!"

As the trio of bumbling roadies finished their song, Clary's violin bow ended up poking Mull in the eye as he danced around with his conducting wand. The dark-haired human stumbled until he fell backward off the stage into the crowd watching. I couldn't believe my eyes, their raised hands carried him around, and he eventually ended back up onto the stage. "I have to try that," Maul grunted.

"You'll make a big impression!" I said, looking over his large frame.

The night ended on a high note, and the promoter hired the trio of roadies to headline the following year. From what I had seen of their stoogery, though, it was an accident waiting to happen!

Entry 36

One night, outside the city of Tidepool, as the band and I sat around the campfire, we saw a determined looking halfling rogue tiptoeing toward us from the woods. He approached and pick-pocketed me with a grin, before padding over to Peavus and doing the same thing. We had quit talking, at this point, and just watched the bold little guy make his way over to Maul, who swatted him like a mosquito.

"Where am I?" he asked twenty minutes later when he woke up.

"Well," I began. "You're still at our campsite. You're lucky my bass player didn't rip you in two!"

The halfling winced as he touched his red, swollen face, now remembering the slap. "Gee, thanks," he stuttered.

"Why would you walk up and try to rob us like that in broad moonlight?" I asked, holding out my claw and helping him to his hairy feet. "By the way, my name is Scales, and this is the Marshtones."

The halfling looked at us and shrugged, not seeming to recognize the band. "I'm Bill Bowman," he began. "I don't know how you saw me; I was completely invisible."

"No, you weren't," everyone replied simultaneously.

Bill frowned and held up his left hand. There was a shiny gold ring on it. "It's a Ring of Invisibility," he explained. "There's no way you should have seen me!"

"Do you mind if I take a look at it?" Peavus asked.

The halfling looked reluctant to hand it over, but one look at Maul slowing rubbing his hands together as if warming them up changed his mind rather quickly.

Peavus held the ring up in the firelight and looked at the inscription on the inner band. "Ronko Ring of Thievery. Steal in Visibility" he read. "Umm, I think you misread this."

Bill Bowman snatched the ring and angrily tossed it into our campfire. "No wonder I keep getting beat up! I should have destroyed that cursed ring a long time ago!"

Entry 37

One of our most interesting tour stops was in the city of Irkruffle, in the province of Slaphammer. It was at a factory called the Magic Box. We didn't expect much pay for this particular show, because it was run by wizards, who tend to be tight when it comes to money. We played anyway, because we had nothing better to do and we had heard it was during a major celebration. Apparently, the wizards had saved the town from some horrific threat. I didn't pay much attention, though; I was just worried about getting our song list right.

I knew this group specialized in inventing all sorts of magic items for adventurers, so we figured we'd make them happy by singing songs about these powerful treasures. "I see a lot of pointy hats in the room tonight," I said from the makeshift stage they had set up for us. "I hope the band and I can dis-spell any frowns and turn them upside down, haha."

After my joke fell flat, I thought it best to jump into the music. "Well, you know there are worse things than a joke falling flat," I stated.

"Like going through a dungeon, coming face-to-face with a scary wraith, and getting your life force drained out!"

"It happened to me," shouted an old-looking wizard from the back. "Look at all my wrinkles. I'm only twenty-three!"

"Well," I said. "I hope the Ring of Moonwalking was worth it."

The crowd laughed and I felt a little better. "Our next song is called *Wraith*, and it goes like this...

(Sung to the tune of Faith by George Michael)
Well I guess it would be nice
If you could slice my body
I know not everybody
Has got a weapon plus +2

But you better think twice
Before I tear your heart away
And all your life I'll drain away
Just by my fingers touching you

Oh but I
Need to feed off that fear emotion
Throw your beating heart onto the floor
Oh when that blood flows out
Like a draining ocean
Well I'll turn a strong man into a baby
By draining all the years away

'Cause I'm bad wraith
Mmm A horrible wraith
Eyes melting from your face
'Cause you got et' by a wraith, wraith, wraith....aaaaah!

Gravy,
That's what I call your soul
I could eat another bowl
You'll soon be turning blue
Zombay!

Get out of my way
I swear I'll save the brains for you
Cuz even the undead have a pecking order too.

Before this liver
Becomes a third course
Before you fill your pants once more
Oh maybe you should reconsider
Your foolish notion
Well I know you came for gold see
now you leave your shape through the wall

'Cause I'm bad wraith
Mmm, A hungry wraith
Plucking eyes from your face
You got drained by a wraith, wraith, wraith....aaaaah!

We got a good round of applause after that song, and we bowed thankfully. "This is going better than I thought," I whispered into Peavus' ear.

When the noise died down, I thought I heard a faint sound. It sounded like tiny hands clapping slowly. I dismissed the odd sound and introduced our next song. "You know," I began. "Magic users are important, but they say a party isn't a party, until there's a rogue in it. Why? Do you ask? Well, there's poison traps, locked doors, and worst of all, *Falling Into Pitz!*"

(Sung to the tune of Puttin' on the Ritz by Taco)
Sprung a trap and I just don't know what to do
Lost my grip so now I'm throwing fits
Falling into Pitz

Opening in the floor makes me secretly wish
I could've did the splits…
Falling into Pitz

Dressed up like a shiny armored trooper
Scrape me up with a scooper (super scooper)

Just my luck, I fell into one with a spikey tip
Like mutton on a spit
Falling into Pitz

Have you seen a secret switch?
Or button, lever, to help us with
Our half-blind rogue said coast was clear
Now we're tumbling through the air
Big splats and lots of hollers
Impaled on spikes with broken collars
Writing down this rhyme, during this horrible time

If you're broken, bloodied, and snapped in two
It all depends on how you hit
Falling into Pitz

Dislocations, traumas, flatlined, and drooling spits,
Writhing around and having fits
From Falling into Pitz

Bottom of the pile is kind of hard to take
Flattened like a fully armored pancake (armored pancake)
Hope you brought a wedge, fulcrum, and armor oil
and spatula in your mitts
Falling into pitz

Crawling 'round in a bloodied stupor
In a pit that smells like a dragons dooper (super dooper)
If you're black and blue it's because of a trap that you've missed
You've fallen into pitz!

The crowd went bonkers and was jumping about to the rhythms of our instruments. I was delighted that these wizards appreciated our music! We did another bow to the sound of applause and even some whistles! Again, when it died down, I heard the slight sound of a slow, tiny clap. This time, I noticed it came from a table of magic items that were stacked up. I swear I saw a small green eye blink from inside one of two small boxes.

"Encore! Encore!" the crowd shouted.

I ignored the distraction, did a quick countdown, and the band broke into our final song without hesitation. We hoped that this would bring the house down. It was a song I had written about an *Invisibility Cloak*, because I wanted to disappear one night off the stage at an orc tavern in Moonwink.

(Sung to the tune of Invisible Touch by Genesis)
Well, I've been guarding this treasure for so long
But thinking nothing, nothing could go wrong, ooh now I know
They had a magical ability
To blend in with the trees
And now it seems I've failed, failed at my job

They must have worn an invisible cloak, yeah
They snuck in and grabbed right hold of the gold
They must have worn an invisible cloak, yeah
Stole all the loot and pawned it off to a shop

Well, I didn't even see them; I only know they came
And right under my nose, now guess who gets the blame, and now I cry
How could they steal so much?
They wore something mysterious
Sidestepped my trap, now it's me, falling in it.

They must have worn an invisible cloak, yeah
They snuck in; gems vanished into thin air
They must have worn an invisible cloak, yeah
My dungeon boss screamed and pulled out all his hair

He did not like losing, and dungeons aren't a game
Now, what do I tell the wife,
I've lost my job again, and now I know
They used a magic ability
To take everything they see
And now I'm filing, filing for unemployment!

They must have had an invisible cloak, yeah
If I ever find them, I'll kick them in the behind
They must have had an invisible cloak, yeah
Stole all the loot and pawned it off to a shop

While singing the song's last chorus, the wizards were dancing in front of the stage with wild abandon. One of the younger wizards bumped into an older one, and the older human lost his footing, fell backward, and crashed into the table holding the magic items. Suddenly, there was a huge gasp, and the group lost all interest in our music. "The boxes!" one cried out. "The Shrink boxes are broken!"

The old wizard held up two small boxes that had been smashed open. "They're empty!" he mumbled sadly.

All of a sudden, the wizards were running about the area looking for something on the floor. The band and I just stood there looking at one another, not knowing what to do. Finally, after a few minutes, a younger wizard with dark hair handed us a light sack of coins and told us we could go. "We've got a mess to clean up here," was all he said before turning to leave while shouting. "Great show, guys!"

We were happy with that, so we packed up our gear and left while the wizards continued their frantic search. "That was fun," I cheerfully stated as I patted down our horses, Haul and Oats. "Let's hit the road."

"Wait a minute," Maul stated, holding up a finger. "Me hear something."

We all stopped what we were doing and listened. We could hear a tiny voice saying, "Help me. Help me!"

Ghasper floated down to a bush by the building's exit door, where we had come out. "Unnh," he groaned, pointing to a spiderweb, low in the branches.

We all gathered around and witnessed a crazy sight. It was a small, bald, ugly humanoid trapped in the web. A nice-sized spider was just about to snag the struggling creature. "Mmm...juicy," Maul said as he plucked up the spider and ate it.

I plucked the humanoid from the web and held him up in my palm. "Me thank you," the creature said. "Me owe you big time!"

"Not a problem," I replied. "My name is Scales."

"Me name is Zham Leaf," it squeaked. "Me was chasing Dragonbait through town when got caught in trap set by wizards. Me got shrunk and put in special box."

"It looks like they cast a shrink spell on him. The magic should wear off soon," Peavus replied. "He'll be back to normal soon."

"Then me get revenge!" Zham Leaf squeaked, shaking his tiny fist.

"Alright," I said, setting him on the ground. "Just stay away from those spiders."

I turned to Peavus and added, "The name Zham Leaf sounds familiar to me, and he looks familiar."

The little guy started shimmering with blue light, so I assumed the magic was beginning to wear off. "We better get to the next show," Peavus said while climbing back up into the wagon. "Colonel Crom booked us at a bed and breakfast place in Tidepool, called the Bed & Pan Inn."

As we rode away, I turned to Peavus, "What did we make?"

Peavus emptied the bag with our payment into his hand. "Two gold, ten copper, and a handful of IOUs."

I knew the guys were disappointed, but I remained hopeful. "Hey, there are IOUs, so maybe we can come back and collect later."

After saying that, we heard the screams as the figure of Zham Leaf grew taller than the trees behind us. He was a fog giant and was now bashing the factory with his fists screaming, "Where are you, Dragonbait!"

"I thought I saw him before!" I exclaimed, looking back as we rode off. "He was a smashing success at the Battle of the Bards!"

"He doing a lot more smashing now," Maul commented as a wizard's arm flew over his head. "Me dig his new beats!"

Entry 38

Trashing campsites is a well-known occurrence with many musical acts in the Unremembered Realms. There are countless wild stories about bards being escorted out by the rangers who usually run these places. One group I knew, called the Litterbugs, would leave garbage all over their campsite. No one dared say anything to them, though, since they were a trio of singing bugbears with a slight temper. They would rip their accuser's limb from limb and devour them.

The Marshtones and I try our best not to be a nuisance, but we will sometimes get thrown out for a messy campsite for one reason or another. Once, we were traveling through the Province of Moonwink, and we were besotted by hungry vamplings, which are vampiric halflings. I hardly slept a wink because of the noise of Maul slapping the little pests all night. The pesky little creatures don't like the taste of lizardmen but kept trying to bite our half-ogre while he sat by the fire. Peavus used the last of his repellant spells on himself and Rhody, so Maul was left swatting at them as they buzzed around.

The problem was that he crushed quite a few before they gave up and left, leaving a bunch of their bloodied bodies around his squatting log. When a ranger approached that morning, we got a ticket for littering.

"I told you to throw them into the woods!" Peavus griped.

"Me forgot," Maul sighed. "Got any itching cantrips?"

Another time, we got in trouble for having a food fight. We had just finished a show at the Sidebucket Tavern, and Maul, being overly excited, decided to stage dive onto a table where two illusionists were sitting. They tried to cast a giant pillow spell but weren't fast enough, so Maul crashed into them. The two survived, but barely. Maul apologized for breaking many of their bones, but I could tell they were still feeling sore from the look on their faces. "Cleric..." one mumbled.

Later that night, the band and I had just settled down around the fire with our usual allotment of preferred foods when strange things started to happen.

As I tried to stab my food with a fork, a small cherry tomato jumped up from on top of my salad and bit me in the snout! It hurt so bad my eyes watered! Maul, Peavus, and Rhody laughed as I struggled against the red, juicy terror! That is until their roasting bird jumped off the spit and yelled, "Your goose is cooked!" before biting Maul on the bottom!

Then, the bread rolls on the table leaped in the air and hurled themselves at Peavus, who unsuccessfully tried to dodge them as they struck him about the head, leaving trails of butter as they flew around him in a doughy maelstrom. Rhody, on the other hand, was attacked by a pile of angry potatoes. "Not the eyes, not the eyes!" he screamed as they flew at his face, bouncing off him this way and that.

"Food fight!" yelled out one of the illusionists from their hiding spot in one of the bushes around us.

The two fell out from their leafy coverings and were rolling around on the ground, laughing. "Hey!" I yelled as I swatted at some croutons dancing up my arms; as I hit them, they exploded with a crispity crunch, and it hurt! I ran over to the fire with the rest of my bowl and threw it in; I heard the shrieks of the lettuce as it curled up into angry brown niblets before jumping from the fire and running around my feet!. "Me going to slap you!" Maul hollered at the illusionists as they stood up, stuck their tongues out, and ran off back into the woods.

At that moment, the food stopped moving and fell onto the ground. When we looked up from our mess, there was a ranger standing there with his arms crossed. "Let me guess," he angrily began. "You're bards!"

Entry 39

It was a dark, cloudy night, and we had set up our tour wagon for the evening in the province of Darkenbleak, just south of the Temple of Temperamental Evil. Rhody was feeling a bit jittery when he went to bed in his section of the wagon. So, it was no surprise when we woke up to hear him screaming. "I saw a ghost!" he stuttered nervously. "There's a floater in here!"

"Ghasper's a ghost," I reminded the dwarf. "You probably just saw him."

"No, no, no. Ghasper's a friendly ghost," Rhody explained. "This one growled."

We all looked at Ghasper, who just shrugged. "Well," Peavus began. "That could have been Maul's stomach. Do you want me to play you a magically enhanced lullaby?"

Rhody looked frustrated. "I'm not hearing things!" he grumped, crossing his arms. "And I'm not sleeping in here when there's some foul spirit in here waiting to swallow my soul! No offense, Ghasper."

Our drummer just shrugged at Rhody and watched as the dwarf walked through him to grab his pillow and blanket. "I'm going to sleep outside tonight; I'll feel much safer!"

We knew there was no arguing with Rhody once his mind was set. Besides, we were tired, and this wasn't the first time the dwarf weirded out on us. "There's a small tent in our gear wagon," I reminded him as he left.

"It's dark," he grumped, "but I know where it is. Good luck in the haunted wagon!"

When we woke up in the morning, we went out to find the dwarf fast asleep. "It must have been dark last night," I said, shaking the dwarf awake. "Because this isn't a tent."

"What? Hunh?" Rhody said, rubbing his eyes.

"Me underpants!" Maul yelled as he stepped down from our wagon. "Rhody ruined me underpants!"

"I wouldn't totally blame him," Peavus whispered to Ghasper, who held his nose.

The dwarf hollered and clambered out from his makeshift tent. "Who put the dirty laundry next to our camping gear!" Rhody yelled. "I need a shower!"

"Me underpants have holes from the stakes," Maul said, holding up his garment.

"He means additional holes," Peavus whispered to Ghasper again, who chuckled.

"At least my soul wasn't eaten by the growling ghost," Rhody stated, trying to regain his composure.

Maul's stomach let out a long growl at that very moment. "Me so hungry, me could eat a dwarf!"

"There it is! There's the soun...." Rhody hollered before stopping abruptly, realizing what he had just admitted.

"Looks like you got to the bottom of it, Rhody," Peavus laughed.

"He sure did," Maul said, holding up his tattered underpants. "Did they pass sniff test?"

The dwarf stomped off in a huff and took one of the longest showers in the history of the Unremembered Realms.

Entry 40

Life on the road can be difficult, especially when it comes to dining. Whenever we pull our tour wagon up to a ride-through window, we never seem to get what we want. I remember one night, at MacGregor's, the teenager taking down our orders was having a hard time with the simplest of requests.

"I'm sorry, sir," the pimpled elf kid said. "We don't' serve pickled bugbear livers."

"What!?" Maul angrily remarked. "And you call yourself a fast-food restaurant?!"

"I'll take a Big Guy Salad with extra mushrooms," I said while looking at the order list, as Maul pondered on something else. "And, um, sprinkle a few halfling toe croutons in there and an ice water, please."

"We don't have halfling toes, sir," the kid would look at me frustrated. "That's gross."

"Don't knock it," I stated, but then Peavus shot me a look. "Oops, I forgot my diet. Ugh. Just throw on some larval moss then…."

"Cool ranch or raspberry dressing?" he asked.

"Raspberry, of course," I replied. "Cool ranch is gross."

"Do you have any turnip pudding?" Rhody yelled from the back. "Oh, and three basilisk eggs, over easy on wheat bread."

"We don't carry Basilisk eggs anymore, sir," the teen replied. "All our suppliers got turned to stone."

"What in the realms," Rhody grumped. "Then give me the wheat bread and a box of salt. I'll catch a basilisk myself!"

"Unnnh," Ghasper said over my shoulder.

"I don't know what that means," the teenage elf said to me. "I don't understand deadese."

"He says he wants an ingrown carrot with picklecheese dipping sauce," I clarified.

It was about this time that the humans in a wagon behind us were squeezing their horn, "Hurry up, we're on our lunch break!"

"Me be right back," Maul growled as he clambered out of the passenger seat.

After a few screams and a couple of honks, things grew quiet, and Maul returned. "How did it go?" I asked.

He handed me a metal horn with a squeeze ball on the end. The metal part was all bent in the shape of someone's face. "We not hear more complaints," Maul grinned.

I ordered Maul the Macgregor Special, which is a bucket of mystery guts. He always enjoyed them, plus they came with a prize inside. In the end, we all ate and made it to the next show. Still, I'm always amazed by how these modern eateries can't seem to get the most basic of foods.

Entry 41

One of the first bands I had ever joined was the Wonderbolts. We were all young and eager to play and would take just about any gig. We mostly jammed out in the woods for friends, but we would luck out and snag a gig at a hall or dungeon every now and then. Back then, I only played rhythm lute, and our singer, a human with slicked-back hair named Daxx Amore, crooned along to whatever music we played at the time. The rest of the band included a Pythagorean named Eugene on bass, a dark-cloud elf named Dark Lee on lead, and a gnoman drummer named Yamahaman, who only knew how to play one repetitive beat.

Our most memorable show was at Grotto Luke's Dancing Sphere, a place run by an evil wizard of that name. I guess Grotto Luke loved to torture, kill, maim, and most of all, dance. Once arriving at his dungeon, the nimble-footed mage led us down many corridors until we reached a large room illuminated by magical lights. Suspended from the ceiling, was a large silvery ball that reflected all the multi-colored lights coming from around the room.

We played all sorts of songs that night, but the one I was most proud of was a song I wrote called *You Ate My Heart*, which went like this:

(Sung to the tune of You're In My Heart by Rod Stewart)
I don't remember which crypt it was
When she stepped out from the gloom
Everything seemed kind of hazy
Her tomb sign had read "Big Daisy."

Green hued skin and smeared lipstick
She belched out 'betically
A and B, C and D
Which spells abcud, don't you see

To my surprise, one of her eyes
Winked out a maggot at me
Her fashion sense was a mu-mu dress
And a floral print so horrible

Large framed dead lady with rotten breath
Tried to stick her claws into me
Her other sunk in eye almost hypnotized
Sorry to stab you, mon ami

You ate my heart and drained my soul
My hair's gone white now I look old
You are a monster you are a ghoul
Lit-er-al-ly

Her waist size was immeasurable
Her victim pile immense
She was ageless, timeless, ugly, and mindless
With an odor that caused offense

She was a tragedy, a curse to me
A flesh consuming plague
She ripped off my arm and then my leg
A buffet is what became of me

You ate my heart and drained my soul
My hair's gone white now I look old
You are a monster you are a ghoul
You drained my soul

All the monsters slow danced to this while Daxx crooned along to it perfectly. Grotto Luke enjoyed the song immensely and wiped a tear from his eye before applauding wildly. "Beautiful!" he shouted to us from the crowd. "And now, for the encore!"

Daxx looked at me and shrugged. We hadn't planned on an encore, but we figured we could come up with something. "Hey, why is everyone leaving?" Dark Lee asked us.

"I don't know," I said, watching everyone run for the exits and slam and lock doors behind them.

As we looked around, we noticed that a dark area near the ceiling held an almost unnoticeable balcony that circled the entire room. The crowd had gone up to it to watch us. At first, we weren't concerned, but then we heard gears under the floor start to move. "Whoa, whoa, whoa," Yamahaman stated, leaving his drum kit and hiding behind me.

Rising from a new opening in the floor, just under Grotto Luke, was a giant, overfed jelly cube. Floating inside the creature were the remains of what looked like other bards and their instruments. "Why are you doing this?" Daxx yelled up at Grotto Luke. "We thought you liked us!"

"Oh, I do!" the wizard laughed while removing his hand from a lever that had opened the sliding floor tile. "But I save a lot of money on entertainment this way. Plus, I get to keep whatever gold you have, since it doesn't dissolve!"

Angrily, I looked around for my spear, but then I realized the wizard had made everyone check their weapons at the door. "Great," I said to Daxx. "We have no way to fight back!"

"We're doomed! I knew it!" Dark Lee said with a frown. "We're all gonna be jelly drops in a few hours!"

Just then, an idea popped into my mind. "Hey guys," I said, beckoning them into a huddle. "Do you know how they say music calms the savage beast? Well, listen…"

I whispered my plan, and we all got our instruments ready, once again. "This last song is dedicated to all our fans here tonight," Daxx said. "It's a catchy little tune about something we all have dealt with at some point. So, I hope you can relate."

With that said, we played the catchiest song we knew, called *Hey, Druid*.

(Sung to the tune of Hey Jude by the Beatles)
Hey, Druid, go take a bath
Don't make bubbles under the water
Remember to scrub up really well
Then you will begin to smell much better

Hey, Druid, don't walk in front
Because we're downwind, in the order
You forgot to loofah up all your skin
Now we're prayin' for rainy weather

And anytime you feel like casting blame,

Hey, Druid, please refrain
Because your excuses are all lame
For we all know that you are a fool
Who needs a dip in a pool
Whose only magic item is a ring around the collar.

Nah, nah nah, nah nah, nah nah, nah nah

Hey, druid, you let me down
You learn lame spells when gaining levels
How is talking to plants going to help us
A magic gardener is what you are there

We're passing out when you come in,
Hey, druid, we're beggin'
Would you like a squeaky toy to bathe with?
And on our nose is a clothespin +2
Your initials are PU
The exit sign is above the doorway

Nah, nah nah, nah nah, nah nah, nah nah yeah

Hey, Druid, you smell so bad
Are those pit stains on your leather
Remember to cast deodorant spells
Then you'll de-smell, and make it better, better, better, better, better... oh!

Nah, nah nah, nah nah, nah, nah, nah nah,
Hey, Drudy, drudy, drudy!!!!!

To our amazement, the jelly cube hadn't moved, but stayed where it was, swaying to the music. The crowd above danced on the balcony singing the nah, nah, nah, nah chorus and waving their arms. It was at that point that I grabbed a cymbal from Yamahaman's drum set and flung it as hard as I could at one of the beams holding up the balcony just above the gelatinous monster.

Being a cheapskate wizard, I deduced that Grotto Luke probably bought these support beams from the Balsadoom Forest, which had the cheapest, most easily breakable wood in all the Unremembered Realms. It didn't hurt that I was an expert in thrown weapons, either. Being a trained lizardman warrior from the swamps of Widowsmarsh paid off, sometimes.

Grotto Luke looked shocked as he plummeted face-first into his pet jelly cube! Others fell as well, either on it or around it, breaking their bones. Survivors on unbroken parts of the balcony ran out through doors on the upper level, shrieking in terror. "That was a killer encore," Daxx said, high-fiving the band.

A few minutes later, we had piled up some bodies, while the jelly cube was distracted by devouring its lunch and used them to climb up enough so we could reach the remaining bits of balcony and escape. Sadly, Yamahaman had to leave his drum set, but that was okay. It was cool that he was willing to sacrifice his skins to save ours!

Entry 42

After a wild show at the Belching Dragon Tavern in Skull Hollow, the band and I were out in the back helping Rhody load gear into the tour wagon. Everything seemed to be going to plan until Maul stated, "Aw, that be a shame."

We all looked over and saw a disheveled-looking ogre sitting down and leaning against the back of the building. He was holding a sign that he made that read, "Will work for guts."

"Just ignore him," Peavus said. "You're only going to encourage him to keep begging."

"Please, mister," the ogre grunted. "Could you spare any guts? Thudd be so hungry."

"Just give him a little of your guts, Peavus," Maul said. "You have two kidneys."

"No way," Peavus shot back. "Teach him to go out and get his dinner. You know what they say: give an ogre a bunch of guts, and he'll eat for a day, teach him to get his own, and he'll eat forever."

"Yeah," I said, agreeing with Peavus. "That makes sense."

"But he has sad face," Maul groaned. "Me can't take sad face."

"Then give him some of your guts," Peavus said to Maul.

"Me be half-ogre," Maul replied. "That cannibalism, methinks. That be gross."

Just then, a kobold ran out from the door and pointed at us, laughing, "You guys stink! I've heard better sounds at the dentalists office!"

I let comments like this slide off my back and down my tail, but Maul gets angry. So, the big guy took a swing at the little pest, but it ducked out the way, easily escaping the blow. What he didn't escape, though, was the Gust of Wind spell that Peavus cast, knocking the creature backward and into the waiting arms of the ogre beggar.

"That took a lot of nerve to come out and say to us," Peavus said, watching the ogre eat the obnoxious kobold.

"It also took a lot of guts," Maul laughed after hearing the ogre beggar let out a loud belch.

Entry 43

The first time we played in a Battle of the Bards with Maul was at the Passthrew Tavern in Daggerfoot. I remember it fondly, because we had won, even though it was in an unusual way. We were a little late, but Maul seemed in high spirits as we pulled into the back parking lot to unload our gear. We could hear the two other bands as they warmed up their instruments. "Me go first," the half-ogre chirped happily.

I had never seen Maul this excited before, so I said, "Sure," and he leaped from the wagon and ran in.

The rest of us went to the back of the wagon to help Rhody unload gear. During our preoccupation, we hadn't noticed that the music had stopped. By the time we got to the loading doors, Maul had appeared holding a bent-up trophy. "We won!" he stated triumphantly, holding it in the air.

"Hunh?" I stated. "How could we have won? We never even got to play."

"Play?" Maul asked. "What you mean?"

"It's a battle of the bards, Maul," Peavus said. "Where the best songs win."

Maul's face scrunched up as he was thinking. "Uh oh," he said. "Me misunderstood. Me thought it was battle."

I got a sinking feeling that maybe we should pack back up and leave. "You want me to go back in and apologize? Hey, Rhody, grab mop."

Before we left, we made sure the unconscious people inside were okay and left some gold on the counter for all the damage. "How did that guy end up in the stage lights?" I asked Maul as he stood on his tiptoes to get the guy down.

"You not want to know," Maul replied with a grin, obviously relishing in the memory.

After packing up and getting into the tour wagon, I noticed that Maul was still holding the trophy. "Hey, I know you're proud of your accomplishment, big guy," I said. "But you should probably give that back."

Maul looked a little crestfallen but nodded in agreement. "You right," he said before throwing it through the tavern's unopened window.

After the sound of breaking glass, we heard a scream, then a thud. "Me feel much better now," Maul beamed as he snapped the reins. "Me like doing the right thing!"

Entry 44

While shopping at the Dragondrop Mall for new wardrobe ideas, we started hearing rumors. A clothing store worker told us that a dark cloud elf named Sorrowman had secretly taken over the mall, and he ruled it with an iron fist. All the gnome shop owners seemed helpless against him, and for some reason, obeyed his every command. We found this rumor odd but kept shopping.

Peavus needed some new platform shoes, so we headed over to Boot Locker. It was the same thing over there; everyone seemed sad or nervous. Ghasper indicated the same thing was going on when he was browsing in All Things Past. "This Sorrowman must be powerful," Peavus stated as a worker slid on a sequined 5-inch riser with spurs.

"He has a magical red, glowing eye that floats above the fountain in the center of the mall," the gnome worker explained. "He is constantly watching."

"Sounds lame," Maul stated, sniffing a pair of galoshes. "Me would get bored."

The gnome shook his head. "That's why he always has a stage set up off to one side. That way, he can watch the latest bands."

"We could do that," I said. "I wonder how much this Sorrowman pays?"

It wasn't long till we had made our way to the center of the Dragondrop Mall and were looking upward at the big glowing eye. It glanced at us for a moment, then turned its attention back to the band that was playing some boppy fluff for all the tweenagers in the audience. Surrounding the fountain base, was a dozen muscular orcs holding some sharp-looking halberds.

Onstage, were five human assassins crooning and making dance moves in sync with one another. The banner behind them read, "The Backstab Boyz." Their song went like this:

(Sung to the tune of Nothing But A Heartache by the Backstreet Boyz)
I'm on fire!
Ow, I'm on fire!
Down in this cave
I did not see the dragon, hey!
I should have worn glasses
I didn't see the spark
Then the flame
The king said have it your way
Tell me why
Ain't nothin' but some heartburn
Tell me why
Ain't nothin' but some heartburn
Tell me why
I never want to hear you say
Let's explore this old cave

Sorrowman's magic eye seemed happy with this music and jiggled about to the rhythm above the foundation. Tweenagers screeched while their parents sat in the back, covering their ears. "I know what would cheer these shop owners up, our music!" I declared. "Not this stuff!"

"I don't know," Peavus stated. "All these tweenagers sure do like the poppy songs and fancy dance moves. I mean, no offense to anyone in the band, but I wouldn't consider us heartthrobs. "

Maul stopped picking his nose for a moment and stated, "Says you. Me big heartthrob!"

Ghasper groaned in agreement with Maul, then flexed a ghostly muscle. His transparent attempt at being eye candy for the ladies wasn't working, and I could see right through it.

"So, what do you suggest?" Peavus asked. "I'm not sure Sorrowman is going to let us on stage with any of these guys."

I told them of my plan, and they reluctantly agreed. After finding a space by the restrooms, we awkwardly practiced our synchronized dance moves. It was a lot harder than it looked. Maul kept elbowing me in the eye, and I kept stepping on Peavus's right foot. "You guys look like you're having convulsions," Rhody laughed from his seat on the floor. "We're going to need a cleric after this!"

After our rehearsal, we went over to Aberzombie & Stitch to pick up some modern duds. "This is embarrassing," Peavus grumped. "These are just matching street clothes. Where are the sequins and face paint?!"

"We can go back to normal after the gig," I said, tucking my sleeveless tunic into my blue denim trousers. "All the kids are wearing this stuff."

"I don't see why I have to dress like this," Rhody grumped. "I'm not even up on the stage!"

I told him it was for solidarity, but honestly, the rest of us just wanted to laugh. Besides, he would be less likely to tease us about this later. "I do like the shoes, though," Rhody stated, admiring their white leather and height around the ankles.

Feeling newly confident, we went around to the back of the stage when the band finished their encore. There was a sad-looking gnome there signing up the next acts. We were stuck behind two other bands, momentarily, until they kindly allowed us to go forward when Maul growled at them.

We took the stage to the now quiet audience and waved at the big glowing red eye. "Hey, kids," I began. "We're Scales & The Marshtones. We're a hip new act, and we hope to get you hopping! Hit it, boys!"

We struck a pose, then began with a song I had written for just such an occasion as this. It was a tune I had composed on a sunny day at the beach, and it allowed each member to rap about their part in the band. It was called *This Lizard Bands Live*.

(Sung to the tune of This Beach is Live by the Surf MC's)
In the taverns I play, gotta stay in the groove
Because when you're green and scaly, they tend to hate you
Throw your gold tips here in the hat
Don't never want to hear boo's, from the back
All the lizardettes wag tails and blow a kiss
I'm the S to the C, A L E S!

Then Peavus started to sing:
My name's Peavus C; I play a mean axe
Castin spells when we need them to cover our tracks
I use a finger slide, don't fret, relax
Because everybody knows Peavus C isn't whack!
Peavus C!
Peavus C!
Peavus C!
Stay busy!

Then Maul jumped in:
Me be Maul and me slap heck-u-leers
Me blood starts to boil when hearing those jeers
One stack, two stacks, 3 or 4
Me stacks em' like cordwood for an encore
Warshburn keeps rhythm with the band
Even with a throat in my hand
Me been around the realms slapping grins and smirks!

Then I cut back in:
Ghasper is our drummer from the plane of death
Not a sound he makes because he has no breath
The sound's not there when he beat the skins
And when he's in the groove, his groans begin!

Then Ghasper cuts in:
Uhhhhhnnnnnnn!!!
Uhhhhhnnnnnnn!!!

Then I jumped back in to finish it off:
Yeah, we're still on tour
I know you need some merch
And I know everybody needs a shirt
Homeboy Rhody has discounts
Colonel Crom Parker paid us what?!

Here it is, you know
Ghasper
Maul Chaffer
And Scales
featuring Peavus C
....Sliding from the G!

The tweenagers didn't move to the sound, but the shop owners and the Eye of Sorrowman seemed happy. We heard a loud gong that shook the whole mall, and a large set of double doors opened behind the stage. An older shopkeeping gnome named Nissa Nackle Nim approached us. She went right to Peavus, squinting as she looked up at him. "Hey, good looking," she said. "Are you Scales?"

"I am," I said, amused by Peavus's squirming as the elderly gnome took his hand.

"Sorrowman wants to see you," she said, winking at Peavus. "Let me show you to his office."

She also handed poor Peavus a business card and wiggled her eyebrows at him. He just sighed and let her lead him along with her wrinkled, age-spotted hand. The rest of us followed chuckling. The gnome led us down a long hallway, which led to an ornate door with a dragon and medusa-head knockers. She lifted one of the iron rings that went through them and banged gently on the door with it. "Come in," came the sound of a man's voice.

Nissa opened the door and led us in. The office of Sorrowman was luxurious. The tiger skin carpet felt soft under our feet, and the furniture in the room was carved of black walnut. Sitting behind a highly polished desk, was Sorrowman, the dark cloud elf. He had long white hair and wore black clothing covered with a white robe. "I appreciate your music," he began. "It sounds different."

"Thanks," I replied. "We heard you recently took charge of things, and we're hoping to get gigs here, once in a while."

The elf had large dark circles under his eyes but continued to smile. That's when I noticed the shiny gold ring around his finger; it seemed to draw our eyes to it. "You can play here, all right," Sorrowman said in an enchanting tone. "But it will be for free!"

The ring was now glowing, and I felt unable to stop myself from nodding my head in agreement. I could see through the corner of my eye that Maul, Peavus, and Rhody were all doing the same. Sorrowman stood up and walked over to the group. "You see, fellas," he began to explain. "I had gone to a pawn shop a while ago to sell the last of my items. I was going to Desperation Point. I was so depressed that all I wanted was to treat myself to one last meal, then end it all."

We were frozen as he walked around us. "But there was a fight inside the shop after I walked out," the elf continued. "After some loud crashes and screams, this ring came rolling out. When I picked it up, I noticed the words engraved in it, 'One Ring to Rule the Mall.' When I arrived here, to get my last meal at the Food Court, I found out that I had power over every living soul in the building!"

With that said, he tilted his head back and let out an evil laugh. The merriment didn't last long, though, because he had walked in front of Ghasper, who was not a living soul. The undead druid didn't usually like to drain the life force from people, but this time he didn't hesitate. He reached through Sorrowman's chest, straight into his heart! The older elf's white hair stood directly on end, and he fell unconscious onto the floor!

I felt whatever hold the ring had over me let go. "Phew," I said gladly. "Thanks, Ghasper."

"Unnnhh," the ghost replied, giving me a thumbs up.

Maul, no longer in good spirits, picked the limp elf off the floor and was getting ready to strangle him. "Wait," I said. "If you kill him, that might ruin any future chances of ever playing here, again."

"But me want to wring his neck," the half-ogre grumped.

"I have an idea," Peavus chimed in. "Let me see the ring."

Maul took the ring off and handed it to Peavus. Our lead luteman reached into his pocket and pulled out a metal etching device and some spell components. After a few magic words, the ring started to glow green, and Peavus started modifying the phrase. Within a few minutes, he finished the task. I squinted to look at the new wording. It read, "One ring to rule the mallow."

"I don't get it," I told Peavus.

"Well," he replied. "I couldn't change the words, so I added two letters. I figured this would shift his ability to control people of the mall to now being the absolute tyrannical ruler of all marshmallows."

"Unnnhh," Ghasper moaned, nodding in approval.

"That's right," Peavus stated proudly. "Let's see him take over the world with an army of squishy treats!"

Things worked out for the people of the Dragondrop Mall after that. Sorrowman was still in charge, but had lost his iron grip. People reported that he had a much softer, sweeter approach, which was fine by us, because in our opinion, the realms needed some more of that.

Entry 45

Peavus had always told me that we should avoid playing at the Doubledeal Casino in the Province of Rustwood. He was constantly reminding me that LaFarina, the halfling owner, was mob-connected and we'd come out on the short end of the spear. Sadly, I let my desire to play for bigger crowds get the better of me, and I signed up with her for a week's run of shows.

The morning before our final show, we heard a scream come from Maul's bedroom in the tour wagon. We all dashed in to see what was happening. Maul was sitting on the edge of his bed in his pajamas, hugging the severed head of a bugbear. "She came! She came!" he cried out happily.

"What?! Who came?" I asked, rubbing sleep from my eyes.

"The Gut Fairy!" he squealed. "Me knew she was real!"

Peavus looked at me, shaking his head, and whispered, "I don't think this is the work of a fairy. I think LaFarina is trying to send us a message. It is payday after all."

I nodded in agreement but trying to convince Maul of this fact would be next to impossible. For as long as I'd known him, he'd told us fireside tales of the Gut Fairy and how it flies into random ogre homes leaving guts and all other assortments of innards for good boys and girls to snack on.

"Anyone for breakfast?" Maul said, standing up and holding the bugbear head by the nostrils. "Me know an excellent recipe for this. Mmmm, just like Grammaul used to make!"

Sighing, I nodded in agreement. I wasn't about to burst Maul's bubble. Besides, if we weren't getting paid, we might as well have a good breakfast.

Entry 46

The day Ghasper joined our group was one that I will never forget. We were traveling through Sunkensod on our way to a gig at the Kettleblack Tavern. The sun had just set when Maul asked that we stop at the nearest graveyard. The big guy tended to do this often, so Peavus and I assumed that our bassist wanted to pay his respects to a lost relative.

Maul had only been gone a few minutes when Peavus and I noticed a large, dead tree next to us. Its top half had fallen over, and all that was left was a rotting base. It stood about ten feet in height, and there was a large knothole. "It's hollow," Peavus commented, looking inside, checking for wild animals.

After twenty minutes or so of exploring, we decided to practice a few song ideas. Rhody even found an apple tree and fed Haul and Oates while we played. Everything seemed peaceful, but I had an awkward feeling like we were being watched. I kept looking over at the dark knothole. Whenever I glanced over at it, I swear I saw a pair of glowing blue eyes before they faded off. "What do you want to rehearse next?" Peavus asked.

Snapping out of my distraction state, I replied, "Since we're by a graveyard, how about the song, *A Zombie's Point of View*?"

Peavus laughed and did the opening slide on his strings that led into the song, and I sang:

(Sung to the tune of Electric Avenue by Eddie Grant)
Out in the street there is violence
And an excellent reason to run
Undead are here for some noshing
And our brains make them groan "Yum, Yum."

Oh no, have you ever seen things through a zombie's point of view
And zombies never tire
Oh, have you ever seen things through a zombie's point of view
And their lobotomal desire

Looking around for cleric
Or even a barbarian
Because in the eyes of this horde
I look like a dog in a bun

Oh, have you ever seen things through a zombie's point of view
My mind is their papaya
Oh, have you ever seen things through a zombie's point of view
Chasing short ones through the shire
Oh no, Oh no, Oh no, Oh no

Anti-paladin had raised them
Because some girls had called him a creep
Hordes growing like multiplication
Now those chicks don't let out a peep

Oh no, have you ever seen things through a zombie's point of view
I think they ate my squire
Oh, have you ever seen things through a zombie's point of view
And for dessert they ate my friar

Out in the street
Lots of brains to eat
Shuffling of feet
Mind meat is their treat

Oh no, have you ever seen things through a zombie's point of view
When living was your prior
Oh no, have you ever seen things through a zombie's point of view
You will when you expire

We would have started another song, but Maul came charging out from around some crypts and interrupted us. "Well, me see enough! Let's go!"

"Whoa!" Rhody shouted. "Watch out! It's a vampire!"

Levitating toward us from the panting half-ogre was a fanged human with glowing red eyes, and he did not look happy! "Prepare to die, bards! Nobody defiles my crypt and lives!"

Peavus and I scrambled for our weapons, preparing ourselves for an attack. "Whoa, there, mister," I said, holding my claws up. "We didn't come here to cause trouble. Maul just needed to pay respects!"

"Is that what you call what he left in the corner of my crypt?!" the vampire seethed. "The smell is atrocious!"

I turned to Maul, who just shrugged. "You told me you had to relieve yourself of a burden, Maul," I stated, "I assumed it was through grieving meditation!"

"Me did," the half-ogre shrugged. "Me didn't see his remains; it was dark in his crypt."

"Well, I saw yours!" the vampire spat. "And now I'm the one who is grieving!"

"Why are you using crypts, Maul?" Peavus asked nervously. "The woods are just over there!"

"Me don't like animals watching, especially squirrels," Maul replied through clenched teeth. "Squirrels always be watching...."

"So, you're telling me we're all going to die because you're embarrassed that a squirrel might see your bum?!" Rhody stated angrily. "Thanks a lot!"

"It vampire's fault," Maul reasoned. "It says John on crypt door, what me supposed to think?!"

"It says John Doe," the vampire stated angrily. "Can't you read?!"

"Me mispronounced his last name," Maul chuckled. "Me thought it said...."

Before the half-ogre could finish his sentence, the vampire shouted out in rage and flew at our group. Before he could reach us, though, he stopped, just a few feet away. He was looking at something behind us. "Oh, uh, sorry, man," John Doe said, holding up his palms. "I didn't mean to cross your turf."

"Uunnnhhh," groaned a voice from behind us.

When we all turned around, we could see the floating form of a ghost. It had a goatee, some robes with fringe on the arms, and a cool bandanna. "Uuunnhhh," it groaned.

I didn't understand him, but apparently, the other undead could. The vampire nodded and held up his hands. "But, but, but…."

The ghost groaned again, then crossed his arms. John Doe rolled his eyes and kicked at the dirt below his feet. "Ghasper likes the cut of your jib," the vampire explained, rolling his eyes and sighing. "He wants to jam with you."

The thought of a ghost playing with us was a bit freaky. We all looked at each other and shrugged. Without saying a word, we knew better than to say no. There was no point in being attacked by a vampire and a ghost! Something in my heart told me that this particular spirit was different, though; Ghasper seemed friendly.

Sensing our apprehension, Ghasper groaned to John. "There's no reason for stage fright," the vampire told us. "Ghasper was a laid-back druid. He played bongos on the side to make extra cash, and then, like most drummers, he died."

We all nodded. "Most of our drummers die, too," I stated.

"They buried him a long time ago, then planted a sapling. It grew into this tree," John continued. "Then, during a big storm, it was struck by lightning, and it awakened his spirit. He's been playing bongos for the undead around here and entertaining us ever since."

With that said, Ghasper started wailing on his bongos. None of us could hear him, but the vampire was snapping his fingers to the silent groove. "Hey," Maul said. "Me can't hear anything!"

The vampire laughed. "That's because his sound is only audible on the Plane of Death. You have to be dead or undead to hear him."

I figured maybe this ghost was our ticket out of this predicament, so I thought of a song that everyone knew. "Hey, Ghasper," I said, "Do you know the song *Potion of Spider Climb*? It's an oldie but goodie."

He nodded his head, and we played after a quick four-count:

(Sung to the tune of Love Potion Number 9 by The Clovers)
I hooked up with a party at the Dragon's Tooth
We heard a rumor from a halfling youth
We traveled over desert and swung jungle vine
To find the mountain, we knew we had to climb
But it was easy cuz I had my bag of tricks

And the little bottle that I hid in it
Then we walked vertically, straight up the side
Thanks to the liquid magic known as Potion of Spider Climb

We had found the treasure room but fell in a pit
The dark cloud elf in the party said, "Well, this is it!"
That's when I turned around and gave them a wink
I held my nose; I closed my eyes, I took a drink

Then the cleric, rogue, and the knight
All climbed back out into the light
That's when I knew that we would all be fine
Thanks to the liquid magic known as Potion of Spider Climb

Peavus busted out in a short lute solo; John Doe quickly joined him with a pretend air lute, then I started singing again.

I held my nose; I closed my eyes, I took a drink
The glow of treasure burned so bright
We started stealing everything in sight
We took all the gold and jewels from that treasure mine
Thanks to the liquid magic known as Potion of Spider Climb

John Doe applauded and said, "You guys have perfect timing!"

I couldn't tell if that was a true statement, but a few skeletons that had clackered up nodded in agreement. "Well, Ghasper," I said. "All our other drummers tend to die, but I don't think you'll have that problem. Would you like to hit the road with us? At least the undead in the audience will appreciate us."

Ghasper gave the thumbs up, reached down into the tree stump, and pulled out an ethereal gear bag. We all turned to leave, but the vampire blocked our path. "Listen, guys," he explained. "I hate to drain the fun out of this, but your bassist left a pretty big mess in my crypt. So, I'm going to have to drink a little of his blood to make up for it."

"Me take full responsibility," Maul stated. "Have your fill...."

We were all shocked at Maul's statement, then quickly figured out why he was being so generous all-of-a-sudden. When he bent down to expose his neck for the vampire, the sunlight he was blocking burned the vamp, and it ran off screaming! With all that had happened, nobody noticed the sun had broken over the horizon, except Maul. "Me could feel sun on me back," Maul laughed, "Hope he enjoys new tan!"

Entry 47

"What did the Colonel say the name of this place was?" I asked Rhody as we rode along in the tour wagon.

"The Friendly Undead Music Place," the dwarf replied front the front. "Or the FUMP, for short."

Maul chuckled, "You be short."

Rhody ignored him and continued, "I guess it's the hot new place to play."

"I hope they are friendly," Peavus chimed in. "The thought of being eaten alive or having my life force drained onstage is not why I signed up to be a bard. No offense, Ghasper."

Our drummer groaned and nodded in agreement. I was a bit nervous, too, but Colonel Crom Parker said the patrons at this place were avid music fans and that all our songs would fall on dead ears, which, in this case, was a good thing. Our last show at the Broken Glass Tavern in Cullenwell didn't go so hot. Peavus cut his foot on the floor, Maul sat on a gnome couple he hadn't seen, and I accidentally had bitten the town's halfling mayor on the leg.

On our way to the FUMP, we gave the Temple of Temperamental Evil a wide berth. Rumor had it there was a staff revolt going on, and I didn't want to bump into any angry monster employees who were picketing. We ran into enough of those at our shows. The Friendly Undead Music Place was to the east of the temple and sat along the coastline of the Elflantic Sea. On a clear day, you see Baremoon Island from there.

When we arrived, we saw the remains of a medium-sized city with a lot of undead milling around. Rumor had it that this was once an up-and-coming city, but an evil cleric named Pandermoan had destroyed it, then raised its population back to unlife. I guess he was trying to build an army but died after being stabbed in the head. The undead army forgot their cause and formed this ghost town.

I didn't sense any bad vibes as we rode into the area. As a matter of fact, skeletons waved hello to us, a banshee shrieked in delight, and a ghoul ran up and gurgled for our autographs! They were all thrilled to meet Ghasper and vice versa. I could tell that the FUMP was a place where we would have fun, and I was right. The minute we set up at the music pit in the town's square, a vast crowd had gathered and were cheering, groaning, and dancing along to the large variety of songs we played. For our encore, we played a tune I wrote about a magic item called the *Deck of Multiple Things*, which gives you powers or curses, depending on which card you drew, it went something like this:

(Sung to the tune of Everything You Know is Wrong by Weird Al Yankovic)
I was raiding a dungeon north of Dockport
Alongside a dwarf with a bad hairpiece on his head
When we found a chest behind a secret door
And a glowing deck of magic cards appeared before our eyes

I guessed I should pick a card, like the one on top
And what happened next was hard to believe
Because it made all of my hair fall out
But I grew two feet taller than I was before

I drew another, and all of my armor disappeared
And I stood there in my heart print boxer shorts
The laughing dwarf just looked at me and shrugged

Every card you've drawn is wrong
This deck has many things for which to long
And every card you seem to try
Somehow ends up a total disaster
Every card you've drawn is wrong
Some cards are cursed like evil spawn
And with each pull of another
You could grow another head or dozen

It was the dwarf's turn, so he drew a card
And was covered with lots of gems and jewels
And soon he could see the redness on my face

And steam coming from my ears literally

So, I got mad and hit the deck
Causing a bunch of cards to land face up
What happened next was hard to report
As I felt my body begin to contort
As I changed into a mallard duck with a unibrow
And the dwarf looked at me so hungrily

And so I ran around flipping cards with my beak
And the magic cards sparkled like fireworks
Giving the dwarf super strength while I got heartburn
All the while, he was flexing and yelling

Every card you've drawn is wrong
This deck has many things for which to long
And every card you seem to try
Somehow ends up a total disaster
Every card you've drawn is wrong
Some cards are cursed like evil spawn
And with each pull of another
You could grow another head or dozen

We received a standing ovation as the song ended, and as we took our bows, we were approached by FUMP's mayor, a weird-looking elf who had become a lich. He wore a floral shirt and still retained most of his mustache and long curly hair. He wore an accordion slung onto his side with a strap and shorts that showed off his bony knees. "Boy, oh, boy, I loved that last song," he said, shaking my hand. "I'm FUMP's mayor. My name is Yankolich."

His skeletal hand still had some flesh on it but was cold. The colorful green glow emanating from his eye sockets was bright and cheerful. "Thanks," I replied. "You have quite a town."

"Listen," Yankolich replied. "Would you mind if I made a parody of that last song?"

"What's a parody?" I asked, looking at Peavus.

"It's where one bard takes another bard's song, keeps the music, and changes the lyrics to make them funny," Peavus replied. "It's all in good fun."

"Wow," I said. "That's brilliant. Why haven't we done something like that?"

The weird elf Yankolich was thrilled and even played a rendition of our song on his accordion, which we found to be quite ingenious. We played at the FUMP dozens of times after that. Yankolich even cast a spell on the band, allowing us to understand Deadese, the language of the undead. It was nice to be able to understand what Ghasper was talking about, now! The Friendly Undead Music Place was a good time, and it was cool playing somewhere that we knew would lift spirits.

Entry 48

A tour stop that I remember well was when we played at the One Star Tavern. It was dim, dank, and dreary. The food was awful, and the audience was scarce. The only two people there, besides the staff and us, were a sleeping dwarf and a halfling cleric. The dwarf had a toupee that had flopped off his head and into his bowl of soup. The halfling stood right in front of us, smiling the whole time.

After our set, the pudgy little guy introduced himself as Padre Pat. "I love your style," he commented. "I like that you have a lot of originals."

"It's just a shame there's no audience," Peavus stated sadly. "At least you were here to enjoy it."

"I agree," I said. "But nothing beats playing in front of large numbers."

Padre Pat leaned forward over the table we were all sitting at and said, "Ditch this place. I know another cleric named Dooganhouse. He's putting together a bash down in Old Country Village, not too far from here. He's looking to recruit more talent."

"Me like the term, bash," Maul said, raising an eyebrow.

Although we were booked at the One Star for three more nights, we decided to check out this mysterious new opportunity. The tavern owner only grunted at us before walking off and muttering about all musicians being ingrates. We didn't mind too much, the pay was just the leftover food off the tables at night, and I didn't feel like squeezing the soup out of the dwarf's toupee, again.

We arrived at Old Country Village later that night and noticed the place was empty, except for a stage in the middle of the village with some metal fencing around it that formed a cage. After we parked the tour wagon and approached the cage, another halfling cleric ran out of a nearby building to greet us. "Did Padre Pat send you?" he asked excitedly. "I pay him well to bring in new talent."

We assumed this was Dooganhouse, so I reached down and shook his small hand. "I'm Scales, and these are the Marshtones."

He seemed to be impressed with us, especially Maul. "What a big guy you have!"

"The better to smash hecklers with," Maul stated. "Me heard there would be bash. But me not see it."

Dooganhouse laughed. "My, my. You're going to be an excellent recruit! Er…I mean…Padre Pat did a great job recruiting you for the Starvation House benefit today!"

The Starvation House sounded familiar, but I couldn't place my finger on it. "Cool beans," I replied. "When can we start?"

"Well," Dooganhouse replied. "It's almost dinner time, so I'd suggest sooner than later. Go ahead and start playing when you're ready. If you play, they will come."

Peavus gave me a look, but I shrugged it off. I love playing charity events; the crowds are a lot nicer than those at taverns. By the time we were all set up and tuning our instruments, we could see the forms of people in the distance. So, we broke out into our first jam, and even Rhody stayed in the cage with us to play tambourine. Our first song was about a dungeon party who constantly fought over treasure; it was called *We Infought All Night Long*.

> *(Sung to the tune of You Shook Me All Night Long by AC/DC)*
> *It was a long campaign with a weary team*
> *A human, elf, dwarf, and even halfling*
> *We killed a green slime or two then wiped our shoes*
> *Before killing the dragon while it snoozed*
> *The halfling barbarian took more than her share*
> *Of all the treasure*
> *She challenged me to fight when I said, "Hey, that's unfair!"*
> *Then we both got blasted*
> *By a fireball casted*

Smelled our behinds burning
For gold, the elf was yearning
And we, infought all night long
Yeah, we infought all night long

Now I'm watching my back in the marching line
I don't trust anyone; they want what's mine all mine
I deserve more than my share; I lied when I declared
Let's split evenly
But then they came back for more
The dwarf cleric used his mace to smash my face
Then I put on a haste ring to take another swing
I grabbed a bag of loot to face another boot
It loosened my tooth
But it was worth it, yeah

And we, infought all night long
Yeah, we infought all night long
I'm going to knock you out
And we, infought all night long
Yeah, we infought all night long

By the time the song ended, people seemed to be coming from everywhere. "Hey!" Rhody shouted. "These aren't normal townsfolk; they're all zombies!"

The dwarf was right; every single one of them had a mindless stare and was moaning, much like some of the late-night tavern audiences, except these were the genuinely undead! "We're surrounded, Scales," Peavus hollered, running over and holding the latch down on the cage door. "We're trapped like rats! I think that halfling priest sold us to Dooganhouse for zombie chow!"

Then it dawned on me, this wasn't the Starvation House charity; it was the Starvation Army! It's a charity organization run by evil clerics who are trying to increase the size of their undead horde. "If me find that Padre Pat," Maul began. "Me will slap his face off!"

You might think that was just an expression, but we have all seen Maul do just that, literally! "What we do now?" Maul said, while using his finger to poke a zombie's eye out through the cage.

"Maybe a song will calm them down," I suggested.

Peavus didn't look confident, but we decided to give it a try. I remembered a song that I hoped would get us some sympathy from Dooganhouse. "Let's do the song about the frustrated cleric, *No More Mr. Cure Light.*"

(Sung to the tune of No More Mr. Nice Guy by Alice Cooper)
I used to heal everything
'Til I lost hope in my team
They'd dimension door little old ladies
Or steal candy from goblings

I disapprove of all their capers
They have been too mean
Their alignment isn't going good
And I'm quitting the team

No more mister Cure Light
No more healin' naughty teams
No more mister Cure Light
I'm about to split the scee-ee-eene!

A gnoll bit me on the leg today
They laughed till they cried
The wizard left me out of the protection circle
And I was nearly fried

I went to the temple incognito
I've been so ashamed
Traveling with these murder hobos
It has ruined my good name

So, I told them:
No more mister Cure Light
No more healin' naughty teams
No more mister Cure Light

I'm about to split the Scee-ee-eene!

Hundreds of undead swayed to the music and Dooganhouse held up a burning finger in solidarity. He was using a Fingerfire cantrip like Peavus does when starting our campfires. The evil cleric wildly applauded when we finished and shouted, "That was wonderful! I can't wait for you to join my monster team!"

"Well," Peavus said, "it was worth a shot."

"Zombies sure are dumb," Maul chuckled as he poked out more of their eyes. "Not have much brains. Maybe that why they like eat others' brains."

"That's it!" I shouted, having a eureka moment. "We must get rid of our brains!"

Peavus and Rhody looked at me like I was crazy, but Maul nodded in agreement. "Yeah," he said, all excited. "Let's chop off our heads and sneak them out!"

"Um, that's not what I meant, Maul," I said to the half-ogre. "But that can be Plan B, okay?"

Maul seemed pleased with that, for the moment. Then, I instructed everyone to empty their pockets. I had some picks, a vial of scale oil, and a handful of fish head cough drops for when my voice gets raspy.

Maul had a rubber band, a half dozen mystery teeth, and a small scroll with a drawing of his mother on it that read, 'Me miss you.' It always perplexed me that his mother was an ogre and his father the human. I felt it safe to assume his father was utterly blind or insane. I tended to figure the insane part, which would explain a lot.

All Rhody had was part of a comb, some string, and a half-eaten potato chip. "I was saving it for later," he explained before popping it into his mouth with a crunch. "But there's no time like the present!"

That left Peavus. He pulled out a small black book ("It's for the ladies," he explained), a firecracker, and the best thing of all, one Potion of Invisibility.

"I was hoping you still had that potion," I grinned while holding it up. "Because I have a cunning plan!"

I instructed Ghasper to fly back to the tour wagon and prepare Haul and Oats for a quick getaway. So, he floated through the cage and the horde until he reached our ride. Then, he gave us a thumbs up. "What now, Scales?" Peavus asked.

"Rub this Invisibility potion on your head," I began. "Really work it in."

Everyone shrugged but did as instructed. After a few seconds, our heads disappeared from sight! I could hear laughter coming from the empty space above Peavus's neck. "This is brilliant!" he said.

"Voila!" I proclaimed proudly. "We no longer have brains!"

A hush fell over the horde, and the zombies started shuffling away. Dooganhouse was furious. "Don't fall for this trick! They still have brains!"

A few zombies groaned as they walked by, but none of them seemed to be listening to the mad cleric. Ghasper pulled the wagon up, and we quickly packed our gear. "Don't worry," I shouted to Dooganhouse, "While we don't expect a payment from you for the show, you can expect a visit from local constables, who will be very interested in your little operation!"

The angry cleric ran up to our wagon and started casting a spell but soon realized his mistake. The whole band laughed as we watched a very unusual sight. A headless half-ogre jumping down from the wagon and punching the cleric so hard that his head actually disappeared!

Entry 49

The one day the whole band dreads is laundry day. For some reason, we always have the worst luck with it. First, Maul will haul out the cauldron when we find a good river. Then, Rhody starts the fire and gets the water to a good boil. Last, Peavus casts a good suds cantrip that gets bubbles up everywhere.

The band usually ends up sitting around in our undershorts playing cards or a few songs while our dwarven roadie stirs the pot. This routine is all fine and dandy, but once-in-awhile, things go awry. Once, we were almost attacked by an orc raiding party. We had heard them coming, so we snatched our drying clothes off the line, so we weren't fighting in our skivvies. That's when we realized the water temperature had gotten too hot and all our clothes had shrunk!

The orcs were so busy laughing at our tiny outfits that we could barely move around in that they let us go and thanked us for the laugh. It didn't help that we had a show that night and had to play in those same clothes!

Another embarrassing incident was when we encountered a couple of halfling barbarians named Hank and Frank. They relished in their taunts after Peavus accidentally threw a pair of his new red socks into his laundry basket and forgot to tell Rhody. All our laundry came out a bright pink! I don't know how, but even Ghasper's ethereal robe was that way, too! "Look," Hank said to Frank, as they stood by our campsite, "A girly band."

Frank laughed and pointed, "Yah. Where are your ribbons and pigtails?"

Maul growled at them, "Quiet, little creeps or me crush you like bugs!"

Hank and Frank both started flexing. "We'd like to see you try," Hank said, between huffs and puffs. "My arms are weapons of mass destruction!"

"That is right muscle-kin," Frank added, showing off his legs. "I will crush their delicate, sissy heads between my glorious thighs. They will break like rotten eggs, and the birds will feast on their brain yolk!"

They would have stuck around longer, but I felt my stomach rumble. "Listen, you two. There's a cauldron right here. Why not jump in for a bath?"

I said this while putting on a pink bib and licking my lips. That's when it occurred to them that I was a lizardman, and halflings were probably my favorite food. "We will let you go, this time," Hank said as they backed away. "Be thankful we only taunted you with our advanced intellect and superior muscles!"

"Come back," I pleaded mockingly. "I do like a low-fat halfling steak, medium rare!"

Another time laundry had gotten us into trouble was when bugbears surrounded us. Luckily, we had time to pull our now dry clothes off the line and get into a defensive position. There was a half dozen of the creatures, and they came slowly at us in a group. That's when Peavus grinned and pulled a scroll from his pocket. "It's a good thing I picked up this Fire Scroll!"

We all sighed with relief, but then Peavus frowned. "Oh, great," he exclaimed. "I left it in my pocket, and it was in the wash! All the ink is smeared!"

"Try it anyway," I shouted while holding up my spear to the approaching monsters. "Or we're in trouble!"

Peavus read the scroll as best he could, sometimes guessing at the words. When he finished, the whole area glowed blue, and bubbles started rising from the ground all around us. Luckily for us, the bugbears found this highly amusing and forgot about us as they ran around popping bubbles and giggling. I don't know what had happened with the magic, but the spell never wore off of the area. Later, we found out that the locals had named the place Welkshire, which means Land of Bubbles.

Entry 50

One of the most memorable shows we ever did was in the town of Dustbin at the Alamode Tavern in the southwestern portion of the Barrendry Desert. While playing a thumping bass solo, a bat flew up in Maul's face. The audience gasped as Maul grabbed it from the air and bit its head off. The crowd went crazy, and our bass player became a local hero. The band thought Maul was eating a typical snack, but I guess this wasn't your average bat. It turns out that it was a vampire who had been tormenting the town for months.

After Maul bit the head off, the body transformed back into its human form and fell to the floor with a thud. When Maul finished chewing, he burped, looked down, and said, "Me not finishing that. Me on diet!"

Entry 51

Every year, we look forward to the Druidic Jamboree at Freedom Rock, which is an island to the north of Watercliff. The place has been refuge to the tree-hugging spell casters for as long as I can remember. There, the druids can hang out, share spell recipes, and speak of peace.

The concert was a must for Ghasper. He'd groan on and on excitedly about it as the time of year approached. Don't get me wrong, we enjoyed it, too. Druids were pretty laid back and weren't phased at all that Ghasper was a ghost. They appreciated that he was still a druid at heart and that his former life wasn't a thing of the past.

The first act on stage was called Mana Mana; which, consisted of a trippy-looking gnome with two kobold females on each side. The only song they sang entailed the gnome shouting the name of the band.

"Mana mana!" he'd sing.

"Doo doo doo doo doo," the gals would harmonize.

"Mana mana," he'd repeat, as they'd do the same.

Then, the gnome would skat, "Um, num, do dat duh do, dum dat doo num nuh."

The kobold girls would shrug their shoulders before the gnome would sigh like they should know where he was going with the song. Then, he'd pipe in with another, "Mana mana!"

The kobold girls would harmonize with him, again, "Doo doo doo doo doo."

This song went on for a few minutes. As bizarre as this number sounds, it seemed to get stuck in your head and was highly entertaining. I have to admit that I was a little bit jealous of this musical masterpiece.

A druid named Drubbins stood next to us, shaking his head. "None of that made any sense."

"It doesn't matter," I explained. "Entertainment is entertainment."

When it was our turn up on the stage, we decided to do a song Ghasper wrote about a popular druid spell called *Stanky Cloud*. It went like this:

(Sung to the tune of I Love It Loud by KISS)
Hey hey hey hey yeah
Hey hey hey hey yeah
Hey hey hey hey yeah
Hey hey hey hey yeah

Let's go; we don't have to be afraid
Footprints lead to a mystery cave
ranger promised we would be safe
And we believed it

Old guy, looking all innocent
Hey Man, did someone have an accident?
If so, better change underpants
A druid just cast….

Cloud, he cast Stanky Cloud,

Right between our guys,
Cloud, he cast Stanky Cloud,
We got burning in our eyes

Turn it off; we start begging him
Pinched nose, want to breathe again
Why did we have to find
A smelly old druids camp

Thick flies, no bathing alibi's
Peeled onion, just so I wouldn't cry
Downwind, that's where we will fly
Old druid cast…

Cloud, he cast Stanky Cloud,
Our lunch begins to rise
Cloud, he cast Stanky Cloud,
We should deodorize!

Hey hey hey hey yeah
Hey hey hey hey yeah
Hey hey hey hey yeah

As we sang the last part with the audience, I could see the curmudgeonly Drubbin shaking his head, again. Just then, an ogre emerged from the woods with a band of orcs. Even from a distance, I could see the bloodshot eyes of this enormous creature and his extra-wide frown that was broken up by two large, lower fangs. The music stopped as one of the druids screeched at the sight of them.

"Party's over, losers," the ogre stated loudly. "Me name is Themann. Me taking over pathetic island. Clear out or die!"

A discussion broke out among all the druids, as we stood on the stage wondering what to do next. There were a large number of druids here, but Themann's troops were numerous, as well. Plus, they looked ready to fight. After a minute, two druids walked up on the stage and waved for everyone to quiet down. I recognized them as Flip Flop and Jinglemilk; they were the ones who had hired us to play this show. Flip

Flop raised two fingers in the air and shouted, "We're not going anywhere," the druid shouted with a smile. "This is Freedom Rock!"

"Yeah," Jinglemilk agreed before shouting, "Turn it up, Themann!"

The audience let out a roar, and Flip Flop turned to us and shouted, "Kick it!"

Without missing a beat, we burst into *Fight For The Life of Your Party*.

(Sung to the tune of Fight For Your Right by the Beastie Boys)
They drag you to the battle, man, you don't want to go!
You ask the knight, please? but he still says, no!
You missed a saving throw and dropped your sword
Our wizard just lost his head, and the ranger got gored
You gotta fight, for the life, of the party

The fighter sees you shaking, and he says, "No way!"
Then that hypocrite screams and runs away
Man, fighting monsters is such a drag
Yet gimmie all the gold in a magic holding bag (bust it!)
You gotta fight, for the life, of the party!
You gotta fight

Don't step out of this armory if that's the chain you're gonna wear
It's got a flap in the back, called the Moon of Derriere
Our monk bites his nails, saying, what's that noise?
Aw, just what I thought, it's some beastly boyz.
You gotta fight for the life of the party
You gotta fight for the life of the party
The party!

The druids went crazy over the song and danced around Themann and his orcs. When the song ended, Themann growled and marched up to the stage. "You call that music?" he stated, more than asked. "Get out of way!"

The audience looked at one another as the ogre, and some orcs, took the stage. The Marshtones and I stepped off to allow Themann room to do whatever he had planned. The monster signaled to his orcs and they rhythmically started making noises with their mouths. Themann immediately started rapping words to the tune, and this unique song style caught the druids off guard. Themann began to bounce to the lyrics and started shouting:

> *(Sung to the tune of I'm the Man by Anthrax)*
> *Now we're monsters, and we make hits*
> *Your fat lip will soon be split*
> *The sound you hear is what we like*
> *We'll smash your skull and turn out your....*
> *Lights!*
> *Themann, what's the matter with you?*
> *Me killing with rhymes, and the truth*
> *Me big club beat the beats, the beats you beat*
> *It hard to smile when yo' spittin teeth*
> *So listen up because you might get flat*
> *Hit the road lizardman band or take a.....*
> *Stool!*
> *Wham! There goes the beating!*
> *Get off the stage, me in your face*
> *Kick you and band in outer space*
> *Clear out druids, understand?*
> *Don't you know,*
> *Me am Themann! Me am Themann!*
> *Me taking over island, in command!*
> *Me am Themann!*
> *Listen up!*
> *We've got real def rhythms and fresh new jams*
> *And me break all your legs and chop off hands*
> *So pocket that fireball and better figure to skate*
> *Themann's here now; you better*
> *Escape!*

When the ogre finally stopped, he struck a pose with his hands in his armpits while orcs around him crouched, throwing up their hands in unique gestures. The druids broke out in wild applause! Even I had to admit, Themann brought something to the stage that was magical. The ogre was a bit taken aback by the amount of clapping, and even did a bow. "They like me," he said, getting teary-eyed all of a sudden. "They really like me!"

A large, bug-eyed orc with no fingertips pushed through the back of the crowd holding a sword, and jumped up on stage. "We here to kill these losers. Enough with this nonsense!"

Themann nodded approvingly while wiping his nose with a sniffle. "You right, Nubbs. Let's get down to business!"

The crowd gasped as Themann turned to face the audience. They all let out a cheer when he held up his arms and shouted, "It Freedom Rock, turn it up, man!"

He then picked Nubbs up and threw him into the crowd, which caught him and surfed him away from the stage with their hands. The audience roared their approval as Themann and his band broke out into a new song while Flip Flop and Jinglemilk danced around him on stage.

"That's not real music," Drubbins the Druid complained. "I must say something to him!"

"I'd just go with the flow," Peavus warned him. "He isn't so bad. His songs are rather catchy."

"I'm sure he'll appreciate an honest critique," the druid claimed confidently. "Themann looks reasonable."

Later, after the show, we found Drubbins moaning while hanging from a tree by his underpants. The foolish druid received a brutal wedgie and a scroll jammed halfway down his throat. "I warned him," Peavus said, pulling out a Healing Potion.

Maul and I helped get Drubbins down. "That's one way to get one of Themann's songs stuck in your head."

Entry 52

If you think taverns can be rough to play, you have never been to a Graysquawk Adventurers Retiree Party, or GARP, for short. These elderly folks formed this organization to get together in the woods and dish about their glory years of battle. We wouldn't play them at all, but they are over with rather quickly.

The night usually consists of a few gray-haired barbarians trying to outdo each other with feats of strength. One might pick up a log, while another will try to beat him by picking up a large rock. These trials are usually followed with a quick healing spell by a clerimedic and some magically-enhanced muscle ointment.

The mages aren't much better. Their fireball shooting competition usually ends with someone's bottom on fire, because they cannot see where they are shooting, due to their cataracts. Their Light spells aren't much more than a dim flicker and their Lightning Bolts don't do anything more than give each other a bad case of static cling.

Thankfully, they quit letting the rangers show off what was left of their archery skills. Let's just say the shooting of an apple off someone's head was more like an Adam's apple, in most cases. Druids seem to fare the best of all the retired classes. All they do is walk around, showing off the various types of molds they have grown between their toes.

"How's the pudding?" I asked from the small stage while the Graysquawk crowd ate their three o'clock dinner.

None of the old-timers replied, unless you count the flatulent dwarf at table number two. "Well, it must be so tasty you don't want to stop eating," I stated, trying to make the best of the situation. "My name is Scales, and this is my band, the Marshtones. Before we start playing, I'd like to point out that the old monk at table five has passed out into his bowl of mush. Someone should help him out."

As a couple of helpers made their way to the table, I turned to Peavus. "Maybe we should open with a song with which they can identify. Let's try Old Djinn."

"Nice choice," Peavus commented before sliding his fingers up the strings of the lute to get the tune rolling.

Maul kicked in on his Warshburn bass as I began to sing our song, *Old Djinn*.

> *(Sung to the tune of Cold Gin by KISS)*
> *My healer's dead, and I'm so tired*
> *We could use a spell to build a fire*
> *Behind the secret door, the lights are out, yeah*
> *The treasures gone, I'm down and out*
> *Ooh, it's old djinn time again*
> *It's lamp I'm always rubbing.*
> *It's old djinn time again*

You know it's the only thing
That gets us our treasure, ow
It's time to leave and stab another orc
Inside a cavern with a treasure hoard
Haha, the cheapest electrum is all I need
To get me back on my steed again
Ooh, it's old djinn time again
You know he'll make my party win.
It's old djinn time again
He's blue-skinned with big earrings
If only it didn't foul up our wishes, ow!

Being one of our favorite songs to play, we moved about the stage and did some cool synchronized moves. By the time the song ended, we had paused in cool poses awaiting a standing ovation. Instead, all we got was the single clapping of a pimple-faced half-orc busboy.

"Where did everyone go?" I asked him after noticing all the tables were empty.

"It's Friday night," the kid answered. "They left for the bingo hall."

Sighing, I turned around to tell the band to pack up. That's when I noticed Peavus running for the door. "Hey," I yelled out. "Where are you going?"

"My daubers are in the wagon," he yelled back. "I'll be done quicker than you can say 'Knock On The Door'!"

I always forget that Peavus has a fascination with things that only the elderly enjoy. From his cravings for dry white toast to using obscure phrases from 40 years ago. He also thinks wearing black knee-high socks with his shorts in the summer is unbelievably hip. Peavus' greatest treasure, though, is an ancient artifact called "Snortmirth's Jokebook", which contains endless puns that leave you begging for less, like, "A skeleton walks into a tavern and orders a lemonade and a mop."

Entry 53

To most people, Maul seems like a frightening, intimidating monster who can lay a bass rhythm like nobody else. But most of them never see how thoughtful he can be. For example, when knocking someone unconscious in the street, he'll gently lay them down in the gutter, so they won't get run over by passing wagons. Or when he's yelling at the library about them not having enough picture books and punches holes in the walls instead of ripping all their lungs out. But most of all, he always takes care of and feeds our cat, Ziljan.

For some reason, the cat seems to amuse him. The rough half-ogre is always sneaking treats for him. Maul doesn't like it when anyone messes with the cat, either. I remember one time when a tavern owner stopped by the camp to discuss a contract and kicked Ziljan, telling him to "Get out of the way, you rotten cat!"

I've never seen underpants stretched over a human's head and to his back, again. It looked pretty painful, so I bent down to help him out, but stopped when I heard him gurgle, "W-w-why don't I ever wash these things....".

I never thought I'd have a clue as to why Maul was so fond of the cat, but one night at a show, I figured it out. As we finished a number, someone started booing us from the back. That's when Maul took out a sling, reached into a small pouch on his belt, and placed something into the sling before swinging it around and scoring a direct hit on the audience member. "Aaah!" he yelled, wiping his face, "Gross!"

"Are those cat droppings?!" I asked Maul, who was standing there laughing.

"Yup," he replied. "Ziljan always makes the best ammo for me."

Entry 54

On our way to Nabiscove, a city in the Province of Moonwink, we decided to cut through the Logfell Forest to save time. There seemed to be plenty of open trails, but we were soon lost after traveling a few hours. Not only that, but the thick foliage covered a lot of the sun, so we began to lose our sense of direction.

"Where's the map?" I asked Peavus from one of the backseats in the tour wagon.

The wizard nudged Maul in the driver's seat next to him. Maul just grunted. "I gave it to Maul this morning when we had our coffee," Peavus sighed. "He said he needed it."

"Don't tell me, Maul," I said, running my hand down my face. "You took it along for your morning constitutional."

"They shouldn't make maps so soft," Mauled muttered, "and absorbent."

"Now what do we do?" I asked the half-ogre. "We're completely lost! Haul and Oats are getting tired, and it's going to be nightfall. Even Ghasper's floated into his urn for a rest."

"Maybe we can ask her," Peavus said, pointing to the darkening trail in front of us.

Standing beside the trail was an elderly human female, dressed in a gray shawl, wearing sunglasses, a dark blue head wrap, and holding a twisty wooden staff. "Who is she?" asked Rhody, appearing next to me.

"Beats me," I replied. "But maybe this little old lady knows the way out!"

Maul whoa'd the horses, and Maul, Rhody, Peavus, and I got out to greet the stranger. "Hello there," I began. "We're Scales & the Marshtones, a friendly group of bards heading toward our next gig. We seem to have gotten lost. Perhaps you can help us?"

The woman looked us up and down, and by that I mean up for Maul and down for Rhody. Her smile grew large, revealing rotten, jagged teeth. "Oh my," she cackled. "I love musicians! They are all so sweet!"

With that said, she pulled down her head wrap, revealing her hair, which wasn't hair at all, but writhing worms! She also removed her sunglasses, revealing her glowing red eyes. "It's a Redusa!" Peavus hollered, but it was too late, we had already begun to shrink! Before we could do anything, all four of us had shrunk to around one inch tall.

"We were hoping to make it big, not small," I squeaked out in surprise as the Redusa's hand came down, sweeping us all up!

We were all in the darkness of her closed palm, smooshed together. "My face is smashed in this hag's sweaty skin," Rhody complained. "It sure is hairy!"

"That's me armpit," Maul replied.

"Argh!" the dwarf cried out in frustration.

"Shh!" I hushed them. "I think I can hear something."

I heard familiar muffled squeaks, one after another. "The Redusa is stealing our tour wagon!" Peavus cried out. "She can't do that! That's illegal!"

"So is shrinking people and probably eating them," Rhody grumped. "I hope I give her gas!"

After what seemed like half an hour, we heard the wagon wheels stop squeaking, and we felt some movement. Then, light broke through the giant fingers as the evil crone tossed us into a small cage that was up on a shelf in her cave. As we looked around, we could see other cages on the shelves with other shrunken creatures of the Unremembered Realms. She even had an itsy bitsy drider crawling around inside a cage a little way from ours.

Surprisingly, the cave was elegant and posh. Luxury furniture lined the room, and expensive-looking lamps kept the place nicely lit. Whatever this Redusa did, she made good money at it. Off to one side was the kitchen, and dead in the center was a large cauldron bubbling with brown liquid. "What is that?" I asked a dwarven monk stuck in a cage next to ours. "It smells good."

The dwarf rubbed his mostly bald head. "I know it does. That's because it's chocolate."

"Chocolate. Me like chocolate," Maul stated. "Maybe she's a good Redusa...."

"Don't count on it," the dwarf stated while pointing. "Watch."

The Redusa went to a shelf, pulled a cage of shrunken creatures from it, and took them over to the cauldron. One by one, she dipped her shrieking captives into the liquid, waiting until they quit wriggling, then laid them out in a nice row on some wax paper to dry. "That's not good at all!" Rhody yelled. "I've heard of death by chocolate, but this is ridiculous!"

The Redusa hummed some unknown melody as she dipped more creatures from other cages while we watched in horror. "Me want to slap Redusa...to death!" growled Maul, shaking the bars of the cage.

I was just about to say something, but then we heard the weird giggling of kobold cublings coming from the cave entrance. The Redusa put on her sunglasses and giggled as she brought a tray of her chocolate treats out to show them. "Who's first?" she cackled.

The kobold cublings danced all around her, handing her money and taking the treats. Then, they started biting into their candy. "What you get, Billy?" one kobold asked another in rough common.

"Me got human," he replied with a chocolately grin. "Their guts are so ooey-gooey!"

Peavus wiped the sweat from his brow. "I hope I'm not ooey-gooey," he snarled, pulling up his tunic, showing his six-pack belly. "All those sit-ups better pay off; I hope I break one of their teeth!"

"Does anyone here have a plan?" I asked the people in nearby cages.

A halfling raised his hand and said, "I've fallen in love with her. I plan on a quick wedding and a long honeymoon. During that time, you could all escape!"

"Listen up, guys," I said to everyone, ignoring the hairy-footed suitor. "Maybe we should harmonize on a song, maybe that will change the Redusa's heart, and she'll let us go."

"What could we possibly sing to a Redusa?" Rhody said. "You know they are pure evil!"

Maul raised both of his fists into the air in a victory stance, "Me know one!"

Within moments, Peavus, Rhody, and I were softly humming as Maul performed one of his famous spoken-word songs, called *It's Not Easy Being Mean*.

(Sung to the tune of It Ain't Easy Being Green by Kermit the Frog)
It's not easy being mean
Having to spend each and every day
Smashing noses on heckling fiends
Just when they think, I couldn't be meaner
Me kick them hard in the spleen or
another place that hurts a lot

It's not easy being mean
Me often called a bad dream
By tavern owners who don't want to pay
Then me gleefully break their legs
Or punch their nose until it bleeds
And if you don't applaud
You'll get me fist in your eye

And when me strum bass up on stage
Me wonder what it would be like to slap your face

Or stage diving down and giving a wedgie
To everyone who didn't buy a Tee

And mean is how me seem to roll
Better get me autograph in the hall
Or you'll wonder how you lost those teeth
And if you do, that's just fine by me.

Believe it or not, the Redusa had heard the song and walked over, listening with a gleam of understanding her eyes. For a moment, the glow softened, and a single tear trickled down her grotesquely ugly face. "That was beautiful," she said. "I've never felt so moved by a song."

"Does that mean you won't eat us?" I asked.

"And miss poppin' that jelly belly between my teeth?" she remarked while pointing at Maul's ample stomach. "No way! I can just taste the gutty nougat!"

She had just started to cackle at her joke when she turned pale white and shook violently! Then, she dizzily turned around to stare directly into the eyes of Ghasper, who had just drained a good bit of her life force. The Redusa's eyes glowed red as the worms in her hair writhed, but her magic did not affect the dead eyes of our drummer. Without skipping a beat, Ghasper grasped her, once more.

She shook violently and screamed before stumbling sideways and falling directly into the chocolate cauldron, knocking it over and spilling it on herself! With a chocolate-covered hand, she reached up in one final motion, but it dropped back down quickly as one last gurgle of chocolate bubbled out of her mouth!

In a bright blue flash, everyone returned to normal size and started cheering. "I never thought I'd be so happy to see a floater!" the dwarven monk remarked, shaking my claw. "My party is never going to believe this!"

Just as we were about to leave, more kobold cublings showed up at the cave door. "What do you kids want? A song?" I asked.

"No," one growled, "more candy!"

I knelt in front of the half dozen or so cublings and flipped my thumb back. "Well, you're in for a treat! There's a life-size chocolate-covered Redusa back inside. Bon Apetit!"

The kobold cublings cheered and ran inside. I could hear the flesh-ripping as we walked toward our nearby wagon. "Well, Ghasper," I said. "You saved the day. How about we treat you out?"

Ghasper groaned his excitement. Peavus agreed and laughed. "Yeah, Ghasper, you really urned this one!"

Entry 55

One of the benefits of being in a band is that the taverns you play usually let you keep all the bottles thrown at you. On top of your regular pay, these returnable items can add up! If the crowd is raucous enough, the value of these will even pay for your band's next meal, which is excellent, even though you might have a few bumps and bruises.

One night, while going through the bottles after the show, I found a note rolled up inside one. "Wow," I replied. "A secret note!"

"What do you think it is, Scales?" Peavus asked. "A treasure map?"

"Maybe free coupon for meat," Maul cut in. "Maybe whole carcass!"

"Mooaannn," Ghasper groaned. "Uhnnnnhhh."

"That would be a dream come true, Ghasper," I replied. "You must be reading my mind."

"What would you do if it was a lot of treasure?" Peavus asked. "I know what I'd do. I'd buy a magical Oat Bag of Holding for our horses and cast a Nitrous spell on the oats. That way, Haul and Oats could go super fast, and we'd never be late for a show, again!"

"That would be a blast," Rhody chimed in as he climbed up the stage. "Unless you were sitting in the driver's seat!"

"What would you do, Maul?" I asked as he sniffed his bass strings.

He pondered over the thought and stated, "Easy. Me buy pet hoppalopper."

"A hoppalopper?!" Rhody exclaimed. "Are you crazy? They are the most dangerous beast in the realms! They can hop up and lop your head off in one bite!"

"Hoppaloppers be fuzzy and cute," Maul explained before a giant smile grew on his face. "Plus, when they lop off someone's head, I can slap it into sky. Maybe hit bird."

Rhody shook his head. "Well, I would buy a turnip farm and put my cousin, Bald Rick, out of business. That skinflint has been fleecing the people of Dockport for years. I can't wait to see the look on his face when I turn up!"

"I'd book us a gig at the Temple of Temperamental Evil," I cut in. "We'd play for free, seeing we didn't need the money, and it would be the biggest blast in the realm of Rippenwind that anyone's ever heard!"

"Let's quit talking and get that note," Rhody stated. "I've got some land to purchase."

I shook the bottle, but the note had unraveled inside it a little, making it impossible to pull out. "Hmmm," I began. "It seems it's stuck."

"Me fix it," Maul stated, grabbing the bottle, then marching off toward the tables and dance area, where the audience had been earlier.

He knelt by an unconscious ranger. It was the same one Maul had knocked out for heckling us earlier. He lightly slapped the man's face until his eyes blinked open. "Huh? Where am I?" he sputtered.

Maul immediately smashed the bottle over the guy's head, knocking him out, once again. Then he waltzed back to the stage, holding the note; the rest of us were shaking our heads. "You know," I remarked. "You could have broken that over a table something."

"Me know that," Maul replied. "Me did that for luck."

Everyone piled around me as I slowly unrolled the note and read it to them. "Your wagon's warranty is about to expire, and for a small fee, you can extend it. Contact Padre Pat at Callcenter Temple to lock in a low rate."

Everyone groaned. We hated getting these scam messages. The worse part about it was this wasn't the first one we've ever gotten; they had been growing in number for months. I always end up reading the notes, even though I know it's a scam. Whenever I see a message in a bottle, curiosity overwhelms me, and I have to pick it up!

Entry 56

I love journal entries, or as others sometimes call them, records. Whenever something interesting happens, I always tell the guys, "That's one for the record books!"

I know others have kept journals of their adventures, but I see myself as a recording star for the music industry in the Unremembered Realms. I figure, who knows, maybe other bards will read the records of Scales

& The Marshtones and one day give writing records a spin! If that ever happened, I'd create a top 100 list of some sort to post on Neverspring's largest billboard!

Entry 57

I was startled from my sleep by horrid cries of anguish. It started with small groans followed by sharp yelps and then long bellows. I pulled the blanket on my swampwater bed over my head and covered my ear holes. The cries were hard to listen to, I didn't know how long the torture would last, but it sounded painful.

I felt terrible, listening to the sobs outside of the tour wagon, knowing that not only was there nothing I could do, but to dare to step out of it with any intention of helping would only put me in danger, as well. I bit at my claw nails, nervously awaiting the next scream, but then there was silence. I peeked my head up from under my sheet only to hear Maul's voice cry out. "Hey guys, come on out, you have to see this!"

I saw Rhody walk past my open door, but I jumped up and stopped him. "Trust me, Rhody, you do not want to see that!"

"It sounds like Maul was killing something big out there," he replied. "I want to check it out!"

"The only thing Maul killed off was his plate last night," Peavus yawned, coming out of his room wearing his sleeping cap and striped pajamas.

"I told him never to fry up roadkill," I said to the others before turning over in my bed. "Especially when it's bloated from sitting in the sun. Serves him right!"

Entry 58

One of the strangest places we ever played was at a village in the province of Winterspring called Mountain Ear. It had only a few hundred citizens, but stands out in my mind because it had a strict constable named Dublin Obervelt. We first had a run-in with this constable when we pulled into town, and the pot-bellied human waved us over.

"Where do you boys think you're going?" he asked while shifting his sword belt.

"We've got a gig at the Echo Chamber Tavern," I explained. "It's a repeat performance."

The constable did not even smirk at my joke and lowered his sunglasses. "Well, lizardman," he said. "We run a tight ship around here, so watch your tail."

It didn't take us long to find out what he had meant, either. The second we pulled in the back alley to unload our equipment through the back door of the tavern, Rhody's humming was overheard by a gnome, who ran off in a hurry. After a few minutes, Dublin appeared with a ticket book and furiously scribbled in it before handing the dwarf a fine. "What's this for?" Rhody growled.

"No humming on Fridays," the constable grinned, rubbing a lower chin. "It's the law."

"But we're musicians," I pointed out, feeling a bit perturbed. "We're supposed to be musical."

Dublin spat on the ground. "Listen," he stated, almost cheerfully, obviously enjoying his power. "I don't make the laws; I just enforce them."

"No, you make the laws, too," chimed in the tattling gnome who stood next to him.

"Well, Pincork," Dublin replied, "It's not against the law to lie, now is it?"

After saying that, the portly human got a wild look on his face. He then pulled out a book and wrote a note in it. Next, he chuckled menacingly. "All right then," Dublin smirked. "No more lying."

After he strolled away, I told the band that we needed to leave as quickly as possible when we finished the show. We were getting paid well, but something told me we'd be losing a good chunk of it to whatever bizarre laws that Mr. Obervelt could ticket us for.

"Me not like fat human," Maul grunted. "Soon, it be slap time...."

"We're not here to stir up trouble," I reminded him. "We're here to stir the soul!"

"Humph," Maul grunted while grabbing his Warshburn bass and heading inside.

It wasn't long before we were finally up on stage and playing our hearts out to a lively audience. It seemed that the people of Mountain Ear were anxious to blow off some steam. There was dancing in the aisles and people cheering in the front row, having a grand ole time. They all sang along when we played one of our most popular numbers called *Green Dungeon Slime*, which went like this:

(Sung to the tune of Sweet Caroline by Neil Diamond)
First square it began, we wandered in the dungeon
Hoping for loot, but we were wrong
Stepped on a spring
And we soon began to plummet
Should have brought a rogue along
Hands, it's on my hands
Oozing out, sliming me, sliming you
Green dungeon slime
Never thought I'd be some monster's food
I'm being dined
Now all that is left is my shoes
But now I
Look to the knight, and I don't feel so lonely
For he too was just consumed
And the clerics hurt
Green slime up to his shoulders
Soon it will spit out both his boots
Run, better run
Oozing out, sliming me, sliming you
Green Dungeon Slime
Slowly 'gested as its food
Things could be worse
At least it wasn't a black pudding
Oh no, no
Green Dungeon Slime
Things didn't work out so good
Green Dungeon Slime
I believe I'm now its food
Green Dungeon Slime
Things didn't work out so good

We were about to break out into another chorus when, suddenly, we heard a bell start to ring, and everyone in the audience stopped whatever they were doing. Every single one of them pulled a small sausage from their pockets, coin purses, or whatever and stuffed them into their left ear. I looked over at the tavern keeper and saw that he was the one ringing the bell. He was looking at us and pointing to his ear as if to say, "Where's your ear sausage?"

The band had quit playing by this point, and we looked at each other and shrugged. I was going to say something to Peavus, but the door to the Echo Chamber Tavern swung open, and there stood Constable Obervelt with a big grin on his face. Everyone gasped and parted out of his way as he whipped out his ticket book and approached the stage. "Wow," he stated. "You guys love to break the law!"

"What?" I asked. "What law?"

"Take a look around you," Dublin stated. "It's 8:00 on a Friday night in Mountain Ear. That means sausage time!"

"That's the dumbest thing I've ever heard!" Rhody shouted from behind a stack of our magically-enhanced Marred Skull amplifiers. "What a waste of food!"

Dublin Obervelt grinned. "Oh, it's not a waste. It's against the law not to eat the sausage afterward, as well!"

"That's just gross," I commented. "Eating a sausage that's been in your ear."

"We're not uncivilized," Dublin corrected me. "You don't eat your sausage. You're required to eat someone else's."

"Eew," Peavus stated, "That's even worse!"

"It's not that bad," a halfling shouted from the audience. "Except for the occasional hair, I love it! And how did you know my name?"

"Me not eat ear hair," Maul stated, "or pay fines. Let me slap this squishy pink human!"

"I wouldn't do that if I were you," Dublin stated, pointing back to the open door of the tavern.

When we all looked, we saw the face of a green dragon peek an eye inside. "This is Bogus," Dublin said. "She is my deputy. She hates it when people disobey my laws, er...I mean the city's, laws."

Patrons ran from the door screaming, pushing their sausages deeper into their ears and hiding wherever they could. I had to admit, the band

and I joined Rhody behind some amplifiers! That is, except for Maul, who marched up to the constable and started slapping the snot out of him!

As Maul did this, the crowd gasped in horror, and Bogus roared outside, shaking the whole tavern! "No, Maul!" I yelled. "Stop!"

Maul then laid a big slap and spun Dublin like a top, who then crashed through a table, breaking it into multiple pieces. The constable lifted his bruised head for a moment, then collapsed into unconsciousness. At that moment, Bogus began to expel some of her poisonous gas breath through the doorway, but she flickered in and out for a moment, then disappeared completely!

"Well, what do you know," Peavus said, standing up from behind an amp. "Dublin is an illusionist!"

"I can't believe it," the halfling named Eew said while chewing the sausage he had uncorked from someone's ear. "Your bass player figured out Dublin's trick!"

"Are you saying you already knew?" I asked the halfling. "Why in the realms didn't you say anything?!"

"And miss out on all the ear sausage?" Eew replied. "Are you crazy?"

By this time, the people in the tavern were surrounding Maul and shaking his hand, thanking him for his good deed. The half-ogre just looked at me and shrugged, like he didn't understand why everyone was so happy with him. I wasn't even sure he knew about the deputized dragon illusion or not. He was just pleased that he got to slap someone.

Entry 59

Like any musician, we've had our fair share of naysayers. Unfortunately for us, one of them happens to be a halfling reporter from Trolling Tone News. His name is Hackett, and he first saw us play at the Wobbletable Tavern in Moonwink. I thought we made a good impression on him, at first, because we spotted him grooving to our song *Skull Cleaver*, which Maul sings. It is a love song about the sword of a lowly Decapitator Barbarian trying to get ahead. Maul always seemed to get emotional when he sang these words:

(Sung to the tune of Dream Weaver by Gary Wright)

Me feel eyes turn red again
And me ready to cause lots of pain
With an aortic fountain spray
Me chuckle and kick head away
Ooh, skull cleaver
You sure can chop the head off of a knight
Ooh, skull cleaver
me believe we can gently slice and dice
Noggin's fly to the starry skies
Cures migraines faster than Aspirin cantrip
Me can be cleric, can't you see?
Why does everyone flee from me?
Ooh, skull cleaver
You seem to be more of a scythe
Ooh, skull cleaver
Me believe you cure for da head lice

I think the problem started when a toothless half-orc waitress the little guy had been flirting with started winking at Peavus. I guess his lute solo during *Great Ball of Fire* moved her soul. I could see the look of rage in Hackett's face as he balled up his small fists before shaking them at us. I found out later what the halfling was furiously writing in his notes when the article was published. It wasn't good.

Once in a while after that, we'd spot Hackett in the crowd glaring at us, pen in hand. I hated this, because no matter how good we'd play, the little twerp would always find a way to put us down. I was so upset I could barely make it through our sets. But, oddly enough, Maul gave me some good advice. "Picture that squab on serving plate with some kale dipping sauce," he whispered to me on stage.

That trick seemed to work well, but it had its downside, too. It is difficult to sing when you're drooling all over yourself.

Entry 60

One of the worst things about being on the road is that you have to face off with random, wandering parties once in a while. These creatures are usually out and about looking for a fight to collect treasure or gain experience in fighting. Half of the time, you can't reason with them; they just come running at you with their weapons.

Being a lizardman who travels with a ghost and a half-ogre doesn't help. Thank the realms Peavus and Rhody are there to step in to calm the wandering party's down and let them know that we are not a threat. We explain that we're in a band, but sometimes, after hearing us play, they decide to attack us anyway!

Entry 61

One day, as we traveled down a trail leading toward Fumblecrit, we came across a group of Thaconian warriors sitting around a campfire, cooking their lunch. Upon spotting us, they leaped to their feet and held up wooden clubs. "Whoa, guys," I said as we came to a halt. "We're just a band on tour, passing through."

After a brief pause, they lowered their weapons in relief. "I wouldn't stick around here too long," a gray-scaled one warned. "These woods are filled with rust monsters!"

When he said that, he patted the sliced-up carcass of one. "They are good eating, though," another Thaconian added. "Good for you, too. Lots of iron."

"You boys hungry?" the first one stated. "We have plenty."

"Sorry, fellas," I explained. "We're booked at the Blacksmith Guild in Fumblecrit tonight. We're the opening act for their main act, Iron Maidens."

"We'll never eat all this," the second Thaconian stated after a burp. "It's a shame, too, since this bugger devoured all our metal weapons and gold."

"I was wondering about that," I replied. "I've never seen a Thaconian fight with a wooden club before."

For those unfamiliar with Thaconians, these were Dragonborn warriors who loved to game, and saw life as just that. They were real number crunchers, always consulting the charts they carried with them. I've seen Thaconians prepping for a surprise attack against an enemy by going over graphs on what they called DM Screens (which stands for Danger Mapping). The leader would usually take a set of polyhedral dice, roll them, then compare them to the numbers on their graphs. If the numbers didn't line up, they would turn around and leave. The downside of being a Thaconian is that you would most likely leave a lucrative dungeoneering adventure empty-handed, or you would be confused during surprise attacks. A Thaconian my father once knew told me it's hard to roll on charts when a Crettin is pounding you flat with the trunk of a fallen tree!

After a short goodbye, we were back on the trail, heading toward what we hoped would be a lucrative convention. We had only gone a little way when Maul, who was driving, had Haul and Oats slam on their brake shoes. Everyone in the wagon was thrown forward, due to the sudden stop. It made me spill the cup of fly soup I was gingerly sipping. "Hey!" I yelled up to Maul. "What is going on up there?!"

When the band left the inside of the magical tour wagon, we all could see why Maul had stopped. He was holding a baby rust monster in his arms. "Look what me found in middle of road, isn't it cute?"

The small creature looked at us with big watery eyes, and our hearts melted. "Those warriors must have eaten its parent; now it is orphan. Me want to keep it."

Everyone looked at each other. "Are you sure you want to do that?" Peavus asked. "It is a rust monster. It will try to eat all the metal we have."

"Me will train it," Maul said, petting its oddly shaped head. "Me promise."

Ghasper groaned in doubt. "I agree, Ghasper," I replied. "That thing is going to grow up to be huge."

"I could learn a shrink spell for it," Peavus said, walking up to pet it. "I could cast it on it every day to keep it small. It is kind of cute."

I couldn't argue at this point. "As long as it gets along with Ziljan, I'm okay with it," I said. "But you have to keep it locked up when we play at the Blacksmith Guild; they hate those creatures."

Maul seemed elated and jumped back into the driver's seat as we all climbed back in. "Me will name you Dustin," he said while setting it next to him on the seat, where it began to pant happily.

Later that night, we were jamming on stage for a lively audience. We were pleased to be the opening act for the Iron Maidens, a top-rated group with blacksmiths from all over the realms. They loved this group, because they were a female metal band. By that, I mean they were five iron golems that magic-users had trained to be bards. Nobody was heavier than these five, and they had to have reinforced stage supports to prove it!

"Is everyone having fun tonight?" I called out from the stage.

A loud cheer came back as an answer. "Before we get Iron Maidens out here, we're going to end our set with a song we wrote with a fellow bard named MC Warhammer, called *Must Forge This*.

(Sung to the tune of Can't Touch This by MC Hammer)
My, my, my, my forge is blazing hot
I make weapons on the spot
Sparks are flying to the beat
Steel is glowing in the heat
Feels so good when sweat rolls down
this homeboy must be a smith, no doubt
and I'm known as such
And my anvil's still hot, so don't touch
(Oh-oh-oh-oh-oh-oh-oh)
I told you, homesmith, I must forge this
(Oh-oh-oh-oh-oh-oh-oh)
Yeah, that's how y'all make a livin', you know,
Must forge this

Holes are burned in shirts and pants
You got the metal in the flame, making it dance
But watch for embers on your seat
Or you'll be up dancing to a different beat
While it's flaming... hold on
Put your rump in a bucket...ssssss...then move on

Cold steel gleaming, on a rack
Not a bit of rust, or a single crack
And this anvil's still hot, so don't touch
(Oh-oh-oh-oh-oh-oh-oh)
Yo, I told you, I must forge this
(Oh-oh-oh-oh-oh-oh-oh)
Don't just stand there like a chump
(Oh-oh-oh-oh-oh-oh-oh)

Whomp! War hammer time!

Special request from a cleric named Fred
Can you make him a mace to bash undead?
With both your thumbs in the air
You promise it'll crush their bones and split some hairs
The weapon is unique, like a flake in winter
But it will make your gold purse thinner

Now shove them out of your shop
Because this anvil's bout to ring, nonstop!
(Oh-oh-oh-oh-oh-oh-oh)
Oh, yeah, I must forge this
(Oh-oh-oh-oh-oh-oh)
Listen up, homesmith, I must forge this!
(Oh-oh-oh-oh-oh-oh)

I was finishing the chorus when we heard a loud shriek from behind the stage curtain. It had a metallic ring and didn't sound like anything we had heard before. The shrieking continued, so everyone stopped what they were doing and raced backstage. When we pulled back the curtain, we saw four of the Iron Maidens huddled up off the floor, on a large table, shaking with fear. Below them, looking up with doughy wet eyes, was Dustin. The baby rust monster had goo around its mouth, as it had just eaten!

"It ate our drummer!" cried out the lead singer of the Iron Maidens in a tinny voice. "It's going to kill us all!"

Before anyone could react, Maul picked Dustin up and carried the little creature. "Naughty, naughty," Maul said softly. "Eating iron people a no-no."

A short time later, we were back on the tour wagon, standing in Maul's room, demanding an explanation. "Me not know what happened," Maul shrugged. "Me put him in wooden cage!"

"But you used a metal lock!" I said, feeling frustrated. "Now we're broke, again, because the guild made us pay for a new drummer to be constructed for Iron Maidens!"

"Me didn't think he'd pick lock," Maul replied. "He one smart baby!"

"He ate the lock," Peavus said, gently taking Dustin from Maul. "You have to keep a better eye on this one!"

Maul sighed. "Me promise, nothing bad will happen again."

Just then, Peavus's pants fell to the floor, revealing his musical note boxer shorts. "My belt buckle!" Peavus griped. "It just ate my belt buckle!"

Entry 62

As usual, due to a lack of funds, we were forced to play yet another show that our manager, Colonel Crom Parker, didn't thoroughly think through. It was deep in the Gungalunga Forest in the Province of Rustwood. Crom told us that it was a monthly get-together of some sort, and there would be big crowds. He had failed to mention that it was a death cult holding monthly sacrifices to a giant red dragon named Briquette.

So, there I was, sitting across a desk in their temple, working out details with the head priest, while the band helped Rhody set up our gear on a platform outside. I wasn't comfortable with the whole scene, but I lived by the motto, "A fan is a fan," so, I sat there listening to the red-robed priest.

I have to say that I was a bit taken aback by his appearance. Apparently, to join this cult, they removed your eyes before giving you a magical one in your forehead that was activated by putting their fingertips together in a circle over it. "How do you see with that?" I asked, finding the non-blinking, golden eyeball unnerving.

"I see clearer now than I did before," he grinned. "Now, if you'll just fill out these forms."

The minute he moved his hands to grab the paperwork, the eyeball disappeared, and he began to shuffle around with his hands on the desk. "I know I have them here somewhere."

I looked at the papers and gently pushed them under his hand. "Ah, here they are," he stated happily, shoving them back toward me, before reforming his hands on his forehead.

"Have you ever thought about joining a cult?" the priest asked. "Because if you did, the Pupils of Briquette have a recruitment drive right now."

I pretended to think about it for a moment; I didn't want to seem rude. "Maybe someday, mister um…."

"Roger," he said, finishing my questioning statement. "We all go by Roger."

"Okay, Roger," I stated as I signed the document. "I'll consider it. But I do have to admit; I find the sacrificing of fellow humanoids a bit off-putting."

"Let me get you a brochure," Roger replied, spinning around in his chair to locate a filing cabinet. "Now, I wonder where I put that file?"

He removed his hands from his forehead, once again, and began scrambling through the file drawers. "Never mind," I said, not wishing to sit there another fifteen minutes. "I got your address; I'll know where to come."

With a relieved expression, he turned around, facing me, once again, with his hands back to his forehead. "Oh, the sacrifices aren't all that bad. It's on a voluntary basis, only, uh, sort of."

"What do you mean, sort of?" I asked.

"Well," Roger explained with a smirk. "You don't have to volunteer yourself. You could volunteer a friend."

He could see by the look on my face I wasn't buying into what he was selling. "Oh, but the bright side is all the rhythmic chanting, good food, and a monthly ritual featuring Briquette the dragon eating someone other than yourself. It's a beautiful thing."

I have to admit that even though I had no plans on joining, all the Rogers we met that day seemed extremely pleasant. Everyone walking by would wave hello, before tripping on something. They even would applaud wildly after each of our songs, even though that meant not seeing us momentarily.

Our stage was set up in front of the sacrificial dais, where Roger the Priest would come out later and ask for volunteers. Right behind us on a pedestal was a giant dragon egg. It rested on a bed of gold coins and jewels. It was about as big as Maul's torso. I tried to ignore it, along with the sacrificial altar, as we played song after song. When we got to our last number, I addressed the crowd. "Thanks for coming out tonight, folks. We want to end our set with an uplifting little song about a lowly waitress whose dream comes true; it's called *An Unearthed Arcana*…and remember, don't sacrifice…your dreams…do you hear me? I repeat, don't sacrifice..."

From their blank expressions, I could tell I wasn't getting anywhere, so, with a sigh, I said, "Hit it, boys."

(Sung to the tune of Copacobana by Barry Manilow)
Her name was Igga, ogga egga
With dreams of power squared, her waitress job couldn't compare
She heard a rumor about some treasure
She found it in the lair, a book just lying there
Its owner was on vaykay
So behind a secret door, with symbols on the floor
She snuck right in with no fellow orcs lookin'
Now she knows some lore!

From an unearthed, unearthed arcana
The book with spells that all can cana
With an unearthed, unearthed arcana
Lightning is flashy and webbing so sticky
With the Arcana... She learned them all...

His name was Bogwind
He was a big Orc
Bugs lived inside his hair; he acted like a derriere
He didn't tip much, sure; his breath reeked of sewers
And on his face ran down a scar
and he stole from her tip jar
Then she let a magic missile fly
and that big oaf died!

From some unearthed, unearthed arcana
A book with spells that all can cana
With an unearthed, unearthed arcana
Lightning is flashy and webbing so sticky
With arcana... Her adventures began...

After an enormous round of applause, we did some bows and then headed back to the wagon. None of us wanted to see what these people did next. "Let's leave first thing in the morning," I told Maul. "After a good breakfast."

"Me get up early and make food," Maul smiled.

The morning rays of dawn hadn't yet broken when I caught a whiff of something delicious cooking. Everyone else had, as well, so we gathered around the campfire outside and ate heaps of the scrambled eggs that Maul was cooking. "I have to say, Maul," Peavus stated. "These are the best scrambled eggs you've ever made."

Maul grinned proudly. "Me agree. But you described the food wrong. It not scrambled eggs."

"Huh," Rhody stated. "Of course, these are scrambled eggs, don't be foolish."

"Nope," Maul stated. "Not plural. This be scrambled egg."

Everyone there did a spit take. "Scrambled egg?!" I said, panicking. "You don't mean…."

"It sure make a lot," the half-ogre grinned, feeling proud of himself, before whispering to me while pointing at his head. "Me use brain."

"Where's the shell? Where's the shell!?!" I began to panic. "Maybe we can glue it back together and no one will notice!"

"Calm down," Maul said, smiling smugly. "Me already thought of that. Used tree sap. Egg shell looks good as new. Me sure no one will notice."

Just then, a loud screech could be heard from the direction of the temple. A fiery flash lit up the sky, and we heard hundreds of screams yell out in agony. Everyone crossed their arms and glared at Maul. "Me guess there won't be an encore."

"Roger that," Peavus agreed, shaking his head.

Entry 63

One of our more embarrassing moments from our Found on the Road Tour is when a couple of the Eldarly attacked us. They are a race of humanoids that appear to be old but are fierce warriors. The main attack these creatures use is surprise. What makes things even worse, is when you report them to a local constable, they laugh at you and think you're a wimp for losing a fight to old folks!

One night, before our big show in Floptover, Maul, Peavus, and I sat around the campfire talking about new song ideas. Maul wanted us to focus on more violent songs, Peavus was writing something from the viewpoint of a snail (it was a slow-paced number), and I was composing a piece about deep-fried halfling innards. I was just about to finish a chorus about cheesy toe sauce when a couple of older humans came out of nowhere. "Excuse us, younglings," the withered-looking female said while supporting herself with her cane. "Is this the trail to Floptover?"

"It sure is, ma'am," I said. "It's an hour by foot or ten minutes by wagon."

The even older-looking male nodded at the woman and said, "They sure do have a nice-looking ride. Maybe they will let us take it."

"Whoa there," I said, standing up. "If you need a ride in the morning, we'll gladly help, but our magic tour wagon is not for sale!"

"Who said anything about buying it?" the man remarked while impressively lifting a giant club out from a sack of holding.

Within the blink of an eye, the Eldarly were upon us all. He was hitting, kicking, and even worse, gumming us! Poor Maul was hit with a Slumber spell before he could even stand up. I managed to kick the male, but before getting to my spear, I was knocked unconscious by a cane with a hard knot on its end! The next thing I knew, I was having cold water splashed in my face. When I blinked my eyes open, Rhody was standing over me.

"You alright, boss?" he asked.

"Where were you, Rhody?" I asked, looking around. "Old people just robbed us."

"I was off in the woods. Nature was calling," he replied. "And believe me, I left a long reply!"

"Please..stop," I said. "I don't want to get any dizzier."

"They took the tour wagon," Peavus stated while nursing a black eye. "I suggest we wake up Maul and head after them."

"This sounds like the Eldarly," Rhody grumped while taking a water bucket over to Maul, who was smiling as he slept. "They are as fierce as they are predictable."

Rhody explained that the old couple was not really old; they were a unique race of humans that only appeared that way. The dwarf also explained that they would be easily trackable.

"Why do you say that?" I asked.

"The Eldarly have strict routines," Rhody explained. "They get up early, drink their coffee at the nearest coffee shop, then have their morning constitutionals before sitting around and complaining of their ailments. Kind of like Peavus."

"Hey," Peavus replied.

"They sure looked old to me," I said, rubbing the bump on my head. "But if they only look old, why do they act like older people?"

"That's their trick," Rhody explained. "Because of their appearance, they were accepted by the elderly of the realms. Over many many years, they just picked up their habits.

"Do you mean to tell me that if we make it to Floptover and we go to fight them for our wagon, they might be mixed in with normal old folks?" I asked, feeling frustrated.

"I'm afraid so," Peavus stated. "We better hurry; poor Ghasper might be waking up soon and will be in for a big shock!"

"Alright," I said, standing up. "Let's hit the road."

After an hour of walking, we came upon the "Welcome to Floptover" sign. The morning wasn't quite over, so we hoped that the Eldarly were still sitting around drinking coffee. It didn't take long to figure out where they had gone. Our tour wagon was parked outside of a Scarbucks coffee shop. When we approached close enough to get it, we saw something that prevented us from taking our precious wagon back. "There are magic locks on all four wheels," Peavus noted, tapping on one. "I don't have a magic spell strong enough to unlock any of these."

"Let's go in shop and smash these elderly," Maul said, smiling.

"You mean the Eldarly," I clarified. "Right?"

Maul shrugged. "Whatever."

"I have a cunning plan," Peavus said. "It will keep the normal oldlings from getting hurt...."

After a short explanation, Maul, Peavus, and I got our instruments and walked into the Scarbucks. Rhody went into Ghasper's room to wake him up and explain the situation. Within no time, we had the owner of Scarbucks agreeing to let us play a quick, free show for all the patrons.

The three of us stood in a corner, since there wasn't a stage, and looked over the gray-haired crowd. There were so many of them that it was hard to tell who the thieving Eldarly were. That's where Peavus's idea would help. We'd play a really old song that only oldlings would like, leaving the Elderly scratching their heads and sitting there with their coffee while the others got up to shuffle around to the music.

"How's everyone doing this fine morning?" I asked while tuning my lute.

Groans about ailments and recent trips to the cleric were most of the replies, so I cut them off. "My name is Scales, and these are the Marshtones. We're going to play a little number about how hard it is to bathe yourself in your twilight years; it's called *Crish Crash, I Fell in the Bath*."

(Sung to the tune of Splish Splash by Bobby Darin)
Crish Crash, I fell in the bath
Yup, it wuzza Saturday night, yeah
Glub, glub, started drowning in the tub
I thought I'd be a ghost that night
Well, I pulled out the plug, like my kids talk about
I check my hips for any cricks
And gave the nurse a shout, and then
A-crish crash, I fell backward in the bath
Well, how was I to know there was a bar of soap right there
I was a-crishing and a-crashing, wailing and a flailing
Bowel moving and a-drooling, dipping and a-drowning, yeah
Bing-bang, then I saw my old gang
Dancing at the pearly gates, yeah
There was Clip clop, the centaurin mage
Hot Top the barbarian who was always enraged
There was Pickpock and Shooby Doo
The dumb thief and my old cleric cut in two
A-well-a, crish crash, I told them about the bath
They laughed and put their dancing shoes on, yeah
I was hopping and bopping, and all the streets were golden
From that crish-crashing, yeah

The rhythmic beat of the song had all the gray-toppers up on their feet and grooving; I have to admit, these old-timers still had some moves left in them! As Peavus predicted, only two hadn't gotten up, and we could now see them clearly; it was the Elderly! They glared at us, knowing that we had found them. They could also see Maul, which is why they didn't quickly attack us, again. But before they could make a break for the door, the second phase of our plan kicked in.

Rhody had slammed the front door open, and in floated Ghasper, who was wearing an ethereal black robe and carrying a scythe (it was one of his favorite costumes he kept for special occasions). The old folks ran to him like they had been waiting for him to show up, leaving the two Eldarly alone and giving them no way to escape! But, as Peavus figured, they wouldn't try to escape; they tried to fight!

As they tried to run up, Maul whipped out his magical music weapon, known as a Kazooka, and gave it a blast in their direction! The concussive musical force knocked the Eldarly duo off their feet, sending them crashing through tables and chairs. They were knocked unconscious! After a quick search, we were able to find the key for the magic locks. The owner of Scarbucks shooed us out of the establishment before running off for the nearest constable station to report the incident.

In the end, it all worked out. The Eldarly were arrested, we got our wagon back, Ghasper signed a bunch of autographs, and we were allowed to play more oldies for all the oldies.

Entry 64

One of the first shows I ever performed as a solo artist was at Heptune's Tavern in Hoptoad, a small city just south of Widowsmarsh. Even though I had been a bit player in other bands, I had finally convinced my father my music was no longer just a hobby. I told him I wanted to take my barding to the next level. He said if I did well at the talent show, he'd give his blessing on me pursuing my dream. I was very excited to put down my spear and sling up Tegus, my trusty lute.

I practiced nonstop, even playing during most of my walk to Hoptoad. I knew it was a small venue, but I saw it as the beginning of a lifelong career. When I got to Heptune's, I was shown to the backstage area where dozens of other performers were getting ready. There were all sorts of creatures applying stage makeup and fine-tuning their acts.

The ones that stuck in my mind the most were a duet called Wight & Zombie, a formerly living couple of married bards murdered by an evil cleric but raised back from the dead. Instead of killing people in dank dungeons, they decided to kill onstage. Later on, they became pretty famous around the realms for their eccentric brand of soul music.

Not all of the acts were music, of course. Some of the entertainers danced, did tricks, or even told jokes. I remember a dwarf named Noneck bombing onstage after a string of weak one-liners. "I've got to steal better jokes," he grumbled after coming backstage, covered with bits of tomato.

My turn was coming up, and I nervously paced back and forth. I could hear the delicious sound of applause as an illusionist named Henning was onstage doing some great tricks. I knew it would be almost impossible to beat him, which made me feel even worse. I'd stop to tune Tegus every few minutes, but I just couldn't get it right; I was too nervous. "You need some help, mister?" a scruffy voice asked from behind me.

When I turned around, I saw a pudgy, light-haired human with thick-framed glasses setting down his magician's wand. He walked over, and with a couple of quick turns of the keys, he had my lute sounding better than ever! "Whoa!" I said in amazement. "You really have an ear for music! I mean, for a mage, that is!"

The wizard just smiled. "My name is Calvin Peabody," he explained while giving my claw a quick shake. "I've been studying magic, but between you and me, I'd rather be a bard."

"So, what is stopping you?" I asked curiously.

Calvin just scratched his head and laughed. "You don't know who my father is, apparently...."

"I'm from deep inside Widowsmarsh," I explained. "We're kind of cut off."

Calvin nodded to show he understood before explaining his dilemma. "My father's name is Houdimli; he is the retired Spellmeister General for the King of Cloverose. He says the life of a bard is too risky."

"My name is Scales, by the way," I said. "And you're not the only one who has a father who doesn't see eye-to-eye."

"The Amazing Peabody!" called out the emcee from the stage. "Come on up!"

Calvin sighed and pushed his glasses up. "I've got to go," he said. "Wish me luck!"

I gave him a thumbs-up as he grabbed his magic gear and ran out to the stage. He didn't notice that he revealed his lute leaning on a wall behind it all. It was a pearl inlaid Stratoscaster, and the fretboard was quite worn. I wondered how good this reluctant magic-user was.

I immediately winced at the sound of booing from the audience. Whatever magic tricks he was doing did not seem to be going so well. I wondered if he was that bad at magic or didn't really care because his heart wasn't in it. Not only that, but Henning the Illusionist was just a hard act to follow. Calvin soon jogged back from the stage, wiping off a few bits of tomato, and gave me a wink as he passed by. I knew it! Magic was not his thing at all!

"Now," the show's emcee voice rang out, "From the swamps of Widowsmarsh, let's give a big round of applause for Scales!"

When I hit the stage for the first time, I felt the warmth of the spotlight hit my face, and it felt great! "Greetings, people of Hoptoad," I began. "My name is Scales, and I wrote a song called *Picked It Up*. It's about a foolish rogue who impatiently picked up a magic item that would have been better left alone. And it goes like this...."

(Sung to the tune of Lick It Up by KISS)
Didn't wait for identification
Now turned to stone from petrification
The potion didn't look right, but you had to taste it
Dividing spoils is when you hasted
Don't start to whine, fool; you did it yourself!

Picked it up, You picked it up, oh-oh-oh (cut in line now)
Picked it up, You picked it up, oh-oh-oh (Woo yeah)
Picked it up, You picked it up, oh-oh-oh (Come on, come on)
Picked it up; you're so dumb, oh-oh-oh (Uh)

Halfway through the song, a few audience members began tapping their feet, while others stared. But just as I was about to go into the second verse, another lute kicked in behind me, filling out my song and embellishing it with some excellent leads. It was Calvin! The audience immediately reacted with applause, and some started moving their bodies to the rhythm! So, I continued...

You picked it up without hesitation
Mentally I think you're on vacation

We all laughed out because we thought it was funny
Picked it up, picked it up
That's one less share, to split the money
I never met such a low IQ elf!

Picked it up, You picked it up, oh-oh-oh (cut in line now)
Picked it up, You picked it up, oh-oh-oh (Woo yeah)
Picked it up, You picked it up, oh-oh-oh (Come on, come on)
Picked it up; you're so dumb, oh-oh-oh (Uh)

When I ended the song, Calvin broke out into a lead that I played along as we faded out. The audience went wild! I couldn't believe it! We both took a bow before walking off stage. "Thanks for the backup," I told Calvin. "We make a pretty good team!"

Calvin nodded in agreement. "Perhaps we should form a band," he said. "You could be the song leader and I could play lead lute!"

I agreed, and we shook on it. "What should we call ourselves?" I wondered out loud. "The Heptunes, after this tavern? Or how about the Marshtunes, since I'm from the swamps?"

Calvin took off his glasses and raised his fist, "I got it! Scales and the Marshtones!"

From that point on, Calvin and I were inseparable. We had even won second place in the talent contest, just behind Henning! Our fathers reluctantly agreed that we could follow our dreams. Calvin was so inspired that he started exercising and grew his hair out. He even liked the stage name I came up with for him, Peavus Calloway. It was a mix of the name of a famous lute company and my uncle Calloway who was one of my inspirations.

The next thing on our agenda was to find a drummer and a bass player. We figured that should be easy enough; after all, how hard could it be to find a couple of laid-back dudes who wouldn't stick out too much?

Entry 65

True fame has always seemed around the corner for the band and me; that's why it is so frustrating to hear famous bards complain about success. Once, we opened for a musical ghoul named Conway Hexx at the Sidebucket Tavern in Neverspring. I was by the back door eating a sandwich when the singer himself came out, stood next to me, and started talking shop.

"You know what I hate?" he groaned. "Having to give so many autographs. I swear, sometimes I want to have some low-level cleric turn me at some point."

"Yeah, well, I wouldn't know." I started to say, but he cut me off.

"Oh and having to wade through my big entourage as they follow me around falling all over themselves to cater to the smallest of my whims," he explained. "I just want some privacy!"

"I'm pretty sure they just admire you for your music and…."

"The chef's in these places never seem to get me," he interrupted. "They make me sandwiches for after the show thinking I'm going to eat them. I don't think they remember that I'm a ghoul and only eat living flesh. I always feel bad throwing it all in the trash."

He didn't notice me drop his discarded sandwich back in the trash can. Opening acts weren't allowed in the courtesy room with the main attractions, so we had to fend for ourselves most of the time. "I just wish, for once, that I would be treated just like everyone else," Conway complained.

Just then, the back door swung open, smashing the flustered singer against the wall. "Where's the trash can sandwiches?!" Maul complained. "Me starving!"

Entry 66

I love Ye Olde Fools Day. It's an annual holiday in the Unremembered Realms that gives everyone a chance to lighten up and not take life, or unlife in the case of Ghasper, so seriously. One year, though, things went a little too crazy. It all started with a yell from Peavus, who had gone down to wash his hair in the river.

"Who did this!" he demanded as he stormed up to the camp.

He pointed to his hair, which now stood on end and was covered in polka dots. Maul, Rhody, and I just laughed. "Don't worry," Rhody said, wiping a tear from his eye. "It wears off in twenty-four hours!"

"You just wait!" Peavus said, stomping off.

And he was serious, too, because when the dwarf brushed his teeth that morning, he didn't know Peavus had hidden some Invisibility Potion in his toothpaste. "What's everybody looking at?!" he grumbled, looking like he had no teeth.

Even poor Ghasper couldn't get away. One of us had put a spell trigger on his urn so that when he opened it to get out, it released a Stanky Cloud spell. None of us could get within six feet of him all day. The poor ghost had to listen to bad gas jokes from Maul, who would wave his hand behind him and say, "me pardon" whenever Ghasper floated near.

I didn't escape the pranks, either. Peavus had enough Invisibility Potion left to slather over my lute, making it invisible! Not only did it make it hard to find, but when I did find it, I looked foolish playing it, like I was air luting. This gag was frustrating because we had a show that night at the Knight Light Tavern in Farlong, and I was not happy that I'd have to play on stage like this. "Don't fret," Peavus laughed. "Just tune it out of your mind!"

Maul thought this was all absolutely hilarious until Peavus snuck up behind him with a Scroll of the Frog Prince and cast it on him. Usually, it would turn a handsome person into a frog, but in Maul's case, it turned him into what human females would consider attractive. "Aigh! Me hideous!" he yelled as he checked a mirror. "Me a monster!"

Later, when we played the show, the audience was quite amused as I strummed and sang along to an invisible instrument, so much so that a bunch of them would mimic me in the front row. Ghasper stayed far in the back with a clothespin on his nose while pounding the bongos. Peavus played red-faced as the girls who would typically swoon over him just pointed and laughed at his hair. On the other hand, Maul was surrounded by all types of girls who couldn't take their eyes off him. There was a nicely dressed one, in particular, who seemed quite smitten with him.

After the show, she approached Maul, escorted by a couple of bodyguards. "Sir," she said to him. "Your minstrel talents and handsome looks have won my heart."

Maul looked at me like he didn't know what to do, so I just shrugged. Secretly, I enjoyed watching him squirm. "I am the Princess of Farlong," she continued. "I believe you would make a suitable prince!"

"Hey, Peavus," I whispered. "Doesn't that spell wear off at midnight?"

"I'm afraid so," he replied.

My mind was whirling. If Peavus had another scroll, Maul could be a prince soon, and we'd have access to playing all the royal courts in the Unremembered Realms! "Hey," I whispered. "You wouldn't have any more scrolls, would you?"

"Sorry, Scales. Ye Olde Fool's Day is only once a year," he explained. "I didn't think I'd need another one."

Ghasper groaned. "I know, I know. It's almost midnight. We better get out of here before things get ugly," I replied.

I whistled to Maul, and he smiled and ran after us as we made our way through the patrons and to our tour wagon. The princess had tried to grab him by the arm, but he pulled away, causing her to slip. As she caught herself, she held onto one of his boots. Due to her tight grip, he had to pull his foot out to get away. "No!" cried the princess. "Come back, my prince!"

Suffice to say; we barely made it out of there. Thankfully, everything returned to normal at midnight, and we got back to our busy touring schedule. Rumor on the road was that the princess traveled all over the realms with Maul's smelly boot, trying to find the foot that it fits.

Entry 67

One time, while performing in the now destroyed city of Emberton, we had been playing a celebration of the city's first year in existence. Little did we know, that the noise from our instruments and the crowd cheering would awaken a sleeping dehydra, named Hush, from its ten-year hibernation. The deadly creature loved peace and quiet, and if it didn't get it, it would incite a riot. As we played that fateful night, the crowd cheered loudly, not realizing they were waking the sleeping monster. It wasn't long before the cranky, bleary-eyed dehydra flew in, with its four heads blasting its breath weapon, which removed all the water from your body, leaving you a shriveled husk.

We didn't know what to do, so we kept jamming. We figured, if we were going to die, we might as well go out doing what we loved- playing music! After most of the destruction and death, Hush finally noticed our stage set up at the pavilion in the center of town. The dehydra landed its massive frame before us and stared at us as we finished our song. "That was a good song," one of the heads said.

"I hated it, Dewbrow," said another. "Let's eat them."

"I liked it, too," one said. "Let's hear some more."

"At least let me dehydrate one of them," one complained.

"Forget that, Scarzo," one said. "We have a bad reputation to uphold. "I say we tear them limb-from-limb."

"Oh, so we're all crazy now? Is that it, Snarlos?" Dewbrow said, rolling his eyes. "Bane Alley seems to enjoy their music."

"We've got a lot more songs," I said nervously. "They say music calms the soul and is good for mental health."

"Come on, boys," Bane Alley stated. "Can't you just feel the noise?!"

"Let's take a vote," Dewbrow said. "That seems democratic."

The rest agreed, while we stood there watching. "Who wants to eat these four bards? Say aye."

Two said aye, while the others stayed quiet. Dewbrow shook his head. "Well, this is just great, another tie. We always end up in a tie! Why did we have to be born with four heads instead of five!"

"Me have a forehead," Maul chimed in. "It above me eyebrows."

Dewbrow lowered his head to Maul. "No, half-ogre. I meant we have four separate heads, and four heads are better than one!"

"But not five," I cut in.

"Twenty is better than five," Peavus spoke up. "I'd do twenty."

"Why not a thousand?" I said. "Let's make it one thousand! You'd be unstoppable!"

"Don't be absurd," Scarzo cut in. "Anything above ten is just a complete waste. Besides that, the top-heaviness would…."

"Just play a song," the one called Snarlos sighed. "Then, can we dehydrate them and go back to bed?!"

"Psst," Peavus whispered to me. "If they are so tired. Let's play a lullaby. Maybe they'll go back to sleep, and we can slip out of here."

"Great plan, Peavus," I whispered back. "Let's do *Torn Between Two Ogres*, but change the ogre part to the hydra's heads."

Peavus told the others, while I started the open licks on my lute.

(Sung to the tune of *Torn Between Two Lovers* by Mary MacGregor)
There are times when a Dehydra has a lot on its minds

Wiping out entire towns is sure is a lot of work
Before you kill yet another, let me say a word, I fear y'all
If you let us all loose, then we'll run as fast as we can

There have been other monsters I've run from, and I've feared
But that doesn't mean I fear you less
And you can't eat all of me; a quarter will be your share
One will get my head, arms, legs, then my derriere

Torn between four monsters, quartered for your food
Will I be eaten raw? Or dipped in BBQ?
Torn apart by dehydras, feelin' like a fool
Giving you heartburn is all that I can do

By the time we finished playing, the dehydra was fast asleep on the ground. As we quietly loaded up our gear and were getting the horses ready to tip-clop out of there, a few survivors came over. "Thank you for helping stop the monster," one whispered. "We'd like to invite you back next year."

"What?!" I whispered back. "Are you crazy?"

"No, sir," another said in a hushed tone. "We already have plans for building New Emberton. It's going to be bigger and quieter than ever!"

"I don't understand," I stated. "Why would you want to rebuild next to the home of a sleeping monster like this?"

"The property tax here is incredibly low," one said. "You can't beat that!"

I took a look at the burning homes and shriveled husks of all the corpses and shook my head. "Whatever floats your boat," I said in amazement. "But to me, it looks like every opportunity around here has dried up!"

Entry 68

The first time I met a Folio Fiend was when the band and I were doing a soundcheck at the Flipside Tavern in Quagholm, which is in the northern area of Sunkensod. We were playing a song called *Elven Chain*, and it went like this:

(Sung to the tune of Purple Rain by Prince)
If you never want to feel no sorrow
If you never want to feel no pain
If you're going off into a battle
You better be sure that you're wearing Elven Chain

Elven chain, Elven chain
Mithral chain and a sword of flame
Elven chain, Elven chain

You better be sure that you're wearing Elven Chain

There's a reason that elves live forever
So go ahead and make one as a friend
Go ahead and throw away that leather
And ask them if they can loan you out their Elven Chain

Elven chain, Elven chain
Mithral chain mined from a cavern's vein
Elven chain, Elven chain

You better be sure that you're wearing Elven Chain

Elf, you know that I know, you know, times are changing
When that ogre cleaved my friend in two
That could have been me, too
You say a party needs a leader
So, if you don't want a kick in the behind
Let's go back to Elvy Wonderland
And get me some of that there Elven Chain

Elven chain, Elven chain
Mithral chain I'm never gored again
Elven chain, Elven chain

    That's when I saw a human wander in wearing a white smock and carrying a leather satchel. He had a ring of white hair around his head and thick glasses with a long beard. He tapped on the table to our music for a few minutes while watching us intently.

Then, the odd human pulled out a thick portfolio notebook from the satchel and began writing things down. "What do you think, Peavus?" I said low enough for the human not to hear. "Think he's a song pirate?"

Peavus shrugged and went into his solo. I looked over at Maul thumping away on his Warshburn bass and noticed him frowning at the man. That's when the human reached into his satchel, again, and sat out a few spell components. Then, he put them together before reciting something we couldn't hear. Suddenly, the music stopped, and I felt frozen in place. Through my side vision, I could see Maul and Peavus were frozen in place, as well. I was hoping Ghasper wasn't affected, but something told me whatever spell that was cast was working on him, too, because he did not appear around me when this human walked up on the stage.

The human giggled as he walked around us, poking us with a quill and studying each of us before writing down notes in his book. "Fascinating," is all he would say.

"What did you do to the band?" Rhody asked, walking up from the back of the tavern. "There better be a good explanation!"

"Oh, my, yes," the man replied. "I've never seen a group of monsters such as this play music together. I'm studying them and taking notes in my folio!"

I wanted to say something, but I was frozen stiff. The only thing I could do was blink. I could see Rhody was red in the face but keeping calm. "Go ahead and make yer notes," he said. "Then scram."

"Oh no," the man replied. "My guild will find this quartet incredibly fascinating. This discovery could be very lucrative for us. I simply must take them with me for further study."

"Why not just buy tickets for the show tonight?" the dwarf asked, hoping to solve this peacefully. "Bring a few mates; I'm sure they'll all have fun."

The Folio Fiend just shook his head. "I'm afraid that won't do. We need to dissect these specimens to find out what makes them tick!"

Rhody could see the looks in all our eyes, and he knew we were not happy. Maul's eyes were completely dilated and were becoming bloodshot with rage. I made a mental note right there about the term "bloodshot with rage" and how that might be a cool song title. When I snapped out of my thoughts, I could see Rhody was arguing with the man. "Listen," he started. "This is my band and my livelihood. You're not going to take them without paying up."

I hoped that Rhody wasn't selling us out. He'd been with us for years, and I trusted him. But maybe after all that time of me talking about our shows being sold out, it affected his thought process. I watched in amazement as the Folio Fiend handed our roadie a sack of gold coins. "Thanks, mister," Rhody said, eyeballing the loot. "This is just what I needed."

When the man turned around to study us some more, Rhody took the sack and smashed him over the head with it repeatedly until he collapsed on the floor. The dwarf gave us the thumbs up before dragging him to a chair and tying him into it. By the time he had regained consciousness, his spell had worn off, and we were standing all around him. "What happened?" he grumbled.

"You swooned at our act," I said with a grin. "That was some kind of powerful spell you cast on us; I've never seen anything like it!"

"I agree," Peavus said. "He deserves a round of applause. Maul?"

The half-ogre cracked his knuckles. "Gladly," was all he said before grabbing the Folio Fiend's chair by the back and dragging him outside as he asked the old guy a question: "You ever hear the sound of one hand slapping?"

In the end, it all worked out. We had a nice bag of gold and a neat folio of monsters that Peavus kept with him so we could learn about creatures in the realms. We even had enough to buy some wipes for poor Maul's hand, which was now covered with snot, among other things.

Entry 69

One race that continues to confuse me here in the realms is the humans. They are unpredictable and always do things based on their emotions. I remember this one young man I met while walking along a trail on my way to Mazenhog. I had left the Marshtones to visit family and was now on my way back to the Clutchseat Tavern, where we had a gig.

This teenage human male was sitting on a fallen tree along the trail and was sobbing deeply. "What seems to be the matter?" I asked, walking up to him.

"I'm in love," he said through some sniffles. "And I never know what to say!"

"Love is easy," I said. "I sing about it all the time."

"So, you've known love?" he asked hopefully.

"Of course!" I said happily. "I have the greatest love! Music!"

The young human started sobbing, again. I patted him on the head with my claw then tousled his hair. "Buck up, kiddo, maybe I can help."

The blubbering stopped for a moment, and the human looked up at me with watery eyes. "Really? You'd do that?"

"Why not," I said. "I've got an hour or two to spare, and besides, I've won the hearts of quite a few lizardettes in my day. Where is this human female?"

I assumed it was a human female because humans were not halflings who would fall in love with anything that breathed. "Her name is Jewels, and she lives in a small fortress with her strict father, just over the ridge."

After a short march through the woods, we came to one of the building's towers. The girl the youth had referred to was sitting in a window, brushing her long blonde hair. I didn't get his fascination with her. She didn't have claws, fangs, or even a tail. I swear I don't know what humans see in each other. I still haven't figured out how the females laid their eggs.

"All you have to do is talk to her in rhyme," I said. "You know, like, your skin is soft like a halfling filet, and your eyes shine like an orcs blood on a blade."

"That's perfect, mister. B-b-but I'm too nervous," he said. "I'm no good at rhymes."

"Here," I said impatiently. "Let me show you."

I stepped out of the edge of the forest, holding my lute so that Jewels could see me. I strummed it a few times, and the young woman smiled and waved. "Wherefore art thou?"

"I'm here to win your heart," I replied. "Hopefully, an orc doesn't come by and rip it out before I finish my song!"

The young lady rested her elbows on the balcony ledge, propping her chin upon her fingertips, which I noticed, formed a heart. I gave a wink to the teenage kid and whispered, "Watch and learn."

That's when I began to sing our song *Run Away*:

(Sung to the tune of Yesterday by the Beatles)
Run Away; we should quickly amscray
We didn't look where we were going, eh?
Oh, I just stepped on a dragon's egg!

Suddenly, I don't want to get bit in half today
There's a shadow growling over me
Oh, I just stepped on a dragon's egg!

What did we do?
I don't know; we better pray.
I heard something squish
Oh, I stepped on a dragon's egg-ay-ay-ay.

Run Away, but we're trapped inside this cave
Finding a place to hideaway.
Oh, I stepped on a dragon's egg!

Did she hear the crack?
I don't know who can say?
Did anyone bring some glue today?
Oh, I just stepped on a dragon's egg!

Mm mm mm mm mm mm mm

When the song ended, I hung my head in a bow as the lady applauded wildly. "My love, my love, you may marry me, my love!"

"You double-crosser!" the young man yelled. "She's my bird!"

"And my daughter!" came a voice from behind me.

When I turned around, there was an oddly-dressed Garbarian quickly approaching. When his fist struck me in the eye, I spun completely around and fell to the ground. Before I blacked out, I could see the young man and the girl run off into the woods together, holding hands. I have to admit, playing the show that night with a darker green eye and a swollen lip wasn't easy. They say love can sweep you off your feet, but I say it's more of a knockout!

Entry 70

I don't usually complain about other acts, but I can't help it when I think of Brundleflea & the Fly Girls. They were a tragic, yet disgusting, act that tavern owners would use to clear out customers at the end of the night. Initially, they were a trio of elven singers from Tidepool, but one day they were captured by an evil wizard who experimented on them.

The magic-using madman turned the lead singer into a weird hybrid of an elf and a flea. Then, his two backup singers were crossed with flies. Their transitions to insectoids were the same; they had bodies of elves, but their heads and arms were that of insects. At some point, a paladin and his crew showed up to rescue them, but it was too late. But at least they killed the wizard before their full transition was complete.

The three bards decided to make the most of their situation and stuck with what they knew best, playing music. Instrumentally, they were still fantastic, playing their instruments with skill and flourish. It was their singing that drove people away. The clicking and buzzing didn't sound well on non-insectoid ears and was highly irritating. Plus, there was the fact that, not only did Brundleflea's voice get under your skin, so would he if you weren't looking. The flea inside him couldn't resist drinking blood. Maul had to swat at him a few times one night to keep him away. On top of that, the fly girls would always creep everyone out because they loved to hang out around the outhouse.

We tried talking to them a few times about trying a new profession, but I understood their reluctance, to a degree. They could not resist the pull of the bright stage lights. They were always buzzing about them.

Entry 71

It's not every day that the Marshtones and I get to be heroes, but the sun shines on every bard's tail, once in a while! Once, we were riding along a trail when Maul thought he heard voices. After stopping the tour wagon, he called for us to come outside to check it out. About ten yards off the trail was an emaciated human sitting on the ground, with his back on a tree stump. We could tell he was a Crimson Roof rogue by his dark brown cloak. He looked as frazzled as he was frail.

Although he did not open his mouth, we heard muffled voices emanating from near him. "Would you…" he paused, catching a breath, "like a free Sack of Holding?"

Sitting next to him on the ground was a leathery bag. It seemed the muffled voices were coming from it. I felt bad for the fellow, so I gave him a drink from my waterskin, from which he drank deeply. "Please," he said, a little more clearly. "It's free."

"I don't trust this rogue," Rhody chimed in.

Then, a voice from the sack said, "Trust him, there's lots of treasure in here!"

None of us liked the sound of that; we were now on guard. "What's your name, traveler?" I asked.

"Aggression," he sighed. "My name is Aggression."

A different voice from the sack said, "His real name is Bailey!"

The rogue angrily grabbed the sack, punched it twice, then threw it into the woods. "Curse you!"

Within the blink of an eye, the sack reappeared next to him. Dozens of voices of laughter chuckled from inside of it. "Let's talk about this," the voices of the sack said in unison.

"That's a Yakkity Sack!" Peavus stated, having an a-ha moment. "Don't anyone touch it!"

"Uhhhhhnnnn," groaned Ghasper, as he floated next to Maul.

"Yakkity Sack's are cursed Sacks of Holding, Ghasper," Peavus explained. "Once you accept one as a gift, they never leave you. The voices never stop talking and drive you insane. Once you die, usually by suicide from their chatter, your soul is sucked into the sack to join the other voices!"

"That's terrible," I said. "Poor chap. How'd you get stuck with this?"

Aggression looked up at us wearily through bloodshot eyes. "A fellow rogue tricked me as we were raiding a crazy wizard's cave. It was rumored to have lots of treasure. We went in expecting a battle, but all we found was the mage's rotting corpse with a wand stuck in one ear and poking out the other. Later, I figured out it must have been suicide because of the Yakkity Sack."

Aggression coughed a couple of times, then continued. "The other rogue had picked the sack up, then shook his head a couple of times, before turning to me and saying, "Do you want this Sack of Holding I found?"

"I thought this gesture was unusual, knowing this rogue as I did," Aggression continued, "but I needed more room for the loot, so I took it. Now I'm doomed to keep hearing these voices until I give this cursed item away! Please, somebody, please take it from me. You can give it away later!"

"Me no want it," Maul stated as he backed away.

"Wait a minute," Peavus said. "I'll be right back."

After disappearing into the tour bus, Peavus came back with a scroll. "Man, I never thought I'd use this!"

"What is it?" I asked. "Magic?"

"Do you remember that my father is the Spellmeister General?"

"Sure," I replied.

"Well, before I left for the road, he gave me a sack of unused scrolls. Here is one that I thought I'd never use; it's called Remove Purse."

"That's a weird spell," I stated. "Who would have ever thought of that?!"

"It says on the label that it was purchased from the Palm Eye Finger Magic Shop in Neverspring," Peavus noted.

"Well, that answers that question," I replied. "I should have known."

"It'll never work," came a voice from the Yakkity Sack. "It's best just to leave us in peace."

"Please!" Aggression spat out weakly. "Try it! You have to stop these voices! Anything!"

Peavus read the scroll, and a green, misty glow surrounded the haggard rogue. Then, he jumped up and ran away from the talkative sack. "Yes! Yes! I'm free!" he yelled joyfully, "I can't thank you enough!"

"No problem," Peavus said, shaking the rogue's hand. "But what are we going to do with that?"

The sack sat quietly on the ground, not making a sound. "Oh, I have an idea..." the rogue said, smiling all of a sudden. "Do any of you happen to have a gift box?"

I just so happened to have one, due to my recent birthday. Aggression opened the flaps, then took a long stick, in which he snagged the sack up before lowering it into the box. "Where are you sending that? To be destroyed?"

"No," the rogue stated as a dark smile came across his face. "I'm sending it to an old acquaintance of mine!"

Entry 72

One of the worst places we play is the Meeplewood Tavern in Skull Hollow. It's a guarantee that you'll be involved in a brawl, at least once, by the end of the night. This gaming tavern takes pride in bad sportsmanship and encourages rude behavior. Its owner, a Rhuddist Monk named Agony, even came up with its slogan, "Where Boardgames Go to Die!"

The elven female monk was fondly called "Aunt Agony" by her patrons, who seemed to thrive on frustration and ill tempers. The feisty elf would only stock poorly reviewed games or old copies of ones that had missing pieces or no rules. Everyone in the band hated playing there, except Maul, who seemed obsessed with the place. One time, he was so excited to play there, he could barely contain himself. "Me ordered new game," he said as we pulled the tour wagon up near the rear entrance.

"That's fine, Maul," I said. "But remember, try to throw bodies away from the stage, not toward it. Replacing all our equipment cost us a fortune last time!"

We grabbed our gear and headed in. We had played there dozens of times before, so when Aunt Agony greeted us with a frown, but Maul with a grin, we didn't feel slighted at all. "Hey, Auntie! Where's me new game?"

"Delivery hasn't come yet," she replied coolly. "It should be here soon. The delivery guy might be late, considering I broke his ankle last week."

Maul laughed and chatted with the Rhuddist Monk as we walked past her. The place hadn't changed much since our last concert. The dumpy-looking stage was near the back. The platform had been repaired dozens of times and was full of cracks and creaking boards. The Meeplewood had a full-time repair gnome named Cobbleskwott, who was constantly on the go fixing everything from the night before. The bald, pudgy gnome was always happy and looking as pleased as punch to be doing this job. The tools in his belt appeared well-used and worn.

On either side of the stage were two doors. One for the in-house cleric named Undead Ted (because he always looked tired), and the other was for the Rules Lawyer who would mitigate game disputes. Unfortunately, this rules lawyer was also a Rhuddist Monk, who loved to start fights for no reason at all. I remembered this psycho from the last few shows; his name was Stryfe.

The rest of the place was filled with tables and chairs that appeared to have been rebuilt about a hundred times each. You could still see plenty of bloodstains where they hadn't bothered wiping it off. You had to watch your step in some areas because you'd slip on a knocked-out tooth if you weren't careful. You'd think you'd get lucky and find a gold one once-in-a-while, but that was rare. Someone luckier had probably crawled around collecting those. We waved hi to Cobbleskwott, then began setting up our gear as he went to unlock the front doors.

A few beat-up-looking humans wandered in and grabbed a game from the collections on the shelves that lined the wall. "Hey, they took our game!" shouted the leader of a small group of kobolds who wandered in after them. "We wants to play it."

The little red creatures wore leather vests that read, "Noobs." The Noobs were part of a more prominent gang that hung around Skull Hollow seeking thrills by finding new things to do. Most of the time, they just liked to irritate others or cause grief, which made the Meeplewood Tavern one of their favorite spots. Within minutes, a brawl had broken out, and a table was smashed. "I haven't even had my coffee, yet!" griped Undead Ted, coming out of his office. He headed over to one of the humans who was nursing a bloodied nose.

When the place filled up and all the riots were in full swing, we started playing through our set like everything was normal. Bottles smashed all around us as we sang song after song. When we got to the crowd favorite, *Instant Harma*, the place was at total capacity. "We all know this one," I said to the enthusiastic crowd, "so sing along if you can!"

> *(Sung to the tune of Instant Karma by John Lennon)*
> *Instant Harma's gonna get you*
> *Gonna knock you right on the head*
> *You better clench your fists together*
> *Gonna leave game night dead*
> *What in the realms are you thinking of*
> *Laughing in the face of that ogre*
> *You're gonna lose a tooth or two*
> *Or get ripped in two, yeah you*

Instant Harma's gonna get you
Gonna punch you right in the face
Better get under a table darlin'
Get a knuckly sandwich taste
How in the realms are you gonna see
With two black eyes, or three?
Who started this tabletop war?
A rules lawyer?!
Well, right you are!

Well, we'll all brawl on
See twirling moons, stars, and other charms
Well, we'll all brawl on
Everyone's fighting on!

Instant Harma's gonna get you
Have you ever stubbed your head?
Better recognize it, brother
Never cheat against undead
Rolled the dice half-cocked
And then you claim it isn't fair
Ghoul complained you skipped his turn
Is that a cleric over there?
Now he's white with fear!

Well, we'll all brawl on
Reap the benefits of Instant Harm
Well, we'll all brawl on
Come on, baby, bring it on!
Yeah yeah, alright, uh-huh, ah

Well, we'll all brawl on
See twirling moons, stars, and other charms
Well, we'll all brawl on
Come on, baby, bring it on!
Yeah yeah, alright, uh-huh, ah!

As we finished the song, the audience went wild, smashing chairs, throwing each other over tables, and forming lines in front of the cleric's office. "Hurry up and heal me, Ted. A bloodied dwarf complained. "I want to get back out there!"

I could see at table twelve that there was a lot of arguing. That's when Stryfe walked up with a rulebook and started making the arguments much worse. "That's gonna be a good one," Maul remarked, "Watch."

After a few seconds of angry words, Stryfe handed the upset gamer the rulebook. When the human held it up to his face to confirm what Stryfe had stated, the monk did a roundhouse kick into the book, smashing the player's face and knocking him backward off his chair.

I just sighed and nodded. Maul laughed so hard he was wiping tears from his eyes. "That funny joke!" he claimed between guffaws. At that moment, a delivery guy hobbled in carrying a box that he dropped off to Auntie Agony behind the counter. She eagerly waved Maul over, who ran to see if it was his new game. He violently shoved people out of the way who were fighting in front of him. One broke a bottle on Maul's head, but he didn't even react; he was too excited about the package. When he returned to the stage, he laid the box on the floor and opened it. "Finally! Me new game!"

It was a large black box with one word written on it, "Fight!". When Maul removed the lid, we could see the items inside, resting neatly in fitted grooves. There was a glass bottle, a brick, brass knuckles, a tooth collector's bag, and a rulebook. Maul grabbed the brick out, testing its heft. "There doesn't seem to be much to this game," I remarked after reading the instructions. "There's only one word in this entire booklet- fight!"

"Game has subtle nuance," Maul stated, getting ready to exit the stage and out into the crowd. "It easy to learn, but strategy and complexity develop over time. Let me demonstrate."

The half-ogre sprang out of our protective cage and ran into the crowd, swinging the brick as he went. Peavus, Ghasper, and I just shook our heads. We didn't understand the game, but apparently, the crowd at the Meeplewood did. In fact, it was so much fun, it left most of them in stitches.

Entry 73

One of the most disappointing shows we ever played was at the Pick & Shovel Funeral Home and Bait Shop in Diggs Deep. Our manager, Colonel Crom Parker, thought it might be a great way to get some exposure, because the dead guy was some local dwarven hero named Kingsfjord. I guess the overconfident fool passed away by getting fried to a crisp fighting a dragon. He didn't want to wait for the rest of his party, so he ran into the room yelling, "Kingsfjord, ho!"

Kingsfjord's ashes were set on the middle of the stage in front of us. One of his wishes was that he be remembered in song, so we were there to lift spirits and sing his praises. The place was packed with lots of the varying races of the realms, but most people were frowning dwarfs, which was nothing out of the ordinary.

"Good mourning, everyone," I said to the audience. "I hope everyone's feeling good. Let's see if we can turn those frowns upside down, eh?"

There were a few mumbles from the attendees, so I pressed on. "You know they say that death is the end, but I wouldn't pay that much heed. Our drummer, Ghasper, has been dead for years, and he's doing great!"

An overweight dwarf, which turned out to be Kingsfjord's sister, swooned and started to faint. "Don't worry, lady. Many womenfolk faint at our shows; it's the nature of being semi-famous."

"We have to remember something about old Kingsfjord, here," I said, resting my left foot on his ash box. "He loved to save money. So, getting fried into a pile of ashes just saved a ton on funeral costs! He would be so proud! We even wrote a song about it called *Cremation*. This one is for you, Kingsfjord!"

(Sung to the tune of Vacation by the Go-Gos)
You said you didn't want any dirt on you
Now you're in a box that probably held some shoes
It was gold you craved
So you waltzed into the cave
Ol' Charguts won't be that challenging, you said
When you said join me in there, I just ran
It turns out you were just a flash in a pan

You'd be alive if you had run
Tell me, folks, am I wrong?
Now folks are here with some stories to tell
We'll ignore the smell
You lived without regret
And now you've urned it, and the will has been read!

Cremations, all you ever wanted
Cremation, from a dragons spray
Cremation, on a quest for gold
Cremations, hoping we're not haunted
Cremation, now a pile of gray
Someone sneezed, and thar' you blow!

There was more to the song, but it got cut off when the crowd gasped as I spun around and hit the ash box with my tail, knocking it over onto the stage. A massive plume of ashes went up into the air, and Kingsfjord's angry sister almost fainted, once more! "Sorry, folks," I said, scooping the ashes back up with my claw.

"Can someone just get these clowns off the stage and read the will?!" the sister yelled as she gained her composure.

The tension was building fast, so I stood up, wiped my claws off on the back of my trousers, and tried to restore the peace with another song. "Sorry about that, miss," I said. "But look on the bright side, at least he won't be able to be raised by some evil cleric into an undead creature, am I right?"

With that said, I quickly hit a few notes of our song about the undead, called *Welcome Back, Plotter*.

(sung to the tune of Welcome Back, Kotter by John Sebastian)
Welcome back
I know undeath is not what you dreamed about
Welcome back
To the cold gray morgue, you laid around
Well, your bodies been all changed
and you shuffle around

And you chew lots of brains
Since you've been above the ground
Who'd have thought they'd raise you
(Who'd have thought they'd raise you)
For an evil clerics harmitsvah?
(An evil clerics harmitsvah?)
Yeah, he needs you a lot
Because he's got an evil plot
Welcome back
Welcome back, welcome back, welcome back
Welcome back, welcome back
Welcome back

The reception to this song wasn't much better. I think the only that kept the greedy relatives of this fallen dwarf from storming the stage was Maul, who just stood there cracking his knuckles. Needless to say, we were barred from playing at the Pick & Shovel, ever again. I didn't mind, though, because Ghasper said Kingsfjord's spirit was floating backstage, enjoying the show.

He couldn't stand any of his relatives and found the whole debacle hilarious. The night's highlight was when Ghasper told me to inform the attendees that Kingsfjord had altered his will before he left. The dwarf wanted his fortune donated to a local dwarven charity that sought a cure for gold fever. About twenty dwarves, including his sister, really fainted after hearing that.

Entry 74

A few months after Peavus and I teamed up, we sat in the Moonring Tavern in Neverspring, going over song ideas. We had individually built up a lot of cool ones over the years, so we decided to compare notes to see how our ideas could mesh. We'd only been noodling over our notes for a little while when a tough-looking bald elf wearing a leather armor jumpsuit approached us.

The armor had sponsorship logos carved into it and was highly polished. Standing behind the elf, was a goofy-looking human wizard who had a frog familiar sitting on top of his head. "Excuse me, gentlemen," the elf said. "My name is Tornetto. I'm a racer with the Boondoggle Enduro, and I'm looking for assistance."

Everyone knew of the great race which happened every year in the Unremembered Realms. Dozens upon dozens of racers would participate in a race throughout all four of the realms. It would start and end in Neverspring. Peavus and I hadn't come here to see the race, but we hoped to get a few small gigs, since the town would be packed with spectators. The one thing unique about this event was the racing wagons. The Boondoggle Enduro's rules were that animals couldn't draw your wagon, but instead, they had to be powered by magic. Most people used modified wagons that were powered by lightning spells. That meant a racer usually had to partner up with a mage, if they weren't one, themselves.

"What do you need a couple of bards for?" I asked. "I only use minimal musical magic, but Peavus here knows some."

"I don't need any magic," he explained. "That's why Froghat is here. I need your music to keep him inspired. He's easily distracted."

Froghat nodded in agreement and did a bow while tipping his frog to us like a hat. "I love music," the wizard stated as he set the frog back down and pointed up to it, "And so does Ozone."

Once we agreed on a price, we followed the duo out of the tavern, and Tornetto led us to a garage a few blocks away. It held about ten or so wagons, which all appeared to be getting their final touches before the race. Tornetto led us to his wagon, which was cherry red, with the number 409 painted on it. "She's real fine," he said, running his hand down it. "I built her myself."

"Is that a dueled exhaust?!" Peavus asked in an awed tone.

"Yes," Tornetto bragged as he started to show Peavus the undercarriage. "See, it leads up to a Hidey-Ho vertical crankshaft with multi-gem powerlifters."

Peavus gave out a short whistle. "I bet this baby flies!"

"That would be against the rules," Tornetto laughed. "But it's close!"

The next day, we met Tornetto and Froghat at the starting line located at the Neverspring city limits. Racers from all over the realms were there prepping their modified racing wagons. Peavus and I had our lutes, and we sat in two comfortable leather seats in the back. Froghat sat in the middle over an open engine gearbox, where he could easily cast spells into the crank system to power our cart forward. Tornetto sat up front, behind the steering wheel. Next to him, sat the navigator, named Crockett. Crockett's race was similar to lizardmen, except they had all the features of an alligator. I was glad for the gator's aid; they were well known in the swamps for their uncanny sense of direction.

It wasn't long before the trumpets blew and we flew across the plain toward the first stop. For the first leg, Peavus and I played dueling lutes. The music was slow, at first, but then became a quick rhythm. Froghat tapped his toes in rhythm while casting spells. "You guys are pretty good," he smiled back at us while his frog chewed on his hair.

We played a few more songs until we hit Nearby Station in Barrendry. They gave small flags to everyone to prove that they had hit the checkpoint. Here, we grabbed a quick bite from our packs and took a moment to re-tune. "C'mon, guys," Tornetto warned. "Keep the music going. Froghat, we're falling behind!"

Crockett checked the map and said, "The next stop is in Amazon Prime, and I just saw a wagon full of dwarves blow past us! There was a tree with an eyeball crudely painted on it."

"We're not losing to dwarves!" Tornetto shouted at Froghat. "Put the lightning to the metal! We've got to reach the amazonian city before they do!"

"You're making Ozone nervous!" the wizard shouted back. "He just leaked on me!"

"Gahhh!" Tornetto shouted before stomping over to his seat and throwing a hand towel at the frustrated wizard.

"Now, let's see," Froghat mumbled. "Was it a sprig of a twig or a centipede's sixteenth leg?"

While he fumbled through his spell components, another wagon zoomed by. "See you at the finish line, losers!" came a shout from a dark-haired cleric. "That is, if everyone sticks around long enough until you finally reach it! Haha!"

The cleric had a wagon full of zombies, and I swear they all seemed to laugh at his joke, which was weird because even a back swamp dweller like me knows that zombies do not laugh. It's like he was using magic or something to make them do it. "What a loser," Peavus chuckled. "I hope we don't lose to that guy."

A few moments later, a loud crack sounded as the lightning spell shot out of Froghat's hand, which caused the wagon to peel out. Peavus and I had to cling to the sides for a moment to catch our balance. We had only played a few songs before Crockett shouted something and pointed to something in front of us. As we skirted the edge of the Barrendry Desert, we discovered a humorous scene. The loudmouth cleric had encountered a flock of vultures who bombarded his crew of zombies, mistaking them for roadkill. In the battle, the wagon had crashed and overturned. The cleric was covered in peck marks and vulture droppings as he tried to fight off the aerial carnivores.

"You may not win the race, cleric," Tornetto shouted. "But you may win the blue ribbon for the best meal served!"

The cleric shook his fist at us and shouted something, but we couldn't hear it because we were too far away. "We should have helped him," Froghat commented.

"Bite your tongue!" Tornetto hissed. "We are in this race to win, not make friends!"

"I am," the wizard remarked, giving Peavus and I a grin.

We just smiled back and launched into our next tune, called *Greasy Lightning*.

(Sung to the tune of Greased Lightning by Jim Jacobs, Warren Casey, and John Travolta)
Well, this spells ampomatic, it's voltagematic, it's electromatic
Why it's Greasy Lightning!
We'll get some hair-raising blasts from this force of nature; oh yeah
(Keep talking, Woah, keep talking)
An amperage injection and a lightning rod, oh yeah
(Get components, lots of spell components)
When cast onto the floor, it will blow you out the door
This power wagon's lit, we'll be jumping lots of pits, greasy lightnin'
Go go go, go go go go go go go go
Go, greasy lightnin', you zoom us up the quarter-mile
(Greasy lightnin', go, greasy lightnin')
Go, greasy lightnin', you're 11 on the power dial
Greasy lightnin', go, greasy lightnin')
Light up the scene, my smile will gleam, for greasy lightnin'
Go go go, go go go go go go go go

We were headed toward the next flag station by the next day, making record time. While Froghat slept, we all took turns using the hand cranks to propel us forward. There would be groups of two; one for the crank and one for the steering while the others slept. We did so well that we managed to surpass a couple of wagons that had parked off to the side of the trails to rest. Tornetto was determined not to lose any ground, no matter what, even if it meant pushing us to our limits.

After picking up our flag, we were headed west to use a little-known shortcut through Bogmarsh that Crockett said would pick us up an extra hour. I didn't mind; the smell of the water was sweet to this lizardman's nostrils. We even passed a couple of hunting spots where my dad used to take me and my cousin Tegus. When we emerged on the normal plains, we spotted a wagon in front of us. It was those pesky dwarves. Their balding leader looked shocked and angry. Even from this distance, we could see him barking orders like crazy. We saw a lot of movement, but I wasn't sure what they were doing.

By the time the 409 caught up, we found out. "Nobody beats the Black Willow gang," shouted the leader at us from the back of his wagon.

We noticed the dwarves had bits of banana stuck in all their beards. "Now, Quade?" one of them asked.

The leader, Quade, smiled menacingly and nodded. The other dwarves started dumping a crate of banana peels out the back and directly in our path! Crocket cranked the wheel to one side, but it was too late, two of our wheels hit the tropical traps, and we all started spinning out of control. Peavus and I quit playing and held on tight as we spun around. "Hold on to your frogs!" the wizard shouted.

He clutched the powered gearbox with one hand and Ozone with the other. By the time the spinning stopped, we all felt like throwing up. Tornetto tried to stand up and yell, but he fell backward out of the cart. When our group got things back in order, the Black Willow gang was out of sight. Tornetto was furious. "We'll never catch up, now," he said, stomping back and forth.

But it turned out he was wrong. The dwarves never considered what would happen if they ate that many bananas while setting up their trap. We all laughed a couple of hours later when we saw their wagon parked near the Muffleman Forest. It was empty, so we assumed they were all in the woods doing their business. When we got closer, we could hear Quade yelling out, "Please tell me somebody brought some bum wipe!"

It was nightfall by the time we reached the perimeter of the Hoktu Mountains. We had already picked up our flag in Mazenhog and even passed two broken down wagons, whose furious captains were now kicking. Tornetto finally cracked a smile. "I'm beginning to think we have a chance," he said, turning back to us. "I think we...."

Just then, a huge boulder slammed into the ground next to us, nearly knocking the 409 over. "Giants!" yelled Crockett.

The navigator was right; we could see giants along the side of the mountain, laughing and hurling boulders at us. Luckily, Tornetto was a top-notch driver and maneuvered us around any falling object with ease. One boulder even bounced over our heads as Tornetto, with precise timing, turned into its direction, predicting where the boulders would bounce. We could tell this was no easy task from the number of crushed wagons and dead bodies we saw.

After this narrow escape, we hoped to rest before reaching the last flag station in Miftenmad, which was the race's final leg. "There's no time to rest," Tornetto hollered at us from the front. "We're too close! We could be crossing the finish line earlier than predicted!"

None of us thought this was a good idea. All of us could see Froghat was on the brink of exhaustion. Even our songs were not keeping him up. Not only that, but our fingers needed a rest, as well. To top it off, Froghat said his spell components were low. "Does anyone have any spare ant livers?" he asked, with bloodshot eyes. "We're getting low."

"What do you mean, getting low?" Tornetto fumed. "You said you stocked extra!"

Froghat opened a pouch along his waist to show him, and immediately, Ozone the frog's tongue shot out and snatched up the last of the ant livers. "Oh!" Froghat remarked. "I was wondering where those were going! Bad froggy, bad!"

Froghat wagged his finger at the amphibian perched on his head, but the frog just belched. Tornetto stepped forward to grab the frog, but Crockett held him back. "Don't do it, boss!" he said. "Wizard's powers can be tied in with their familiars. If you murder his frog, it may weaken him!"

"Listen," he told us all. "We're only five miles from the finish line.

Froghat, please tell me you can cast at least one more spell?!"

The wagon was already beginning to slow down as the last charge wore down. It only took a moment for a black scaled Dragonborn to pass us. Tornetto was furious as we slowly moved forward. After we hand-cranked some more, spectators started to appear along the sides of the trail as we approached the final three miles. "Cast something!" shouted Tornetto at Froghat.

"I can't without any ant livers," Froghat stated back.

"I've got half a pocket of spider tongues," Peavus offered. "Will that work?"

"I don't think so," Froghat stated. "As a matter of fact, it may even…."

"Just use it!" Tornetto shouted. "Hurry! We're closing in on the last mile! We could still come in second…."

Another wagon blew past us. "I mean third!"

Froghat immediately started casting as Peavus and I grabbed the hand cranks to keep us moving. Then, a blue light shot from his hands, and a big chunk of ice appeared over the engine box, freezing the gears. We were within eye shot of the finish line. "Nooooo!" Tornetto shouted, dropping to his knees.

"I was trying to tell you that you just can't switch out the components," Froghat explained as wagon after wagon passed us. "Perhaps we can still push it over the line?"

The wagon's gearbox was frozen, so the gears wouldn't let the wheels turn. "That's impossible," I said. "Unless we had somebody really strong."

Froghat stood up in the wagon and spotted a large human standing in the crowd eating what appeared to be a large box of donuts. "Excuse me, sir? Would you mind giving us a push?"

The tall but rotund man stepped out with a smirk and wiped his powdery fingers on his tunic, leaving long, white stains. "C'mon, Pickenfling," he said to a halfling next to him.

The halfling pulled his finger out of his nose and wiped his finger on the large man's tunic, as well. "Sure thing, Markus," he replied.

With the help of everyone on board, we were able to push the wagon past the finish line. We ended up being seventy-sixth out of one-hundred, which wasn't that great considering that twenty-four of the other racers were destroyed before they could make it back at all. Froghat cheered along with the two helpers as Peavus and I just shrugged. "What are you morons cheering about?!" Tornetto fumed. "We came in last place! A zombie could have won this race better than we did!"

"Well," Froghat stated, grinning broadly. "There's always next year. Right guys?"

Tornetto just yelled into the air. "Aargh! There's not going to be a next year! And you can keep this piece of junk!"

With that said, the furious racer ran off, with Crockett shrugging and following.

We all stood there silent for a minute around the wagon, looking at one another. The big guy named Markus then spoke up. "Umm, Pickenfling and I are forming an all-powerful adventuring party to start raiding dungeons. Would any of you like to join?"

Froghat raised his hand. "Count me in!"

"No thanks," I replied. "Peavus and I are building a band and going on tour."

"You guys are my favorite band," Froghat commented. "You kick out some great jams! Hey guys, I'm giving these two bards the wagon; the gear system is shot, but animals could still pull it."

Markus and Pickenfling nodded. "Sounds good to us," the halfling stated. "But we still need a fighter and a rogue in our party. Let's go put up a want-ad."

The trio marched off with the rest of the dispersing crowd. "Well," Peavus said, patting the wagon. "Looks like we need to modify this thing and buy a couple of horses."

Entry 75

One of the rules I've learned over the years is to always look before you lunge. For instance, we were scheduled to play a show at the Rising Star Tavern & Bakery in the city of Shallowditch. That morning, as our wagon approached the venue, Maul shouted back to us from the driver's seat, "Hey guys, come look!"

When we all came up from inside, we could see a line leading to the Rising Star wrapped around the block. Our jaws dropped due to our excitement. "I can't believe it!" I beamed. "We're going to have a major crowd!"

As we were all going through a happy round of high-fives, Rhody cut in. "Wait a minute," he began. "You know, we agreed to play at only ten gold coins apiece. For the size of this crowd, we should be doing much better than that!"

"I don't know," I told the dwarf. "Maybe we shouldn't rock the rowboat."

"It does seem kind of unfair," Peavus said, eyeballing the length of the line. "That's quite a crowd."

"Me agree," Maul chimed in. "More money needed."

I just shrugged. "Great," Rhody said as we pulled into the back of the venue. "Let me negotiate a new deal!"

"Fine," I said. "Try to work on a good meal, too. I'm getting sick of living off bruised vegetables we pick off the stage."

Rhody marched through the back door with his chin held high while we started to unload. After fifteen minutes, Rhody shuffled back through the door, looking crestfallen. "What happened?" I said, hoping a big smile would cross his face like he was pranking us.

"How much we get now?" Maul asked.

"Five gold each," Rhody glumly stated. "And a pick off of the leftover plates."

"But what about the crowd?" Peavus asked. "The line is out of sight!"

"It's a bread line," Rhody skulked. "It's like that here every morning. People are here early to see if they can get a discount on the day-old bread."

After a big sigh, Rhody started to walk away from the wagon toward the line. "Where are you going?" Peavus asked.

"To get in the bread line," Rhody answered. "I'm not eating any more leftovers from some gross halflings!"

Entry 76

It never ceases to amaze me how frugal wizards can be. Seriously, once we were hired to play a pre-raid jamboree this evil wizard, Nemorex, was throwing for his monster hoard. The Marshtones and I played our regular set, and everyone seemed happy, but after two encores, we decided our job was done and started the process of packing up.

"Wait!" Nemorex yelled from the crowd. "We have some birthdays!"

After a short hesitation, we decided to relent and do a few. The problem was that the wizard wanted it sung to each individual by name. After a few dozen of those, Nemorex pointed to a zombie and said, "Don't forget Grony!"

"He's an undead," Rhody said, clearly perturbed. "He doesn't even know he's being celebrated! Don't be daft!"

"Zombies are people too," Nemorex quipped, crossing his arms. "They have feelings."

"Feeling hungry isn't a feeling, " Peavus said, pushing Grony away, who was trying to bite him.

"It doesn't matter," the wizard replied. "I paid you fair coin, and I want my money's worth. I don't want my undead troops to think I don't care about them."

Maul would have slapped the wizard silly, but his army was too big, so we reluctantly played the birthday song... again. In fact, we ended up playing it around one-hundred times. Nemorex wanted us to keep going, but I was starting to lose my voice. "Fine," he huffed. "I have a recording of the birthday song, anyway."

"What?!" we all exclaimed at the same time, shocked.

He pointed at a tiny Orbit Stone that floated around his head. "My magic stone records music and I can play it back later."

Maul was beet red at this point. "Why not you record the first one and play it back?! Me fingers are bleeding!"

The wizard looked at Maul indignantly. "Are you kidding? I don't want my troops to start saying, 'is it live or is it Nemorex?', each one of my team is special!"

"You do know you're raiding Slaughtergrind Keep in Slaphammer tomorrow, right?" I pointed out. "Most of your horde will be ripped to shreds in seconds!"

Nemorex's expression quickly changed from irritated to curious. "Oh, that reminds me- How much do you charge to play funerals?"

Entry 77

Having Rhody around sure has been helpful to the band. For example, we once played a gig to an unreceptive audience in a dwarven mine. The dwarves were cranky, as always, so it was hard reaching through to them with our music. After our third song, Rhody marched up and handed each of us a sheet of paper. It read I Want A Rock by Rhody Sibilance. After reading the lyrics, I said, "Are you sure this song will work?"

"Trust me," he replied. "I grew up with these hard heads! All they care about is mining. They'll dig it!"

With a nod to the group, we began.

(Sung to the tune I Want to Rock by Twisted Sister)
I Want A Rock! (Rock!)
I Want A Rock! (Rock!)

Break it down, you say
But all I got to say to you is time and time again; I say gold!
Gold! Gold! Gold!
With pickaxe or spade
Well, all I got to say when I'm swinging pick or spade, I say gold!
Gold! Gold! Gold!
So, if you ask me why I'm picky about cavies
There's only one thing for me to bust in two
I Want A Rock! (Rock!)
I Want A Rock! (Rock!)

You think I'm cracking up
But every time I do, I bust more than a move, yes sir, I'm finding gold!
Gold! Gold! Gold!
Turn my fever up
I've been mining for so long I think my gold picking my mind is gone, for gold!
Gold! Gold! Gold!
When I see its shine, I always start to feel so groovy
That's why I'm here with my hardy dwarven crewy!
I Want A Rock! (Rock!)
I Want A Rock! (Rock!)

Rhody couldn't have been more correct. The whole place started whooping and hollering with wild abandon. Shadows danced on the walls as the headlamps from the dwarves moved all about, sending dancing lights everywhere! We ended the song with a big blast from Maul's Kazooka, which ended up being a great finisher, because it shook some rocks off the ceiling, revealing a gold vein. The dwarves considered this good luck and began mining it right away. From that point forward, the miners adored Maul and considered him their golden boy.

Entry 78

Most entertainers in the Unremembered Realms are very superstitious. I'd like to think the Marshtones and I are above all that, but I'd be lying. Peavus won't go onstage without painting on his lucky face stripes. Ghasper seems to have an off performance if he doesn't float in a circle for 5 minutes around a fresh-picked flower. Maul pulls the tongue out of an orc whenever he gets the chance, but I still don't understand how that's supposed to help. It makes him giggle a lot, though.

Me? Well, I have a ritual of baby-talking my lute, Tegus. Peavus thinks this is amusing, but I swear it's not as weird as him having a conversation with his lute. One time, I heard him arguing with it. But when I brought it up, he said everything was fine and that he won the argument. Either way, we treat our instruments like family and never, ever, tune them out.

Entry 79

A common problem on the road in some regions of the realms is undead groupies. These goo-goo-eyed fangirls swarm the stage, and are so in love with your music, that they try to take a piece of each band member, literally! It's not easy being a heartthrob to the undead, especially when all they seem to care about is your throbbing heart!

I don't mind giving out an autograph or lute pick here and there, but I stand firm against losing a finger or two to some pearl-clutching, animated corpse whose eyes pop out whenever they see you. Plus, it's always gross having to watch them pop them back in! Although we don't get too close, physically, to these fans, we do try to answer all their fan mail. This task isn't always easy to do, considering we can barely read their writing because zombies tend to write in a bunch of bloody scribbles.

Entry 80

One of the hardest things about life on the road is the struggle to eat healthy. The band and I do pretty well because of all the vegetables thrown on stage, but that only happens when we're playing. The rest of the time, we're on the road and stopping at Haystations to fuel up the horses and grab quick snacks. While I sneak in the backroom for halfling jerky in the southern regions of the realms, the rest of the band has their own favorites. Peavus loves any concoction that's been in the food warmers for who knows how long; Maul grabs two 25-pound bags of amphibian flavored swamp chips, and Ghasper groans on endlessly about them not having any soul food.

The worst of the worst, though, is Rhody. He has an iron stomach and will hardly turn away anything, as long as he can sprinkle a little of his secret spice that some rogue claimed to have invented. His biggest weakness is what the haystation owners call Road Chum. When any of their foods start to expire, they throw everything into a bucket, mash it all together, and throw it back on the shelf with an "eat at your own risk" warning label. The only thing I have to say about Rhody eating these is that, after he's done, don't sit next to him on the wagon; if so, then you'll be doing it at your own risk!

Entry 81

Growing up a lizardman wasn't easy. We are trained from a young age not to trust the softskins. Our people said they were weak and had no honor. I remember the first day my father sent me into the woods to become a "wandering monster", as the realmsfolk would often call us. I was dressed in my best loincloth, carrying my sharpened spear and a leather pouch holding my lunch. "My son is all grown up," my mother said with tear-filled eyes. "I remember the day you first broke out of your shell!"

"Aw, geez, ma," I complained. "Not in front of the guys."

Other young lizardmen were waiting for me at our door. My mom hugged me, but my dad noticed my One Man Bard button on my leather pouch's shoulder strap. "Is that a pin on your uniform?!"

"I, uh.." I stuttered.

"When I was your age, I was off to war," he began to lecture. "It wasn't long after that I finished my third molting and was out winning hearts, which I promptly brought home for your mother to cook!"

He tore the button off and gave me a quick lecture on liking humans. I just rolled my eyes and marched out. "Old people," another young warrior stated as we marched to the woods. "It's no wonder we're all still living in the swampage!"

Entry 82

Before meeting any Marshtones, I played in a few start up bands, then did some traveling as a solo act, trying anything musical just to earn a few coins. While I'd play the occasional tavern here and there, my biggest venues were campsites. It didn't pay much, but I figured it would give me a chance to hone my skills as a musician. One of the weirdest situations that I got caught up in was when I approached a group of humanoids at night without knowing they were bandits.

"Let's skin him and make a few belts," one human said, holding his blood-stained dagger.

An uglier human stated, "No, he'd make much better boots."

"Whoa, fellow travelers," I cut in, "I'm just a bard, trying to make a living. I came here hoping to entertain you!"

"Your death will be entertaining," a dwarf with a spiked helmet said, holding a mace. "I killed a lot of men today. Your death would make a satisfying encore!"

There were about eight of them in total, and they all started slowly circling me. Out of instinct, I grabbed my loot and started playing the most toe-tapping song that I knew, called *You Cast a Spell But It Ain't Working*.

(Sung to the tune of You Keep Knocking by Little Richard)
You cast a knock spell but it ain't workin'
You cast a knock spell but it ain't workin'
The chest is locked and won't open
Better rest the party and we'll try it again, woo!

You cast a sleep spell but it ain't workin'
You cast a sleep spell but it ain't workin'
The ogre's growling and it ain't snoring
Let out a scream and we start running, ooh!

You cast a light spell but it ain't workin'
You cast a light spell but it aint' workin'
Can't see a thing and we're all tripping
Didn't see the pit and we all fell in, aahh!

You cast a stanky cloud but they ain't cryin'
You cast a stanky cloud but they ain't cryin'
Smells like an onion that's gone rottin'
Flew back to us when it was cast upwind, ooh!!!

My song was working! The bandits were banging their heads with their fists in the air. I didn't know how long I could repeat the chorus, but as I did, I began to move backward, hopefully, to gain a few steps advantage, so I could flee. But it was during this chorus that I saw something strange happen. I spotted a female human with an open umbrella floating down from the sky in the middle of the camp!

My playing drifted off as the bandits all turned their attention toward her. All of them were struck dumb by her beauty. I happen to find humans ugly, with all that hair growing out of their heads and fangless teeth.

"Hello, boys," she said with a perfect smile. "I heard the music and found it delightful!"

What appeared to be the leader of the bandits, a human with a large, pimply nose, stepped up to her, clearly drooling. "Well, well, well," he began. "Look at the bird who just flew in!"

"Close your mouth, fool. You look like a codfish!" the odd visitor said sharply.

"Oooh, burn!" his men all said, laughing.

The man's face became red with fury. "You better explain who you are, woman, and what you're doing here!"

"First of all," she said, flattening out her lovely frilly dress, "I would like to make one thing clear: I never explain anything."

"Oooh," the men began again.

"Shut up, you dolts!" the man said, turning around, yelling at his gang. "Nobody talks to the Shimeny gang like that! Come on, boys, let's teach this bird a lesson!"

With a quick whistle from her, five burly barbarians appeared from the woods surrounding the gang. These men were huge, muscled, and carried blood-stained axes. "It's the Decaptitators!" shouted one of the men before sputtering, "They're bounty hunters that work for...."

"M-M-Merry Loppins," the leader timidly stuttered as she gave a small curtsy and pulled the handle out of her umbrella, revealing a glowing magical blade.

"I'm super fragile-istic," the leader of the Shimeny gang cried, pleading with his hands together. "And not ferocious!"

Without hesitation, Merry Loppins, with a dainty swipe of her sword, sliced the man's head off, and it landed on the ground with a thud. She looked up at me with a twinkle in her eye and said, "Well, sing something, bard. It may just save your life!"

I immediately started playing a song from a musical I had seen; I couldn't remember the lyrics, so I made some new ones up as I went along.

(Sung to the tune of Mary Poppins Chim Chim Cheree)
Shing shiminey, Shing shiminey
Chop chop sha-wing!
Headhunters are slicing
And so I must sing
Shing shiminey, Shing shiminey
Chop chop cher-oo!
Your 'ead will roll off when
They're done with you

Now as the splatter of blood
Grows on the ground
Can't find yer' 'ead?
Check Lost and Found!

They score 2 points when a
A basket's been made
And you've lost your 'ead
To their vorpal type blades

Shing shiminey, Shing shiminey
Chop chop sha-wing!
You should have ducked when
They started to swing!
Shing shiminey, Shing shiminey
Chop chop cher-oo!
Your 'ead will roll-off
And land by your shoes

They choose their targets with pride
Yes, they do
And a noggin' like yours
Will soon fly to the moon!

Their victims all think that
They're cruel and so hard
But they always leave
A get-well-soon card!

One time they made par with
A swing from a blade
The 'ead rolled from the body
And into a grave!

Shing shiminey, Shing shiminey
Chop chop sha-wing!
they can tell your age

By counting the rings
Shing shiminey, Shing shiminey
Chop chop cher-oo!
Your shrunken head is now
On their table for pool!

I was playing my heart out as I watched them dance around to my music while slicing the heads off each one of the bandits. The five barbarians were soaked with blood, but not Merry. When a tiny droplet hit her cheek, she merely dabbed at it daintily with a small kerchief. When her men were done with the bandits, they all turned to me, and one of the big men approached with his axe raised. "Wait, Nektarim!" Merry laughed. "He wasn't one of them."

"How do we know?" he asked, staring at my head. "This one's got a nice cranium."

"He's not mentioned on the Wanted Poster," she stated. "He's not worth a copper."

"Humpf," Nektarim stated, lowering his axe. "I guess. Whatever."

The barbarian stomped off and started collecting the chopped heads with the others of his group. "Gee, thanks, Merry," I said, wiping sweat from my brow. "They captured me and...."

She just smiled, tipped the brim of her hat, and lifted her umbrella. "Now, if you'll pardon me. I've got a pet Hoppalopper at home that needs to be fed."

After opening her umbrella, she gave me a quick wave and rose slowly into the sky. I don't know what other magic was in that umbrella, but I'm glad I didn't find out!

The Decapitators finished collecting the heads into bags, then left the rest. "You can keep the change," one of the barbarians laughed, as he pointed to a corpse that was still spurting blood.

The others laughed, too, so I went along with it nervously, faking a laugh. "I got to get a band," I reminded myself as I quickly packed up my gear. "Or at least a big bodyguard!"

Entry 83

I keep telling Colonel Crom Parker not to book us at any more retirement villages, but he always does it anyway. Sure, the money is good, but the audience never remembers who you are. You can play one set in the morning, and they are cheering you on, but by the afternoon, they have no idea you played there before. Then, these elderlings start booing, and you end up dodging bowls of gruel or false teeth.

Plus, you wouldn't believe how often the older folks cheat at checkers. I've left the gaming tables there many times, annoyed, broke, and smelling of prune-based ointment!

Entry 84

One of the things we get thrown out of taverns for the most is starting a Gosh Pit. That is when the audience slams against each other to the rhythm of our music. Usually, there's a broken nose or arm, and that person yells out, "Gosh, I think I broke something!"

You could say it's their fault, but Maul cannot control himself and usually ends up in the mix with them, causing a lot of the damage. "Me can't help it," he explains. "Me love the sound of snapping fingers!"

"You're supposed to snap *your* fingers," I'd explain, "not other peoples!"

"That dumb," he'd laugh. "That would hurt!"

Entry 85

One day I was shocked to find that I was not the only member of the band to keep a journal. It turns out that Maul keeps one, as well. I found this out because he left it on the ground by a tree where we were camping. I couldn't help myself, so I took a quick peek. "Rat head has good crunch but taste sour," one of the entries read. "Need more salt."

Another entry was too hard to read because of all the long scribbles followed by exclamation marks. By this, I assumed he was mad at something. I came across one, though, that touched my heart. "Joined Marshtones today. Green guy sing good. Can't believe me getting paid to slap hecklers. Oh, and play music, too!"

Entry 86

Sometimes, being in a band of diverse individuals can be frustrating. For example, none of us can hear Ghaspers drums when he plays them because the spectral sound waves can only be heard on the Plane of Death. While the undead in our audience snap along to it, Peavus, Maul, and I can only assume that he's holding a good beat. If we're playing at a cemetery or onstage in the middle of a zombie horde, Ghasper breaks out into one of his out-of-control bongo solos, where he even floats upside down over the audience. These antics go over really well, and the undead often groan in delight.

It doesn't work so well in front of a live audience, because they are like us and can't hear him playing. When he floats out above for his favorite maneuver, they assume he's attacking them! The poor audience doesn't understand that the only softskins he wants to attack are the ones stretched across his ethereal bongos!

Entry 87

One time, while Maul was on vacation, we hired a bass player named Flee to fill in for him for a few shows. The skinny, blond-haired human was incredible! I swear he was strumming notes I've never heard before! The harmonics synced up with Peavus and me wonderfully. At each show he seemed to make us better and better. Not only that, but all the females fancied him, and he was drawing bigger audiences.

The problem was that he liked to brag about his talents and frequently spoke about being the band's star. We tried to explain that Maul would be back soon and that his short stint would be over. "I'll handle that wannabe," the replassist bragged.

We had never mentioned to him that Maul was a half-ogre and that he'd pulverize anyone for just about anything. "You think I'm scared of some musclehead?" Flee explained over lunch at the Badwater Tavern.

"I've fought dragons with my bare ha...".

Flee stopped his lie in mid sentence as Maul walked through the tavern's door. "I wish he'd open it first," Peavus said, shaking his head.

"We'll let you tell Maul he's fired," I said, turning to Flee.

But Flee had flown. He ran so fast, that he jumped through the tavern window, shattering it. "Typical bass player," Peavus laughed. "Destroying everything in their path!"

Entry 88

One of the hardest things to deal with as an artist is songwriter's block. It seems like inspiration just doesn't happen on some days, no matter how hard you concentrate. I got so frustrated the last time it happened to me. We had pulled the tour wagon over along a trail and built a fire to cook lunch. I grabbed my lute and sat under a lovely shade tree to relax, and hopefully, develop a new song.

But it was not going to be, because I kept getting my thoughts interrupted as I sat there. "Hey, Scales," Peavus said, walking over to hand me a sandwich. "Do you remember yesterday, when all our troubles seemed so far away?"

I had almost thought of some lyrics, but now it slipped from my mind because of the disruption. Then, Peavus continued, "Well, now it looks like they're here to stay."

He referred to the small rats who'd gotten into our tour wagon. I knew this because of the rodent in my sandwich. Peavus knew I loved rat hoagies, but I wasn't hungry at that moment, so I sat it down next to me. "That's good," I replied. "It's always nice having fresh snacks."

After Peavus left, I felt inspired by his words. I was about to write a few of them down when Rhody wiggle-walked by in a hurry. "Here I go, again on my own! Going to find a place where I can be alone," he stated. "By some driftwood with a handy pine cone!"

These interruptions were utterly throwing me off my game, so I went and stood by the river we were near and started humming, hoping to clear my head. "Ahem," Maul cleared his throat. "Me needing privacy here."

I was so deep in thought that I hadn't seen him sitting nearby, soaking his large feet. I could see he was holding a letter. "Fan mail?" I asked.

"No," he said. "It from home."

"Is everything copacetic?" I asked.

"Mom is alright, dad is alright, but things seem a little weird," he explained. "Me think kobold home loan officer is giving them trouble. Me tell them to keep up fight, not surrender. Don't give your place away."

"You think your advice will help?" I asked.

"Probably not," Maul said. "Mom will crush little twerp."

I nodded, then excused myself and walked over by the fire and started plucking some strings. Just as a melody popped into my mind, a flying banana hit me on the head! "Hey, hey! We're not monkeys," I exclaimed, ducking another one as it sailed by. "Quit monkeying around!"

Ghasper had started a food fight with Rhody. I have no idea why; I mean, the yellow fruit just passes through the ghost anyway! I sat my lute down with a sigh and gave up on trying to write, at all. Inspiration should come from things around you, so I gave up trying to force it. I grabbed a banana, peeled it, then threw it at Maul's head. After the splat, he turned around, and I pointed at Rhody. After that, I was too busy for anything creative. You wouldn't believe how long it takes to get a mushed banana out of a dwarf's ear!

Entry 89

The entertainment business has its ups and downs. On any given night in a tavern, you can be up on stage singing your heart out with the audience singing along with you, or you may be dodging rotten vegetables. Either way, it's part of the life, and you have to accept it.

One side most people don't see is the cleanup. You would assume that tavern owners have janitors to clean up the mess every night, but that's not always the case. These shrewd business people will sometimes pay the entertainment a pretty penny to do that work. This extra duty is almost always good for Marshtones and me, because we always demand that we get to keep whatever treasures we find.

The valuables could be returnable bottles, gold teeth, or even coins. And I guarantee there's always one dead body left after every show. If it's a wizard's corpse, you don't find much unless they have a valuable scroll or a ring. These types of treasure we can usually hock at a local Flip-n-Wink. Dead rogues typically have the most loot, but they are a rare find. Rogues are generally the ones to start the riot in the first place; that way, they can pick some pockets before leaving.

In the end, we don't do too bad. It's a win-win for everyone, well, except for the dead people. The only hassle we ever get from the tavern keeper is if we don't place the bodies in the designated bin in the alley behind the tavern. They get a hefty fine from Cemetery Waste Disposal if the bodies aren't in properly labeled bin liners.

Entry 90

Sometimes you have to be careful when signing autographs in the Unremembered Realms. At one show, a halfling made his way to the stage between songs and was happily waving a scroll up at me. I gave it a quick signature then started on the next tune. "Thanks, mister!" he yelled before running off.

I felt pretty good about that. That is, until the end of the night when everyone had left. We went to collect our money from the tavern keeper, and he said, "Sorry, Scales, I used your pay to wipe out Robbie the Thief's tab."

The band and I were furious! "Why in the realms would you do that!?" I demanded to know.

"Don't ask me," he replied, "You're the one who signed off on the bill!"

He held out the scroll the halfling had me sign earlier. My heart sunk. I would have sworn an oath to hunt him down, but being a lizardman, I knew identifying him was going to be a problem. I have too much trouble telling halflings apart. Whenever I see one, all I can picture is them on a plate, smothered in padlily sauce, along with a side of sauerkraut.

Entry 91

Not many people can say music saved their lives, but we can! We were lost on a trail north of the Hoktu Mountains when we spotted a cave entrance hidden behind some brush. When we left the wagon to investigate, a wizard jumped out from behind a bush and shouted, "Stand and deliver!"

"We're not delivery people," I said calmly. "We just spotted this cave and thought we'd check it out."

"No, you fool," the wizard shouted. "I mean, give me your goods, or you will die by the magic of the mighty Dabb!"

Maul stepped forward with a big smile. "Me like slapping magic men, me like to stick their wands in their ears."

Dabb crossed his arms and laughed. "We'll see who does the slapping here!"

With a quick whistle, a fifteen-foot tall rock golem appeared out of nowhere and started coming our way. We all stumbled backward in surprise. Fortunately, I tripped and landed on the ground, which made me inadvertently hit the strings on my lute. The rock golem immediately stopped and tilted its head as it looked at me. Then, it stepped closer. I gave the strings another strum, and the magical creature stopped, again, and this time it tapped its foot.

With a quick signal to the Marshtones, they all began playing. The wizard couldn't believe it. His golem loved our music and began to dance around while banging its head up and down. The faster we played, the more it seemed to get in a groove. It danced even quicker to the rhythm. Dabb jumped and dodged, trying to avoid its stomping feet. But it was too late. With a quick twist of the waist and two arms pointing diagonally in the air, the creature stepped backward and directly on Dabb, who was crushed instantly.

With the wizard's death, the magical creation froze in place, no longer filled with life. "Wow," Peavus said, wiping some of the blood spray off his face. "I think that the last song was a hit!"

"A smash hit!" Maul laughed.

Entry 92

I love music, from the writing of the lyrics to the arrangement of the instruments. That's why it puzzles me when a band doesn't take their musical craft seriously and parodies songs of other people's work. One particular group that I know rises above the others in this category. It's a couple of halflings who call themselves the Two Cheeks. I think they chose this name because they like to be cheeky with other groups' songs.

This duo, Pratwhid and Foist, consider themselves a comedic musical act. It started as a trio, but the third member was let go because he continuously erupted on stage with some unscripted improv. But the group continued as a duo writing popular parody tunes such as *Open the Window*, *I Know What You Ate For Supper*, *Let's Peel Paint*, and *Pulled Finger Blues*.

Some people think the Two Cheeks stink, but I have to admit that something about their music passes the creative sniff test. Maul finds them hilarious, but for the life of me, I can't figure out how you can consider yourself an artist when all you do is make funny parody songs about breaking wind. People must like things like that, though, because the Two Cheeks can always fill the room by the end of the night.

Entry 93

One extraordinary memory I have was during Amateur Night at the Big Gong Tavern in Hollowood. The owner, a smug little halfling named Yowza, was the judge and got a kick out of disrupting the contestants with a big gong he had alongside the stage. With each act, he'd pace in front of the gong, waving the gongbonger (as Maul called it), getting hoots from the audience. We watched nervously from the sidelines as most of the bards onstage got "gonged," then verbally berated by the little tyrant.

One act he gonged was a duo of thieves called the Ruse Brothers; Snake and Felwood. They had a bard backup band while they sang, and they sounded fantastic. The two brothers didn't seem too upset after their gonging when climbing off stage. The duo even laughed at all the put-downs Yowza carelessly hollered at them as they left. Later I found out that they used their act as a distraction while a fellow rogue, planted in the audience, went and robbed the till, picked people's pockets, and broke into the Big Gong Tavern's safe.

After each act left the stage in shame, the halfling danced into the spotlight, ready to welcome the next group. All the way there, the crowd cheered, "Yowza! Yowza! Yowza!"

The next act walked out onto the stage, looking sullen. "And now for the hottest new group from Dociletoff," Yowza proclaimed, "The Mixed Emotions!"

The singer, a dark cloud elf, walked up to the front and stated with a frown, "We're so happy to be here tonight."

"Could have surprised me," Peavus muttered.

"We wrote this song, *I Just Want to Give Up*, to uninspire others," the elf continued, "So, if you have a dream, you need to wake up...one, two, one, two...sigh...."

That's when the bards kicked into high gear, playing a fast and catchy tune. My foot was tapping in no time, but the lyrics that he sang didn't seem to capture the spirit of the music. It was depressing!

(Sung to the tune of I Don't Want to Grow Up by the Ramones)
When we raid dungeons at night
I just want to give up
Nothing ever seems to turn out right
I just want to give up

How we got lost in this fog that
Might have monstrous things
Sure do wish we'd leave this pronto

When I see their evil cleric pray
I want him to shut up
Or their wizard casting stanky cloud
I just want to throw up

It seems that folks turn into things
Bitten by other chang-a-lings
The only thing to do is run away-ay

Pantlegs trickling something wet
I just stained your rug
Wanna keep my heart inside of my chest
I don't want it ripped out

I just wanna shout and flee
I just wanna climb up a tree
I know I'm always filled with doubt
I just wanna skeedaddle on out
I just wanna take the quickest route
I'm just about to holler out
I just want to give up

When you say it's fight or flight
I just want to give up
Chased around by skeletal knights
I just want to give up

I'd rather stay here in my room
Not creeping around in dungeon gloom
Spider webs or a scary old tomb, you hear me?

When I get the coward blues
I just want to give up
I'm always shaking in my boots
I just want to give up

I'd rather stay around in my old hometown
Not wincing at spooky old sounds
I don't wanna hear no dying groans
Or have a giant grind my bones
I don't wanna change at a full moon
Or fall in a pit till I go boom
How in the realms can I leave here soon
I just want to give up

    The crowd broke out into cheers after the song ended, and even Yowza was clapping. I must admit this made me nervous about our chances of winning. The dark cloud elf looked over the audience with an emotionless glare and said, "Thanks, I guess," before walking off the stage.

The next act made us feel a little better. They were called the Jive Turkeys, and they wore costumes depicting their favorite bird. Peck, the lead singer, flapped his feathery arms, yelling, "Quack, quack, quack," while the music played behind him. The gonging came quickly for them.

While the Jive Turkeys were leaving the stage, I turned to the band. "Hey guys," I whispered. "Let's do *My Half-A-Ling*. Yowza keeps making me hungry."

"Good idea," Peavus replied. "The crowds love to sing along with that one, and maybe it will make the runt a little nervous."

We took the stage, and I stated, "We'd like to dedicate this song to all the tasty, I mean feisty halflings in the audience."

(Sung to the tune of My Ding-a-Ling by Chuck Berry)
When I was a little bitty 'lerd
My grandmother cooked me a tasty dessert
Mystery meat hooked on a string
She told me it was a half-a-ling-a-ling, oh

My half-a-ling, my half-a-ling
I want you to cook me a tasty half-a-ling
My half-a-ling, my half-a-ling
I want a liddle nibble of a tasty half-a-ling

Then mama took me to Barding Guild
They tried to teach me some musical skills
Every time my professor would sing
I'd let out a belch that smelled of half-a-ling-a-ling, oh

My half-a-ling, my half-a-ling
I want you to cook me a tasty half-a-ling
My half-a-ling, my half-a-ling
I want a liddle nibble of a tasty half-a-ling

Once I caught one climbing the garden wall
It slipped and had a terrible fall
It fell so hard; I heard dinner bells ring
And fricasseed up that juicy half-a-ling-a-ling, oh

My half-a-ling, my half-a-ling
I want you to cook me a tasty half-a-ling
My half-a-ling, my half-a-ling
I want a liddle nibble of a tasty half-a-ling

These little beings are not too bad
The tastiest little treats I've ever had
With the proper prep and good seasoning
You must simply try a taste of half-a-ling

My half-a-ling, my half-a-ling
I want you to cook me a tasty half-a-ling
My half-a-ling, my half-a-ling
I want a liddle nibble of a tasty half-a-ling

    The crowd sang along merrily through the whole song, and I kept licking my lips at Yowza whenever he'd march over to the gong. His eyes would get wide then he'd sit back down. All I could picture in my head was a nice juicy apple in his mouth, surrounded by a variety of dipping sauces. I was surprised the audience could hear the song at all over the rumbling of my stomach!

    In the end, it worked out well for us. We got second place, just behind the Mixed Emotions, and we made some gold, too! We congratulated them, but they just frowned and nodded. They almost seemed happy.

    The best part of the night, though, was when we found out Rhody had sold a bunch of our merch. "This one wizard, with a frog familiar on his head, bought a tour tunic, a Tote of Holding, two helm bands, and a Mug of Refilling!"

Entry 94

    Dealing with Ghasper's stage fright is never easy. At the beginning of each show, we have to explain to the audience that he's a laid-back ghost who only wants to entertain them, not drain them of their life force. Usually, they warm up to him after I tell a few of my jokes. I know they must be liking them, because they tend to groan along with Ghasper at all the punchlines. What I don't understand is why Peavus and Maul groan along, too.

Entry 95

One night on the trail, the band and I sat silently around a campfire. That is, until Maul started to brag, "Me can break bones with me bare hands. Let's see anyone top that!"

Rhody put down his half-eaten basilisk leg, picked a bit of meat from his teeth, and said, "I have an iron stomach. I can eat almost anything!"

We all knew this to be true. We had seen him consume even the most disgusting food set in front of him. I swear there must be a small Jelly Cube living in his stomach.

"Ungh," Ghasper groaned, bragging about his talent.

"Of course, you can float through doors," Rhody said. "Wooooo, I'm a ghostie. Come on, Ghasper; you're so transparent!"

Everyone chuckled at that comment, except for our floating drummer, who just stuck his tongue out at the dwarf. I didn't think anyone could top any of these talents, but Peavus jumped to his feet and cracked his knuckles. Our lead lutist grabbed a cup of water and drank enough to fill his mouth. He then sat the cup down and cupped his hand before sticking it in his armpit. The flatulent noises he made with his armpit were amazingly musical. This man was a true bard, indeed! The most jaw-dropping part, though, was every time he lowered his arm to make the noise, the water from his mouth exited through his tear ducts like tiny fountains!

We all had a good laugh before everyone turned to me. "I have the most incredible skill of all," I proclaimed proudly. "Because I was raised in the swamp, I'm able to hold my breath underwater for twenty minutes!"

I could tell everyone was less than impressed, so I followed that statement up with, "That means I can survive in the bathroom after Maul's done for the same amount of time!"

Everyone rose to their feet and gave me a standing ovation, even Maul!

Entry 96

After participating in the Boondoggle Enduro race, Peavus and I stopped at a stable called Poppa Rocks. It was owned by a retired dwarf miner named Iggy, which was short for Igneous. He was thin, for a dwarf, and had a scraggly white beard. I guess the people of Neverspring referred to him as Poppa Rocks because he was so old and he could name any stone you showed him.

"What can I help you fellows with?" he asked from behind his counter.

"We just formed a band not long ago, and now we have a tour wagon from the big race," I explained. "We need our wagon modified, so it's back to normal, and then a couple of horses that can pull it. They don't need to be fast, but strong would help. We plan on hauling a lot of stage equipment."

We agreed on a price, and a couple of days later, Peavus and I were headed east, being pulled by our new horses, Haul and Oats. "This sure beats walking," I remarked to Peavus as he held the reins. "We could be all over the realms in no time flat! We could play any anywhere and everywhere!"

"How about Shadenfroy," Peavus asked.

"Huh?" I replied. "Where is that?"

He pointed at a sign nailed to a tree behind a lot of foliage. It was hard to see it, let alone read its weathered lettering. "Wow, you have good eyes," I said. "Shadenfroy it is!"

The trail had grown over, and it was a bit of a mess. But Haul and Oats stayed the course, and within an hour, we reached what was one of the smallest towns I had ever seen. In the middle of it all, was a flowing fountain, but it looked like it received no maintenance at all. Moss was growing all over it, and bits of the stonework had collapsed.

What was stranger was the people we saw. At first, they looked normal as anyone else, but after a few moments, we noticed they all had blank, emotionless expressions. We said hi to a few of them, and they looked at us blankly, without ever blinking. Then, they would slowly nod before heading off to do whatever they had been doing before we showed up.

"This place is creeping me out," Peavus whispered. "Maybe we should just turn around and split."

I couldn't argue there; the whole vibe of the place was freaking me out, too! "I agree," I replied. "Let's get out of here."

By the time the wagon had circled the fountain, we were surrounded by dozens of people. More than a few had sharp-looking swords. We slowly raised our hands and descended out of the wagon. The people never said a word; they only prompted us forward with their weapons. Soon, we were guided to a jail cell in a small building not far from the fountain. Sitting in the cell, was a dwarf who looked at us with relief.

After the people had gone, the dwarf spoke to us. "You're not like them," he said. "I can see it in your eyes."

"No, we're not," I answered. "Neither are you. What's going on in this town? Some kind of evil magic?"

"I don't know," the dwarf replied, stroking his beard. "All I know is that my cellmate, an elf named Len, was taken out of here yesterday. Today, he was one of the ones that led you in here. Now, he's as mindless as the rest of them."

We all paused for a moment to look at what was obviously the town constable, sitting behind his desk across from our cell. He was staring at us blankly. "Don't worry about him," our cellie stated. "He's always like that. I still haven't figured out why or what's going on in this place. I wandered in a few days ago, only to be shoved in here with Len. What's your story?"

"We are a couple of bards and we formed a band," I said. "We were hoping to tour the realms and become big stars, like Elfis or One Man Bard."

"I thought you two were musicians!" he grinned. "I could tell by the lutes strapped to your backs. I've always wanted to learn how to play, but I've got two left hands. By the way, my name is Rhody, and I'm at your service."

"This is Peavus Calloway, and I'm Scales. Hey, you want to hear a song?" I asked.

"I'd like that," Rhody replied. "Maybe it will relieve the tension. I'm starting to go stir crazy!"

"Hey, Peavus. Let's do the new song we wrote for playing at gaming taverns, *Dice, Dice Baby*." I said while pulling my lute down to my lap and starting to strum.

(Sung to the tune Ice, Ice, Baby by Vanilla Ice)
Alright, stop, collaborate and listen
This DM's back with my brand new vision
Something grabs hold of you tightly
Through tears, you ask, will it bite me?
Will it ever stop? Yo, I don't know
Roll those dice, and make a saving throw
Dexterity check, there you go
Light up with rage when you fumble
No chance, throw dice across the room
I brought a dice jail, hee hee they are doomed
In a cage, on the thirteenth level
Chained to a wall, sitting on gravel
But the shackles are loose; you might escape
You better roll good, cuz' these guards don't play
If there's a problem, yo, you best solve it
Check out the graph while my DM resolves it

Dice, dice baby
P'hedral Dice, dice baby
P'hedral Dice, dice baby
P'hedral Dice, dice baby
P'hedral

Yo man, let's order a pizza
Call up to your mother
Dice, dice baby, to roll, to roll
Dice, dice baby, to roll, to roll

As we played the song, the constable across from us got a weird look on his face. He smiled broadly as a large black bug squeezed its way out of his ear. It was covered in pink goo and little sparks of electricity moved over it's body as it ran across the desk. Then it crawled down to the floor, and headed our way. Then the constable closed his eyes and collapsed onto his paperwork.

When the bug ran into the cage with the three of us, it started dancing wildly. We watched it for a moment, then, Rhody stepped on it, sending little sparks out from under his boot. "Gross," Peavus commented as the dwarf scraped its guts off his heel.

"You know what I think that was?" Rhody said, looking up at us. "It was an Electric Bugaloo!"

"Well, whtever it was, it knew how to shake a leg," I stated. "A whole bunch of them!"

"I've heard tales about these insects," the dwarf replied. "They burrow into your brain and slowly eat it while you are their mind slave! Apparently, they have a thing for music!"

The constable began to groan and lifted his head. "Ugh," he said, wiping the pink slime off his ear. "What happened? What are you three doing in there?"

After our explanation, he hurriedly unlocked the cell, and we set a plan into motion. Peavus and I stood outside cranking out good tunes, while Rhody and constable beat all the insects streaming toward us with their boots and big rocks. "Keep on rocking!" Peavus shouted as the dwarf killed bug after bug, which sent sparks flying with each hit.

After we finished playing, the whole town woke up, as if they had been in a weird dream. Peavus and I were hailed as heroes, and we were given a place to stay while we put on shows all week at Ye Olde Skool Tavern, which was their only real establishment besides than the jail.

We packed up after the last show, and Rhody approached us. "Hey, you guys looking for help? I'm not a bard, but I'm handy with tools. I can fix almost anything."

"Can you do laundry?" I asked, pointing to bug goo stains on my shirt.

"Stubborn stains are the enemy of my dwarven people," Rhody said with a far away look in his eye as he held his hand over his heart.

"Really? Is that true?" I asked.

"No," the dwarf laughed. "But if there's coin in it and I'm allowed to complain, I'm in!"

Entry 97

Only one band in all of the Unremembered Realms has the distinct honor of taking on Big Tech and that is the Marshtones! Let me explain.

One of the bigging headaches that all bards have to deal with is song theft. Sometimes, the songs we write and sing get borrowed and played by other bards, especially if the tune can get a crowd on its feet! Most often, one bard asks another for their permission, which is a thoughtful thing to do. But other times, songs are stolen and then claimed to be original work, which is uncool, especially if they made it more popular than you!

The worst case was when two weird Metrognomes from Omer, named Wawa and Flange, built a mechanical giant and called it Big Tech. This oddball metallic creation could capture the music it heard and play it back! I don't understand gnoman technology, but this feat upset many bards who would lose gigs because tavern owners would hire Big Tech, instead of the bands, themselves. The two gnomes would play these "recordings" at taverns for half the cost of what a band would charge. The gnomes, dressed in all black, would sit inside this machine, crank spinning what they call "record discs," which contained the music.

Because of its size and metallic composition, Big Tech was almost physically unstoppable! That's why Bards, like myself, ended up petitioning to have the kings and queens of the four realms put a stop to this infernal machine. But the Metrognomes beat us to them. The little pirates gave them a percentage of the profits, which they happily claimed as royalties.

Then, one day, it all came crashing down for Big Tech and its two pilots. We had just set up our gear at Purgewater Lake for the multi-band festival they held every year, and we heard the thump-thump-thump we all dreaded. "Oh, great," Peavus stated from next to me on the stage. "Another visit from Big Tech!"

As the towering machine approached, we could see Wawa and Flange staring smugly at us from behind the glass portion of its chest. It stopped just behind the crowd, then Wawa turned a crank, opening the window. "There will be no need to thank us after we have stolen your music, lizard band," Flange stated emotionlessly. "The gold we earn from your harmonies is thanks enough."

The crowd said a long, "oooooh," and looked at us. "Fine," I replied angrily. "Let's just get this over with."

"Hold on minute," Maul said. "Me forgot good luck charm."

The half-ogre jumped down from the stage and ran to the tour wagon. A few moments later, he returned wearing a backpack. "I didn't know you had a lucky charm, Maul," I said while watching him grab his

Warshburn bass.

"Me ready now," Maul said with a grin and a wink.

With that said, we broke into the starting tune we had just written called *Tavern Wall*.

(Sung to the tune of Bathroom Wall by Faster Pussycat)
We found your dungeon on the Tavern Wall
It revealed the secret doors and all
Got a party, set a date
Hey there, baddie, I just can't wait
Found your dungeon on the Tavern Wall

We picked the lock right there on your door
Rogue undid the weak trap on the floor
What a poorly run dungeon; what can I say
Was this drawn by an ex-employay?

Found your dungeon on the Tavern Wall
We're going to raid it; there's no time to stall
It turns out it wasn't such a secret after all

Answered the door in a growly voice
We looted the place down to the joists
Illusionist with a fake cold of cone
We disbelieved now we're raiding his home

Found your dungeon on the Tavern Wall
We're going to raid it no time to stall
It turns out it wasn't such a secret after all
Found your dungeon on the tavern wall
Boy, am I lucky that we swung by for a call

The crowd danced and sang during the song, even whirling themselves around the front of the stage. This reaction to our music made Wawa and Flange extremely happy. So happy, in fact, that they left the window open on Big Tech as they pulled levers, turned dials, and pressed buttons to "record" our music. They were doing dance moves as if controlled by an Electric Bugaloo, one of the realm's most annoying but deadly insects.

None of us noticed that Maul had jumped down from the stage during all the commotion and ran up to Big Tech, removing his backpack. With one quick motion, he hurled his pack up into the window where the distracted Metrognomes were. Within seconds, red dust came poofing out of where the gnomes were running their illicit operation.

By this time, the crowd and the rest of the band had fallen silent as we watched what was going on. The two Metrognomes climbed down from inside the machine, coughing and nearly falling. "Das machine is kaput," Wawa choked.

The crowd parted ways as the machine seemed to crumble to fine red dust and collapse. Its head rolled to the front of the stage. Its cold metal eyes stared up at me blankly. "What secret technology have you used against us," Flange asked Maul. "We must have your secret, sir. A mind like yours is rare!"

"Me know that," Maul replied, pointed to his head, and whispered back. "This is where me keep brain."

Then, Maul let out a whistle, and Dustin, his pet Rust Monster leaped from inside the fallen machine and into his arms. It licked his face happily, wagging its tail. Wawa and Flange sighed before sadly shuffling off into the red cloud to pick through the wreckage of Big Tech.

Entry 98

Many people ask me how I come up with inspiration for my songs. I suppose it's the same for all bards; it is mostly from life experience. Songs such as *Full Moon on Monday*, *Spelunky Tunk Girl*, and *Don't Raid the Town* are more introspective numbers influenced by the dangers of life on the road.

I also write love songs when I'm in the mood and thinking about the lizardettes I've had to leave behind because of life on the road. Some of those ballads are *Cold Blooded*, *My Heart will Molt Again*, and *My Lute Gently Weeps*.

Of course, there are plenty of feel-good gaming jams, such as *I Got Friends (In Gaming Places)*, *Roll 20 for Me*, and *Crit Me with Your Best Shot*.

I write these when I'm in a good mood and ready for fun.

Sometimes, a song will come out of nowhere or be influenced by something I see. An excellent example of this is when I wrote *When Dwarves Cry*. I came up with this tune after watching Rhody throw a fit at the complaints window at the Doubledeal Casino in the Province of Rustwood. I guess you never know when inspiration will hit you. All you can do is hope you make a good saving throw versus musical fumbles.

Entry 99

One of the reasons I like to be onstage better than I like being in the audience is because I have a hard time adjusting to the demi-human world of the Unremembered Realms. Deep down, I'm just a good ole lizardman from the swamp. An example of me having a hard time with this is when Peavus and I went to see a play at the Ladida Theater in Hollowood.

We both snuck in snacks in magical Sacks of Holding. Peavus had his favorite, hot-buttered popcorn, and I had mine, a beehive. Most humans and others don't understand that bees are a sweet, crunchy snack to lizardmen. They can't sting our tough skin or our thick tongues. Their constant stinging feels like a refreshing oral massage. Apparently, softskins do not find these buzzing snacks delightful; it only took about thirty seconds for the whole theater to clear out screaming after I plunged my claw deep into the hive.

When we got back to the tour wagon, the rest of the band asked how the play went. Peavus said, "I gave it an A+, but Scales gave it a bee, lots of them!"

Entry 100

Maul had only been a band member for about a week when we learned just how crazy he could be. One night, as we sat around a campfire in the Tanglewood Forest eating our dinner, a bunch of glowing eyes started to appear all around us. Peavus had been telling one of his stories when he suddenly stopped. A deep growling could be heard emanating from the darkness all around us. "Why you stop telling story?" Maul said, sounding perturbed.

"I think we have company," Peavus said nervously.

Maul immediately stood up, marched into the woods, and began pummeling whatever creatures were making the racket. Peavus and I were both wide-eyed as we watched Maul appear from out of the dark forest. He still had a large dead wolf clamped onto his leg, which he kicked off without even looking. "Okay," he calmly stated as he sat back down. "Tell rest of story."

"Um," Peavus started. "Weren't you afraid? Those animals could have ripped you to pieces!"

"What?" Maul replied. "The little doggies? That be a laugh!"

"You didn't know what was out there," I cut in. "How do you know it wasn't a dragon?!"

"Easy," Maul replied calmly. "If it was dragon, it would have eaten me!"

It didn't make sense to Peavus or me, but it occurred to both of us that it was nice to have Maul on our side.

Featured Artist
Josh Will

Weird Elf Yankolich

See more of Josh's great art at: www.joshwill.com

Official Road Crew

Scales and the Marshtones couldn't have got this book on their merch table without the support of these awesome supporters on Kickstarter! Thank you for your contributions, you are now offical roadies for the Marshtones! Now, let's hit the road!

John "Aces of Death7" Mullens
Aubrey Dee Sweeney
David Holzborn
Ark the Legend
Chris Johnson
Eron Wyngarde
Terri Connor
Balki
Kurtis Primm
Nonie Osantowski
Scantrontb
David Swisher
Doug "Dhomal" Raas
Brian Williams
Jessica Marquardt
Raphael Bressel
Mitch Megaw
Sgt Pepper
Michael Kingswood
Dan Kawecki
Steve McEntire
Dancing Dan
Bill Brasky
Mary Putnam
Javier A Verdin
Andy Schiller
Gary Trowbridge

This book is independently published, it would be
a huge help to the author if you could please take
a moment and review this book on your favorite book
site. Please give this book series a mention on
your favorite social media as well.

THE UNREMEMBERED REALMS™

ALSO AVAILABLE FROM
THE UNREMEMBERED REALMS™
BOOKS:
JOURNAL OF AN OUTLAW: BOOK ONE
JOURNAL OF AN OUTLAW: BOOK TWO
JOURNAL OF AN OUTLAW: BOOK THREE
JOURNAL OF AN OUTLAW: BOOK FOUR
JOURNAL OF AN AWFUL GOOD PALADIN: BOOK ONE

GAMES:
THE FORBIDDEN TREASURE OF MIFTENMAD
THE FUMBLECRIT WARS
GAMBLE AT THE GALLOWS
MERCH MADNESS
THE TEMPLE OF TEMPERAMENTAL EVIL

MUSIC:
SCALES & THE MARSHTONES CD

JOIN THE EMAIL LIST FOR PRODUCT UPDATES
AND BOOK SIGNING LOCATIONS.
WWW.THEUNREMEMBEREDREALMS.COM
AND FILL OUT A SHORT SIGN-UP FORM.

ARE YOU READY TO TAKE YOUR DUNGEON CRAWL TO THE NEXT LEVEL?

Drakenstone is magnetic stackable dungeon tiles with the highest quality on the market. Whether your delve is big or small, the only limit of size and configuration is your imagination!

The magnets embedded in the high-quality resin pieces make it so you can click them together in any pattern you choose. The squares in the tiles are the perfect size for miniatures, and the tiles can be rearranged in hundreds of ways! They are all cast with a granite look so they do not have to be painted! All the dungeon tiles are hand-crafted by artist Andy Schiller in the USA. Shop the extensive collection at: www.drakenstone.com.

DrakenStone

www.drakenstone.com

Dungeon Hobby Shop Museum

Are you looking for a place to purchase your favorite Unremembered Realms books, games, music, or more? Look no further than the Dungeon Hobby Shop Museum in Lake Geneva, Wisconsin! This is the very building where E. Gary Gygax formed TSR and launched the Dungeons and Dragons game role-playing system that changed the world!

The museum is a great place to visit and see where it began. You can even play games there as well. Not only can you see all the versions of D&D from the past, but you can pick up new games and books from the future gamers and authors that they help promote! They even have an annual convention with appearances from big names of D&D's past, present, and future!

www.tsrmuseum.com
DHSM: Facebook: www.facebook.com/TSRHobbiesMuseum
TSR Con Facebook: www.facebook.com/TSRCON

ABOUT THE AUTHOR

Mick McArt is the author the Unremembered Realms comedy fantasy series of books. He was inspired to write the books and create this world because of his love of Dungeons & Dragons. Mick is also an illustrator and author of children's books, his most popular being the "Tales of Wordishure" series.

Thanks to massive support at his book signings and crowdfunding on Kickstarter, Mick has also become a game designer, with a number of games being composed based on the Unremembered Realms.

Micks family include his wife Erica, and their children Micah, Jonah, and Emerald. They currently live in Midland, Michigan. Mick earned a Bachelor of Fine Arts degree from Central Michigan University in 1997 and a Masters degree from Saginaw Valley State University in 2006.